REFLECTIONS
BOOK TWO OF NOVELLA/NOVEL DUET #1
COMPANION TO *BRIDGE TO MY HEART*

#2

The

Prospector

and the

Widow

BY

Award-winning Author
CAROLYN TWEDE FRANK

The Prospector
And
The Widow

Carolyn Twede Frank

Published by AugustWise Press
Copyright 2019 by Carolyn Twede Frank
ISBN 978-0-9852513-8-3

Acknowledgements and Author's Note

Thanks to my husband for our road trip to the remote Four-Corner area of the United States and our visit to Natural Bridges National Monument. I also want to thank him for his full-fledged support in writing *this* romance novel. (He is not a fan of the genre). I also want to thank the park ranger at the gift shop at the monument. He opened my eyes to a relatively unknown character in Old West American History, Cass Hite. Hite discovered the three natural bridges in the park. He also ran a placer gold mining operation on the Colorado River in the late 1800's. While at the gift shop I purchased a biography of him, and by the time we arrived home from our trip I had finished the book and fallen in love with Cass's unique story. Except one thing. I hated the sad ending. *The Prospector and The Widow* is a fictionalized version of how I envisioned the story playing out, including an ending I so very much wanted as I read the biography.

Chapter 1

1889

Sarah sprinkled a handful of earth into the grave. The dirt felt dry, lifeless, like this desolate spot of the Utah Territory where they lived. The small clods pattered against the top of her husband's pine casket in muted tones, landing on two other offerings of soil. As the third wife, everything in life for the past nineteen years of her marriage had felt muted. Why should this day be any different? She glanced to the side at her sister wives. Nyda's eyes brimmed with tears, her handkerchief already soaked. Being his first wife, she'd been with Jacob the longest, thirty-six years. She'd known him the best. Edna, his second wife, knew him almost as long. She had her handkerchief handy, constantly dabbing at her eyes.

Sarah rubbed against one of the sagebrush bushes dotting the tiny Hanksville cemetery. The plant's rich aroma bothered her nose and tempted a sneeze. She reached into her pocket to confirm the whereabouts of her handkerchief. Still folded neatly in fours, it rested amongst the pleats of her black dress. It would likely remain there for the rest of the day, unused. She stepped back from the grave to give the Hansen children, all twenty of them, a chance to add their handfuls of dirt. This might take some time.

As always, her two children stood at the end of the line. Cleon and Clara glanced shyly at her as they inched forward. She could hardly believe they'd already grown into their teen years. Bless their hearts, they loved their father despite the limited time he gave them.

Sarah chewed on her bottom lip. She shouldn't begrudge her late husband. He was a decent father. And a good provider. Maybe not even that bad of a husband—as far as a polygamist husband went. But their marriage was not the one she'd envisioned, or dreamed of as a young girl. She'd always wanted a handsome young man of her own to sweep her off her feet like her father had done to her mother.

She and Jacob had never bonded. The fact that he was old enough to be her father certainly hadn't helped. Theirs was not a marriage of love, but one of necessity for her and a case of charity for him.

Nyda stepped to Sarah's side. "Did you forget your handkerchief?"

"No." Sarah patted her pocket. "It's right here. I'm one to hold my tears inside."

"Yes, you were always one to hold things in." Nyda's mouth straightened into a flat line. "I remember when you joined our family—with that long blonde hair of yours, you were such a pretty young thing." Nyda dabbed her red eyes with her handkerchief. "Jacob thought it was a shame that your beauty was tainted by that continual pout you wore."

Sarah's eyes remained on the children taking their turns at the grave, listening to Nyda with only half an ear. The sight of Jacob's thirty-two-year-old son, Jesse, at the front of the line combined with Nyda's words and twisted Sarah's insides with a familiar pain. The pain had been the source of that "continual" pout, and here it came again. She felt as though she belonged in that line of children more than with her sister wives, being only slightly older than Jesse.

"You hardly said a word to any of us that first year," Nyda continued. "I could have helped you adjust a little easier if you had."

"Maybe so," Sarah said merely to be agreeable. Sarah had just lost her parents and had become Jacob's third wife at the tender age of fifteen. She hadn't felt like opening up.

"Let's not have a repeat of that first year you joined our family, or seven years ago when we moved here, okay?" Nyda's eyebrows puckered like they always did when she dished out advice.

Sarah reached into her pocket, clenched her fist around her handkerchief, and pulled it out for Nyda to see. "Okay."

"Good." Nyda blew her nose and walked away.

Bishop Smoot dedicated the grave after all the

children had sprinkled their last respects onto their father's casket. He added nothing more about Jacob Hansen. Everything there was to know had already been said earlier during the funeral service. After his prayer, he turned and faced the gathering of mourners.

"The Relief Society sisters have prepared you all a fine meal. It's waiting back at the big house."

Nyda wiped her eyes, put on a composed face, and stepped to the side of the bishop. "Make your way back over to my house when you're ready," she said. "Take the time you need."

Two boys took off toward town at a sprint.

Nyda called after them. "Children, don't run! This is a solemn day and should remain such until sundown."

"Sorry, Ma."

"Sorry, Grandma."

The two boys slowed, and several more children joined them. Soon the adults trickled away from the cemetery.

Sarah chose to remain a little longer, strolling past the handful of headstones, kicking at the occasional rock that got in her way, contemplating her time spent married to Jacob. Those days had not been all bad—and she'd likely not have survived without him. Could she survive without him now?

She made her way back over the reddish-brown dirt piled to the side of the grave and peered down one more time before they came back to fill in the hole. She couldn't honestly tell her late husband that she'd miss him, but she could definitely tell him how grateful she was to him for Cleon and Clara and helping her provide for them the past eighteen years.

"Thanks," she said softly to the casket.

She sensed someone move to her side. Glancing up, she noticed Edna standing there and that everyone else had left except for a man grazing his horse on a patch of spring grass east of the cemetery. He appeared to be a stranger—had to be. She knew everyone in town.

Edna touched Sarah's arm. "I wanted to say my final goodbyes too. Without the crowd." She smiled at Sarah as if wanting to comfort her and then peered into the grave. "Goodbye, Jacob. I'll miss you. Fifty-six is much too young to meet your maker."

"That it is," Sarah responded.

Edna wiped her eyes. "But I suppose God knows best."

"Yes, I suppose," Sarah said, not really agreeing, but like always, appearing to. Her guess was that God had nothing to do with Jacob's death—or the lack of being spared from death. Her husband had been unwise in early spring and had stayed outside too long in the cold tending his cattle. He'd battled with the effects of scarlet fever for the last two months.

"It shall be difficult—getting along without him." Edna sniffed. "And lonely."

"Yes, I suppose."

There was, however, some level of agreement this time. Sarah knew it would be difficult to get by without the small allowance Jacob gave her from time to time to purchase a new pair of shoes for the children or other necessities. He had, however, built her a comfortable two-room log cabin on the edge of town when they'd moved here seven years ago with five other families, all fleeing, trying to hide out in this harsh, out-of-the-way place from those who would abolish polygamy. She assured herself that she'd already thought this out. She and her children could survive if she tightened her belt on what minute spending she did do and sell eggs, and maybe some of the fruit from her trees, for what little income she needed in the future.

As for being lonely, she was already accustomed to that pain. When she was fourteen and her mom passed away during childbirth, Sarah had felt her first pangs of lonesomeness. Just like all of Sarah's four other siblings, her new baby sister hadn't survived either. A year later when she lost her father to a wagon accident, she'd felt as though every shred of good in her life had abandoned her. The lonesomeness overwhelmed her.

And then she married Jacob three months before she turned sixteen.

The lonesomeness had remained. He took care of her as much as any decent person who hadn't married for love could, yet finding her place in his household never emerged. She didn't fit with the other children. Nor did she fit with the adults.

And it was not what she'd wanted to do.

Others had determined what was *best* for her. That's when she'd learned to bottle up her feelings and just let those around her make decisions for her. Now it was second nature for her to make choices that pleased others while ignoring her own desires.

"It shall be difficult, living without him," Edna repeated, "but we shall manage. We have each other to lean on."

"That we do," Sarah said, turning her head toward Edna and offering a smile, wondering how much they really would lean on each other, or if they were hollow words.

A glimpse of the stranger's cream-colored hat caught Sarah's eye. He'd moved closer and was now leaning against a lone tree several yards away. "That man over yonder, behind us. He's staring at us." Sarah inclined her chin toward the man.

Edna turned, made a quick glance, and jerked her head around to stare forward, keeping her back to the man. "Pay him no mind, Sarah. He's that prospector who passes through here from time to time. He's as Gentile as they come, and we'd best ignore him."

"So you know him?"

Edna looked at Sarah as if she'd slapped her in the face. "I know *of* him," she said almost as a whisper. "Jacob told me all about him after we'd run into him on one of our afternoon wagon rides some time ago."

Sarah's cabin sat next to the horse trail that led south out of town, and she'd spotted a traveler now and again as she worked out in her garden. Now that she thought about it, she remembered that light beige hat because it looked store-bought and expensive. Sarah's curiosity was piqued. "What did Jacob tell you?"

"Only that he pans for gold on the Colorado River

about fifty miles south of here and the man has no manners, conscience, or respect for God or others. He's set his sights on the riches of the world, he has. Makes a pretty penny, too. Spends it all on women and whiskey on his trips up north."

"Good afternoon, ladies."

Sarah startled at the man's greeting. Wanting to attach a face to the deep voice, she turned.

He no longer stood by the tree, but a mere ten feet away from them and had his hat in his hand. He wore a fairly new red shirt, had a strong build, a handsome face, and appeared to be in his late thirties like her—yes, definitely not from Hanksville. She would have noticed him before now. His eyes matched his voice, deep and alluring. They prompted Sarah to stare. Her eyes met his for much too long. She felt the need to say something so as to not appear rude.

"Good afternoon," she said to dispel the awkwardness.

Edna jabbed Sarah with her elbow. She kept her back turned to the man, but shot Sarah a warning glare.

Sarah leaned toward Edna. "I'm being neighborly," she said under her breath.

"But he's a—"

"He's a neighbor," Sarah finished her sister wife's words, speaking barely above a whisper. Being rude to another person was difficult for her—whether they were God-fearing or Gentile, it didn't matter. She straightened up and looked the stranger in the eye. "Nice weather we've been having for May, isn't it?"

"Yep," the man said. His eyes lit up as if thrilled

she was speaking to him—or at least surprised. "Certainly makes burying a loved one a little easier. Sorry, I meant that a funeral on a sunny day is better to take than fighting the muck and the mud of a rainstorm or the blasted snow in winter. Burying a loved one is never easy. I'm sorry for your loss, ladies."

"Thanks." Sarah failed to see how this man lacked manners or conscience, as Edna had mentioned.

"Who was it?" The man pointed to the grave and then scratched his wide moustache. "The one who passed away? Black dresses. A close family member, I gather?"

"He was my husband," Sarah said, thinking of how all three of her dresses were black—or at least dark gray.

"Sorry to hear that."

She placed a hand on Edna's back that was still turned toward him. "He was her husband too."

The man raised an eyebrow. "Mormons, eh? Should have known. Maybe I did." He moved his hat over his heart, stepped closer, and peered into the partially filled grave. "I was just passing through on my way down south and saw the big gathering of folks here—thought I'd stop and pay my respects too. Anybody who's gutsy enough to brave this God-forsaken corner of the territory deserves my respect." He paused a minute and then stepped away. "Good day, ladies." He placed his hat on his head and then gathered the reins of his horse into one hand. Pulling the animal's muzzle away from the tender green grass, he mounted it in one fluid motion. A moment later, he was back on the trail, heading south.

Unmoving, Sarah stood there at the side of her husband's grave, her eyes for some reason unwilling to look anywhere but at the stranger riding away.

Edna turned around, glanced at the stranger, and then looked at Sarah while latching onto her arm. "I think we best hurry back to the big house and join the rest of the family. No more speaking to men the likes of him." She waved one hand behind her, and with the other hand pulled Sarah toward town. "You're almost like a daughter to me, Sarah, and with you in the grieving, lonely state you're in, I'd hate to see you make a poor decision."

"What are you talking about?" Sarah quickened her step to keep up and then shook off Edna's grasp.

"Me, I'm too old to go looking for a new husband. Besides, there'd be none who'd take me." She touched her fingers to her sagging eye and cheek that had met with a bit of palsy. "But you—you are still young, pretty. You could still bear children. It's natural for you to have a desire to remarry. But whatever you do, don't marry outside the faith—and especially not a man the likes of him."

Edna's comments caught Sarah off guard, and hurt somewhat. Did her sister wife really think Sarah would do such a thing as marry out of the faith? Her concerns had been for how she'd take care of herself and her children. She'd not given any thought to finding another husband, not wanting to be another polygamist's wife. Those were the only men to be had around here. "Don't worry. I'm not even thinking about such thi—"

"You might want to consider moving away from Hanksville. There would be more eligible husbands elsewhere."

"I've got my little cabin with its garden and hens," Sarah said as they left the cemetery, determined to speak her desires for once. A new life lay ahead. She wanted to start it out right—choose her own path. "And I've got my two children to keep me company. I'm content with where I am, but thank you for your concern, Edna."

They walked the dusty road without further conversation. Only the warble of a meadowlark in the distance interrupted the silence. When they'd made it to the edge of town, the lilacs of the Brown family's yard offered their delightful fragrance. Edna picked a cluster of blooms, brought it to her nose momentarily, and then spoke up.

"I was in error to say you might want to consider moving away from Hanksville so as to find a husband."

"Oh, really?" Sarah sighed in relief. She had feared Edna was turning as meddlesome as Nyda.

"Yes, 'consider' was poor advice. I feel you *should* leave Hanksville to find a new husband. There are no marriageable men here, for there's talk that the prophet himself will soon do away with polygamy. If you'd like, I'll send my boys over with our big wagon when you're ready to leave, and we'll all help you move."

Sarah shoved her hand into her pocket where she once again formed a fist to vent her frustration. At a loss for words, she responded simply with, "Oh." This was unlike Edna. Edna didn't meddle in her life.

"I've forgotten something at home," she said,

desperately wanting to be alone for a moment. "Continue on without me. I'll be there shortly."

She waved Edna on and darted back the way they'd come. She didn't want to hear what else Edna might have to say. She didn't need to be told what to do with her life, and she knew how easily she could be talked into things, so rushing off to the isolation of her little cabin and missing the big meal in Nyda's backyard would be more than worth it.

Halfway back down the street, she veered off onto the road that led to her place. It too lay on the east end of town, but a little north of the cemetery. As she approached her humble cabin, a sense of security swelled inside her. This was home. She doubted she'd be making many trips into town, to the big house or to Edna's house, now that Jacob was gone. And she doubted she'd move away in search of a husband.

She had Clara and Cleon to keep her company and didn't need anyone else.

Chapter 2

Cass kicked his heels into Gold Dust and urged his horse faster down the trail, anxious to get home after his hectic trip to Salt Lake City. Never before in all his thirty-eight years had he struck up a conversation with a Mormon woman. He and Mormons got along about as good as his gut and a rotten apple. He didn't agree with polygamy, and Mormons didn't agree with his rowdy life—and he didn't care to change.

Cass slowed Gold Dust to an easy pace once the small town lay well behind. He had to admit, however, that Hanksville appeared a metropolis compared to anything else in these parts, where only Mormons, outlaws, and Indians lived. He didn't fall into to any of those groups—yet he chose to be here.

And why not? Where else could a man be so free to do what he wanted, especially one with an itch for gold and silver in his blood? Where else could he stake claim on a huge swath of land with a sandy-beached river running through the middle and not be bothered by greedy neighbors?

Yep, he had all he needed to be happy.

His mind wandered back to the cemetery, back to the young, blonde-haired widow with the sad but un-teared eyes. What would become of her? She seemed so young to be widowed.

The sun dipped low in the western sky as Cass approached Dandy Crossing and the tiny town of Hite. When he'd been a kid growing up in the gold fields of California, he'd never dreamed he'd have a mining town named after him.

He slowed to a stop and took in the beauty before descending the switchbacks that lowered him down to Hite. The orange-tinged light of evening bounced off the red rock plateau on the east. It looked magnificent, rising a hundred yards up from the riverbed, now infused with even more color. Such views were another reason why Cass loved it here—that and the fact that he owned the only spot on the river for a hundred miles north and south where one could cross the immense gorge of the Colorado.

"Enough gawking. Come on, Goldie, let's get home." He prompted Gold Dust down the steep trail, glancing once more at the two cabins and the three dingy white canvas tents that composed the town.

Once down into the gorge, Cass dismounted and led Gold Dust onto the wide raft tethered to the shore. He slipped the rope from the boulder that held it bound and cast off across the flattest, gentlest spot of the river. The current caught hold of the raft. He struggled for balance and laughed at the thought of his brother calling this rickety collection of logs a ferry. But hey, John had made two bits now and again from the occasional traveler coming this way, wanting to cross the Colorado. A clerk by trade, John didn't have a great mind for the nitty- gritty details of business—even though he ran a store, a ferry, and a post office. It'd been Cass's idea to go up to Salt Lake and officially establish their mining company.

Cass caught sight of two of his men working the river where it had a bit of space to flatten out. "Joe, how's it going?" he hollered as the raft reached shore.

Joe ceased shoveling river sand into the sluice and waved. "Fine. And welcome back, boss."

Cass liked this tall fellow with a crop of constant messy hair the color of the red-rock walls behind him. He was reliable—and the oldest of Cass's crew at twenty-five. Leading Gold Dust, Cass sloshed across the sandy shoreline toward Joe, and Billy—the youngest at eighteen.

"Where's the rest of the boys?" Cass asked, thinking about his three other men.

"Upriver a piece." Joe pointed to the bend in the river that took it out of sight behind canyon walls. "They found another sweet spot up there."

"Excellent." Cass nodded with approval. "How much you haul out while I was gone?"

"At least an ounce, more like two."

Thrilled, Cass looked Joe in the eye, then Billy. "Good work." He felt the itch to stay and help shovel, but he needed to see his brother. "I'll be out here bright and early with you tomorrow." He turned to head up the rise where the cabins and tents stood.

Joe shoveled a scoop of wet sand into the sluice box Billy held. "Don't worry about it, Cass," Billy called out as he passed.

Cass rubbed his lower back with his free hand as he led Gold Dust up the rise to where the cabins and tents stood. "I imagine your back's hurting from the ride too?" He rubbed the ache again, thinking how good stretching out on his bed sounded at the moment. "It's good to be home."

He went home first and put Goldie into the corral, unsaddled her, and rubbed down her golden brown coat. Then he headed over to his brother's cabin. When he stepped inside, he scanned the shelves of the store his brother had set up in the front room. He put his saddle-bags on the makeshift counter and hollered toward the back room where John had his bed.

"John! Get out here. I got you the supplies you wanted."

"Cass!" John's scratchy voice echoed through the doorway. "You darn coot, I was wonderin' when you'd get back!" He rushed out dressed in his usual riveted denim trousers, dirty white shirt, and dark whiskers in need of a shave, and gave Cass a quick hug. "And to hell with the supplies—what about our minin' company? Did you get it all set up?"

"Yep." Cass could feel his face beam. "And I sold our first twenty-five shares of stock!"

John slapped the counter, sending a stack of three envelopes flying. "Yahoo! We're in business! I'll be buildin' another wing to the store before you know it."

"Don't you go cutting down any of those precious trees yet, little brother." Cass plopped into one of the chairs set around the small table John used for poker more often than holding his supper. "We need to hire us some more hands, buy some new equipment."

John lowered into the chair next to Cass. "You're right." He dragged his hand down his face and held on to his stubble-covered chin. "You didn't by chance put one of those help wanted ads in the newspaper while you were up north, did you?"

Cass scratched the skin beneath his bushy moustache. "Blazes! I can't think of everything. I had so much rattling around in my head in Salt Lake. It wasn't easy, what I had to do up there."

"Well, it wasn't easy stayin' down here either." John eyed Cass, his eyebrows drooping. "Doin' your job on top of mine—the boys were complete jackasses while you were gone. Plus, I had to deal with a bunch of damn Indians."

Cass held out his hand to stop John from continuing. "Okay, those men we've hired, I understand. But don't you go cursing my Navajo friends." He lowered his hand. "Was it Hoskininni and his son who came by?"

"How should I know? Those redskins look all the same to me. I just know there was two of them." John stood and stepped over to the makeshift counter. He picked up the big bottle of pickles he kept there to sell off one at a time. He removed the lid and positioned the opening toward Cass. Two pickles sloshed around in a pool of brine. "I assumed they were your friends, the way they came in here askin' for you and then raidin' my pickle jar like they owned it." He set the jar down with a thud, wafting the smell of dill and vinegar into the air. "Those Indians owe me three bits!"

"They don't owe you nothing." Cass pounded the table and stood, ready to get out of there and not hear any more of this bad-mouthing. "You give Hoskininni, or his son, anything they want when they come to visit. Don't matter if I'm here or not." He pulled some coins from his pocket and tossed them on the table. "Here." *Such a measly amount to fret over.* "If it wasn't for those two Indians allowing us this spot on the river, you and me'd surely be working for someone else in some crowded hole-in-the-ground mine farther out west."

"I hear you, Cass."

Cass stepped over to the door. "How long were they here?"

"A full two days," John grumbled. "They kept hopin' you'd show up. It couldn't be more than about a half an hour ago that they finally left."

"Why didn't you tell me this earlier?"

"I didn't think it was important."

"They wouldn't be staying for that long without a reason." Cass dumped the contents of his saddlebags onto the table. Tucking the bags under one arm, he threw the door open with the other. "Can I take your horse? Goldie's had her share of riding today."

"Uh, sure." John raised an eyebrow. "Where you goin'?"

"To see if I can catch my friends."

Cass kicked a rock out of his path and hurried to his cabin to load up a few supplies. On his way to the corral, he wondered if Hoskininni and his son, Tahoma, needed something. Or were they just paying Cass a visit? In either case, he would have liked to see them. In a land where good friends were as scarce as water, he felt fortunate to have found probably the two best ones a man could hope to have. Tahoma had even made Cass his blood brother.

They'd been his only human contact for months when he first came to this corner of the west looking for gold and silver. He had befriended them over time, finding their thinking and his similar—except for one thing: mining.

Cass smiled at a memory.

The old chief had looked at Cass with heavy eyes. "Silver makes white man greedy, cruel in heart. If they know it is here, they will come with guns and blue-coat soldiers and wash over our land like a flood. We will kill some, but in the end they will overpower us and drive us from this land, or put us in cages like cattle. My dreams tell me so."

Cass had remained silent—he knew Hoskininni spoke the truth.

"A brave man you are, Hosteen Pish-la-ki." Hoskininni smiled ever so slightly as he used the Navajo name he'd given Cass earlier on. "We could have killed you when you came on our land looking for silver. But we did not. We like you, like the way you treat Navajo and our land. A foolish man you are, too. You seek silver for wrong reasons. You have lost your way in this world."

"Yet you are still my friend." Cass had added, but wondered what the man meant by that. Cass never considered himself "lost." There was nothing wrong with his passion for mining gold and silver. It was an honest way of making a living.

Cass stepped into the corral to get John's horse, appreciating Hoskininni more than the old Indian could ever know—and not just for directing him to the gold-rich spot on the Colorado.

Cass's saddle still remained perched atop the rail fence where he'd left it minutes earlier. He'd not yet had a chance to remove the bedroll. He placed it on John's horse, secured his saddlebags in place, mounted, and rode off.

He knew well the direction to take, though ashamed he hadn't visited his Navajo friends for some time. Unfortunately, creating one's own mining company took time.

After a good hour on the trail, darkness filled each crevice of the canyon walls and the sandstone's red color faded into shades of black and gray. Cass figured he'd better give up for the night, make camp, and continue his pursuit of his friends in the morning. He continued riding until he found a wide spot in the river bottom and then dismounted. Ready to unsaddle his horse, he noticed a glow of light touching the cliffs downstream. The aroma of roasting fish wafted his way. *Hoskininni*. He climbed onto John's horse and followed the light.

As he came around a bend in the canyon, he spied Hoskininni and his son sitting cross-legged on the riverbank beside a modest fire. Two fish sizzled on a stone at the side of the flames. "Hoskininni," he called out immediately to make his presence known.

The chief looked Cass's way. He wore the usual leather band around his head to keep his long gray braids away from his face. With flickers of orange lighting the weathered face, the old man's eyes communicated recognition. "Hosteen Pish-la-ki." He raised his palm in Cass's direction.

Cass dismounted and led his horse toward the two men's camp. "Do you mind if I share your fire tonight?"

Hoskininni gave a slow nod. "Hosteen Pish-la-ki is always welcome at our fire."

"My father speaks truth." Tahoma swept his palm over a spot of ground next to him.

Cass pulled the saddle from his horse. "My brother said you came to visit. Is everything all right? Do you need more gun powder? More blankets?" He carried the saddle to the spot his blood brother had indicated.

"No, we use our guns little and have plenty of white man blankets." Tahoma helped Cass unstrap the bedroll from his saddle. "It is a question we have for you."

"Question?" Cass rolled out his bed. "Now that's different. But sure, ask away."

Hoskininni looked Cass in the eye. His own bore a heavy expression. "Have you broken our promise made long ago?"

Cass felt hurt they would think he'd do such a thing. But they must have a reason. "Which promise? Wait, no, I have broken no promises."

"My father speaks of your promise not to tell other white man of the gold sand in river."

"I've told no one. It's the truth." That was the last thing Cass would do.

"Nine days past," Tahoma continued, "I rode upriver from your village a far piece and saw many white man digging in sand same as you."

"Are you certain?" Cass's gut lurched.

Hoskininni spoke up with a tenor of authority. "Only Hosteen Pish-la-ki and his friends are welcome here."

"Believe me, I want it to stay that way too. Unfortunately, I only had so much money when I staked claim on that spot of the Colorado. Upriver is still up for grabs as far as the land office is concerned." Cass ached for the old chief and the changes the government imposed upon his way of life, forcing them onto worse and worse land.

"So, they are not your friends?" Tahoma looked at Cass in earnest. The glow of the fire lit his face, accentuating his square jaw and thick black hair that fell freely and reached past his shoulders.

"Nope, they are no friends of mine."

Hoskininni brought his palms together and rested his weathered hands below his chin. "We feared so. They do not respect the river as Hosteen Pish-la-ki does."

"They shoot their guns at us," Tahoma added. "Our people are worried."

Worry clawed at Cass too. "I'll see what I can do. I'll talk to those white men, tell them not to shoot at your people—that you are friendly. And to respect the river, dang their hides."

"Thank you, my friend." Hoskininni offered Cass a piece of roasted fish.

Cass accepted the tasty morsel and shared his dried apples with them. After their lean supper, they talked for a while about Hoskininni's concern for his people, and then crawled into their bedrolls.

Exhausted, Cass figured he'd fall right asleep. His mind, however, refused to relax. While the fire died to embers, his head churned thoughts of confronting those men. As the last of the coals gave up their glow, he contemplated the impact this competition might have upon his newly formed mining company.

When complete darkness engulfed the camp and only pinpricks of light illuminated the moonless sky, his mind finally let go of Hoskininni's words.

Events of the morning crept into his thoughts, and the image of that young widow's face refused to leave.

Why on earth am I thinking about her?

Maybe because she actually talked to me.

A handsome woman like that didn't belong in that town. She certainly didn't belong with any of those other stiff Mormon men who already had themselves a wife—or two, or three—either.

He punched the jacket he used as his pillow to get more comfortable.

"She don't belong with me neither," he mumbled, barely above a whisper. He found it odd that such a thought bothered him.

Chapter 3

October 1890

It had been over two years since Jacob's death—and the big dinner Sarah had eventually dragged herself out of her cabin to attend. She figured there would be no reason to come over to Nyda's house again. But there she stood, behind the big house, mixing up a big bowl of punch made from the apricot nectar she'd bottled earlier in the year. Nyda had insisted that Clara's wedding reception be held on her back lawn. Sarah couldn't refuse the offer. After all, it was the only sizable patch of grass in town, and she wanted Clara's wedding day to be memorable. Unlike her own.

Two of Nyda's grandsons struggled out of the back door of the house, each hefting one end of a kitchen table. Nyda followed a step behind them. "Now be sure to put it square in the middle of the shade of the willow tree. Understand?"

"Yes'm," the boys said in unison.

"And girls . . ." Nyda flagged down two of her

youngest daughters with a wave of her hand. "Come over here and spread this tablecloth neatly on the table once the boys have finished."

"Yes, Mother."

Nyda gave them a straight-mouthed nod of approval. "Hurry. The guests should start arriving in a quarter hour, and we need to get all the baked goods set out neatly." She turned, squinted, and headed toward the old pine picnic table where Sarah worked on her punch.

"Thank you again for letting us hold Clara's reception here," Sarah said as Nyda approached.

"Well, we certainly couldn't have it over at your place, now could we? Unless you were planning on having your guests sit on pumpkins in the place of chairs." Nyda's mouth curled up, obviously amused with her own wit. Her smile faded as she touched the weathered top of the picnic table. "You're not planning on leaving this uncovered, are you?"

"Sorry, but I guess maybe so." Sarah bit on her lower lip. "I've had so much on my plate, trying to finish up Clara's dress in time for the ceremony this morning. I completely forgot a tablecloth."

"Well, we can't have it like this, can we?" Nyda turned on her heel and headed for the house.

A minute later, Edna hurried out the back door with tablecloth in hand. "Here." She waved the lacy cloth in the air. "Nyda said you wanted this."

"Yes, thanks." Sarah lifted her big bowl of punch as Edna spread the table with the cloth.

"It's a big day for you, my dear Sarah, is it not?" Edna removed glasses from a box on the ground and placed them neatly on the table. "Your only daughter just got married. Surely you must be very excited."

"Yes, I am. Thank you," Sarah said, the lump in her throat feeling both good and bad as she swallowed it down. Good because Clara was so happy. Bad because now Clara would be moving out of the cabin.

"It has been delightful as of late while Nyda and I have helped you with the preparations. Nyda was just saying the other day how we've seen you more in the past two weeks than we have the whole two years and five months since Jacob's passing." Edna placed a hand on Sarah's arm. "You really should come over our way more and visit."

Or you and Nyda could make the effort to come over to my cabin. Sarah knew her cabin was out of the way, and was smaller than either of her sister wives' houses, so the responsibility fell upon her shoulders to come into town and pay the visits if any contact was to be made. But honestly, she hadn't felt a need to do so. Besides, she'd been too busy. "Yes, I really should. With Clara gone now, I'm sure I will," she said with hesitation. Calling on her sister wives usually brought with it unwanted scrutiny.

"You be certain to do that, dear. Once Cleon goes away to school after the wedding, you shall be all alone in that little cabin of yours. It's a shame you didn't have more children."

Sarah merely smiled in response. She'd never felt affection toward Jacob. He most likely sensed that—he rarely shared her bed. Not at all after he'd given her two children. It was like he'd made sure she had the love and companionship of her own children to make her happy so he could then slip into the background of her life. She appreciated Jacob for that. Her life *was* her children, but now they were both gone—Clara to marriage, Cleon off to Provo to attend the Brigham Young Academy thanks to some money Jacob had tucked away for this very purpose.

Edna ladled herself a glass of Sarah's punch and took a drink. "Very tasty. Everyone will love it." She drank it down and held on to it. "I'll run and wash this out, then I need to help Nyda with the baked goods. You enjoy the rest of this day, mother of the bride." She winked at Sarah with her good eye and scurried inside the house.

Sarah served herself a portion of punch and then peered over the glass of apricot nectar at Clara as she emerged in the backyard with her new husband in hand. That morning, Sarah's eighteen-year-old daughter had married her childhood sweetheart. Sarah's heart swelled with gladness. James was a local boy, third son of Bishop Smoot and his second wife. Clara certainly made a beautiful bride. *Yes, I will enjoy this day.*

"Mother," Clara called out, glancing from one side of the backyard to the other. "Everything looks wonderful." She broke into a run, pulling James across the lawn with her. The hem of the wedding dress Sarah had made for her ruffled gracefully in the breeze. Once she made it to the picnic table, she pulled Sarah into a hug. "Thank you so much, Mother. This day just keeps getting better and better."

"Oh, really?" Sarah sensed that Clara had more to say.

"Yes! After the ceremony, James's father pulled us both aside. Guess what he said?"

"What?"

"James has been given a small acreage several miles west of town. Imagine that—a place all our own, where we can build a life together, just the two of us. And of course any children who may come along," Clara added with a touch of pink blushing her face.

"Several miles west of town, you say?" Sarah grabbed the table to steady herself. "That's wonderful," she managed to say, truly happy for her daughter.

"I just had to tell you." Clara squeezed Sarah's hand. "I've got to run, though, and greet all our guests now." She swept her hand toward the people filtering into the backyard.

Sarah took another sip of her nectar as Clara rushed off, dragging her new husband behind her. She looked at the influx of well-wishers one by one, knowing for the most part these people enjoyed living the law of polygamy. Sarah had not. She let out a sigh of relief. Just last month, the prophet had issued a manifesto officially banning any further plural marriage in the Mormon Church. Clara would have James to herself. The very idea filled Sarah's chest with happiness.

Tears gathered in her eyes. She tried not to think about the bitter side of those tears—this was after all, Clara's day, a day to celebrate her daughter having been wed to the young man of her choice. But Edna was right. After tomorrow when Cleon went off to school, she'd be alone. And she doubted a visit to either of her sister wives would fill the emptiness.

Chapter 4

December 1890

Cass dreaded leaving the mild winter weather of Dandy Crossing and venturing way up to Salt Lake City this time of year, but he saw no way around it.

John furrowed his brow as Cass mounted up. "You wouldn't be making this trip up north right now if it wasn't for that blasted Adolph Kohler."

"I know, I know," Cass said in total agreement. "That *neighbor* of ours has been like a boil on my butt ever since he's horned in on our gold."

John kicked at the dirt. "He even dares call his digs upstream a city. Crescent City." He laughed out loud, his voice echoing off the walls of red sandstone. "The mouth of Crescent Creek ain't worth the trouble of a name."

"Hey, we've at least got a post office and a store. And we've built two new cabins this year alone." Cass held out his hand, indicating the town of Hite. "You know what burns my butt, along with that big boil Kohler's made grow there?" Cass's gut churned at the disastrous possibilities that lay ahead. The Colorado River Placer Mining Company was sure to run into problems if he didn't nip this in the bud. "That maggot of a man has gone and named his operation the Colorado River and Utah Placer Company."

"How come you never told me this before now?" John handed Cass a bag of jerky.

"I told you the other day, when I first mentioned Kohler. You obviously weren't listening." Cass stuffed the jerky into his saddle-bag.

"Hey, I was busy sorting the mail—I just thought you were talking about our company."

"See, you can barely tell the difference." Cass's gut soured again at the thought. "His stinkin' company sounds practically the same as ours," he spat out his words as he pulled the reins and maneuvered out of the corral. "I best be on my way."

He kicked his heels into his horse and took off toward the ferry. "And that's why I'm takin' you on a trip this blasted time of year," he said to Gold Dust, giving her a pat.

The wind increased as Cass climbed the switchbacks cut into the gorge. He turned up the collar of his coat to cover his neck, wishing he could shield himself from his fears as easily. Kohler would surely horn in on the limited number of investors who were out there. With a title that sounded so similar to his company, Cass guessed Kohler was attempting to take advantage of the success and good name Cass had already established. "But not if I can help it, Goldie."

Unfortunately, as of late, the gold they were finding was not enough to pay the investors they had. "Blast it all, Goldie, the gold's hard to capture. Fine as flour, it is." The only way to increase production was to hire more crews and install more machinery. "That'd take more money." The last few months, they'd had to find new investors to help foot this bill—and pay the old investors. "Me and John can't afford to let Kohler make things any harder."

Once Cass made it out of the canyon, the wind beat at him as if Kohler himself controlled the elements. Thankfully, the air held a measure of warmth absorbed from the sunbaked sandstone and barren red soil. But as he expected, the farther and farther they traveled from the Colorado River gorge, the temperature grew colder and colder.

By the time they reached the point in the trail where he knew Hanksville lay just over the rise of the sagebrush-lined crag, the sun had long set, and he had only the gray of twilight to help him find his way to his usual camping spot.

"Blasted December sun," Cass mumbled to Gold Dust as they passed the Hanksville cemetery in near darkness. "Don't it know we need it to hang up there in the sky just as long as if it were May?"

May. Cass's mind reached back to that day in May two and a half years ago. He'd been letting Gold Dust graze on this very spot while he'd watched a Mormon funeral. A smile pulled at his lips as he remembered how one of the dead man's wives had actually talked to him—and polite-like, too. She was a right handsome woman, as pretty as the other wife was homely. Not that any of that mattered. The woman was merely a pleasant memory, a beautiful face to dream about from time to time when that niggling longing for companionship reared its pestering head.

He shook the image from his thoughts and concentrated on keeping to the trail in the growing darkness and increasing wind.

By the time Cass made it to his familiar spot along Muddy Creek, he had to depend on moonlight to help him set up camp. He staked two corners of his square of canvas into the hard ground and stretched the other end of his makeshift tent up the side of an outcropping of rock. There he tied each corner to the sagebrush growing from the wall as if the stone face was garden soil.

Rain mixed in with the wind and soon poured from the night sky. Cass struggled in the darkness to remove Gold Dust's saddle, slipping and falling to the ground more times than he cared to count. By the time he got the saddle tucked beneath his canvas shelter, rain poured off his hat in a solid stream. Water ran down his back, soaking through his coat and trousers.

Cass blew out a breath of frustration. Building a fire would be nigh to impossible at this point, nor could he change out of his filthy clothes—his spare set would be just as soaked. "Quit your dreaming about something you can't have," he said to himself and climbed into his damp bedroll. As he tried to get comfortable and fall asleep with chattering teeth, his mind drifted to another dream he couldn't have.

The face of that blond haired polygamist widow filled his thoughts.

"Don't mind if I do," he said to himself, indulging in the memory. He was cold and exhausted, without a fire or dry clothes. He needed something pleasant to dwell upon.

***

Cass awoke to three inches of snow covering his tent. At least it had stopped falling, and blue now filled the sky. He welcomed the sun. Its light penetrated his damp, filthy clothing and somewhat dispelled the chill that lingered clear down to his bones.

By the time Cass made it to Green River that evening, the chill and chattering teeth continued to plague him. He immediately took Gold Dust to the livery stable and headed to the Palmer House. The saloons held little appeal at the moment compared to the warmth of a fire and a dry bed.

"Give me your best room," Cass said to Ma Palmer the moment he stepped into the hotel. "One with its own fireplace. And bring me up a tub."

Ma Palmer straightened her back, extending her large frame and ample bosoms even farther. "Land of Goshen! Is that you, Mr. Cass Hite?"

"Sure enough."

"You look like something the cat drug in." Ma Palmer wagged a hand toward the stairs. "Head up to room three. I'll have my boy up there in a minute to start you a fire. Then he'll fetch you a tub and some hot water."

"Much obliged." Cass tipped his hat, and then hefted his saddle with his belongings onto his back and hurried up the stairs.

Cass had barely stripped down to his long johns when a timid knock came at his door. He cracked the door open and peeked out into the hall.

A boy about thirteen or fourteen years of age with messy hair stood there with each arm loaded with wood. A box of matches poked out of his shirt pocket. He tilted his head as if to get a better view of either Cass or the room. "I'm here to build ya a fire, sir."

"Hallelujah." Cass opened the door all the way.

The boy stepped inside the room and went straight to work.

Once healthy flames licked the interior of the fireplace on all sides, he turned to Cass. "So, you're a gold miner?" The boy's eyes widened with noticeable awe. "What's it like, livin' way out there on that big river, finding gold that's just sittin' there in the sand?"

"Well, it's not all that glamorous." Cass draped his spare set of clothes over a chair placed next to the fire. "It's a lot of work, and sometimes the sand offers nothing." He rubbed his arms to get the warmth moving through him. "And sometimes you get really cold."

"Then why do you do it?" The boy's voice rang with curiosity.

"I guess it's in my blood. My pa was a miner. I grew up in the gold fields of California after the big rush of forty-nine."

"So, is your son goin' to be a gold miner too?"

Something squeezed Cass's heart to where it pained him worse than the stubborn chill that refused to leave. "I don't have any children." He plastered a smile on his face to lighten things up. "Maybe that's 'cause I don't have a wife." It didn't help—at least as far as the emptiness that resurfaced in his heart.

The boy must not have had a clue of Cass's pain because he smiled back. "Why, a man like you, with all your gold. I heard you even have your own minin' company? You should be able to find a wife real easy like."

"Well, thank you, boy. Unfortunately, down where I'm from, a good woman is about as hard to find as a good tree." Cass gathered his dirty clothes and handed them to the boy. "Hurry along and fetch me my bath. While you're at it, take these to your ma and have her wash them. I'll send the long-johns I'm wearing down with you after I'm in the tub. I'm willing to pay what it takes," he added, figuring his hard-earned money might as well bring him some comfort right now.

After a warm bath and donning dry long johns, Cass crawled between a set of sheets that smelled of fresh air, figuring he'd sleep like a bear in winter. Mere seconds after he'd nodded off, an annoying tickle arose in his throat and demanded that he cough.

He coughed all night, leaving him exhausted in the morning. He dragged his feet into the dining room, but still wolfed down his breakfast of sausage and eggs. At least his appetite remained healthy. He left his saddle and bedroll in the care of Ma Palmer, taking the saddlebags and the clothes she'd cleaned for him and hurried off to the train station.

The clickety-clack of the train's wheels on the track lulled Cass to sleep now and again. Thankfully, his cough didn't plague him so bad when he sat up. He made it to Salt Lake City by mid-afternoon. Figuring he still had some daylight, he headed straight for the general land office where he'd applied for the mining claim for the Colorado River Placer Mining Company over two years earlier.

Dodging mud puddles, he crossed the street that ran in front of the train station and then headed toward the heart of town. Wind chilled the air. Cass cinched his coat tight at the neck, grateful that at least he was dry. But breathing in the cold air aggravated his throat. A fit of coughing ensued. He leaned against a building until it passed. This round of coughing felt different, deeper in his chest.

A few blocks farther on, he located the gray granite building he was looking for and stepped inside. He took the stairs to the third floor, wondering all the while why a measly three flights of stairs left him winded when he could shovel a mountain's worth of dirt through a sluice all day back home without breathing hard. After a moment to catch his breath, he barreled through the door marked General Land Office, determined to set things straight before they closed in half an hour. Then he was going to enjoy a night on the town.

"I'm Cass Hite, and I need to speak with Mr. Perry," he said to a young lady with her hair piled high who was sitting behind the front desk. "It's urgent."

The young lady stood. "Yes, Mr. Hite. Let me see what I can do." She slipped into a rear office and then returned shortly. "Mr. Perry says he will speak to you." She motioned for Cass to enter the back office.

Cass stepped over to the big desk and the big man sitting behind it. He shook Mr. Perry's hand and sat down in the chair offered him. "I'll cut right to the quick, Mr. Perry. Two years ago, I came all the way up here to Salt Lake City to fill my mining claim rather than taking my chances of having it done right back down in San Juan County. You were the very person who helped me set up the Colorado River Placer Mining Company all official like." Cass pulled his documentation from his pocket and placed it in front of Mr. Perry.

"Yes, I daresay I remember that day, Mr. Hite." Mr. Perry shifted his weight in his chair. "So, what can I do for you this cold winter day? Are you wanting to stake another claim?"

Cass wished. Wished he could have staked a second claim five miles upriver two years ago as well, but he hadn't had the money then. "No, sir. But I want to file a complaint and ask that you require a certain mining company that operates next to mine to change their name."

"Oh, really now?" Mr. Perry leaned back in his chair, a faint smile detectable behind his moustache.

"Yes." Cass wanted to wipe that grin off the man's face—this was nothing to smile about. "A Mr. Adolf Kohler had the gall to name his operation the Colorado River and Utah Placer Company."

"Yes, I do remember seeing that claim come through here this past year from San Juan County. For a moment, I thought it was you and your brother filing another claim until I read a little further. I did find it interesting that Mr. Kohler chose a name so similar to yours." Mr. Perry scratched his bald head. "But the man has every right to name his company whatever he wants, as long as it's not the same as someone else's."

Cass pounded the desk with his fist. "But even you admitted you thought he was us—I mean, you thought his name was the same as ours. Don't you see the problem here? Investors are likely to do the same as you and confuse the two companies. And then they'll invest in Mr. Kohler's company when they meant to invest in ours. Blast it all! There's got to be some kind of law that says Mr. Kohler can't go and give his company a name that sounds so close to ours."

"Unfortunately, Mr. Hite, there is no such law."

"Surely there's something you can do to help me fix this problem."

"Sorry, there is not." Mr. Perry stood and removed a coat and hat from a set of hooks behind his desk. "Now if you'll excuse me, Mr. Hite, it's quitting time. I want to get home before another storm blows in." He motioned with his hand for Cass to exit before him.

Cass hurried out of the office and stomped down the stairwell in front of Mr. Perry. He didn't feel like continuing the conversation anyway. He didn't feel like doing anything—except maybe finding a good place to get a big shot of whiskey.

A gust of cold air blew down Cass's neck as he stepped outside. He buttoned up his coat and plowed into the wind. He headed to the stockade district on the west end of town where the measly selection of the city's saloons existed. "Blasted Mormons!" He would have liked to buy himself a good drink just around the corner—like he could have if he'd been in any normal city—but now he had to walk several blocks.

By the time Cass made it to his favorite place in the city to get a drink and best of all, mingle with his big-city friends and potential investors, his cough had returned. He stepped up to the bar and leaned on it for support.

"What'll you have?" asked the bartender.

"A glass of your best whiskey." Cass looked around for a place to sit down. Normally he could stand all night at that bar, but right now his legs felt as though they'd give out at any minute. At a table tucked in the corner sat Curly and Tom, two of his old friends. The table had an empty chair.

"I'll just take my drink and sit over there." He slapped a few coins onto the bar, grabbed the glass as soon as the bartender had filled it, and headed for the table. A fit of coughing hit as he walked across the floor, causing him to spill part of his drink. He downed what little remained. The burn felt good going down his throat and seemed to calm the cough. He turned back to the bar and pointed to the bottle still in the bartender's hand. "Blasted cough. Just give me the whole thing." He slapped down some more money, took the whiskey, and dragged himself over to his friends' table.

Curly, whose moustache had to be at least twice the size of Cass's and a lighter shade of brown, looked up as Cass approached. "Well, if it isn't our gold-mining friend from down south. What brings you up into the Arctic Circle this time of year?"

Cass dropped into the empty chair. "Business." He didn't feel like going into the details of his meeting with Mr. Perry. He poured himself another shot—he didn't feel like doing much else than soothe his unsettled cough and nerves.

Tom cocked his head to one side and stared at Cass. "Buddy, you look terrible. Did you get hold of some bad booze or something?"

"Naw, I'm just coming down with a blasted cold." Cass held up his filled shot glass. "I'm hoping I can drown my cough with this."

***

After an hour spent in the company of good friends and enough booze to lighten anyone's spirits, Cass expected to feel better than he did. He downed the whiskey in his glass only to have a coughing fit worse than any he'd had all day. "What the blazes!" He filled the shot glass. He was ready to lift it to his mouth when city friend,

Curly, clamped a hand over his.

"Hold it there, Cass." Curly looked Cass in the eye. "I don't think another drink's what you're needin' right now."

"How do you know what I'm needing?"

Curly let go of Cass's hand. "For one thing, you're burnin' up."

After several minutes of arguing, Cass was too exhausted to resist further. He relented and let his friend take him to the hospital.

"The beginnings of pneumonia," the doctor announced after a thorough late-night exam. "The best thing right now is for you to get some sleep and stick to this bed for a few days." He tapped the painted-white wrought-iron bed frame that held Cass prisoner.

As soon as the doctor left, a nurse dressed all in white stepped into the room. In Cass's foggy state of mind, for a second he'd thought he'd died and was seeing an angel. Then he realized angels wouldn't be carrying trays with a pitcher of water or an empty glass splotched with hard water spots. She placed the tray on the stand next to Cass's bed. She poured him some water and handed it to him, along with a little white pill. "Now you take this and drink some water. I'll check back from time to time to see if you need anything. In the meantime, you need to get some sleep like the doctor ordered."

Cass didn't fight. He took the pill, drank all the water, and gratefully drifted off to sleep.

***

After two days in that hospital bed, Cass'd had enough of nurses poking and prodding him like he was a head of cattle. And to try to have a conversation with one of those ladies in the white dresses . . . holy tarnation, he might as well talk to the wall. "Nurses . . . their small talk is about as colorful as their dresses," he said to the man in the bed next to him.

The door to his room swung open and the snootiest of the nurses out of the three who had attended to him walked into the room.

"There are two gentlemen outside who wish to visit you," the nurse said in a business-like voice. "Technically, it is not visiting hours for another thirty minutes. But if you're feeling up to having visitors, Mr. Hite, I could make an exception and let them in."

Cass noticed the door crack open and then saw a sliver of Curly's face. "Can't think of anything I'd like more at the minute." He motioned for Curly and his other friend, Tom, to enter, thinking maybe that stiff nurse wasn't so bad after all.

"You're lookin' better," Curly said the moment he came through the door.

"Must be 'cause I'm feeling a heap better."

Tom followed one step behind Curly. "Is there anything we can get for you?"

"Yeah, get me out of here." Cass looked at the window, noticing yet another round of snow falling from the sky. "I've had enough lying around in this hospital bed. I'm ready to get back home to Dandy Crossing where it hardly ever snows. That's all I need—some good warm sunshine." He looked at the nurse. "Not all your poking and prodding, and watered-down beef broth you call soup. No offense intended. Now, can you fetch me my clothes? I'm going to have my friends here take me to the train station."

"Heavens, no." She brought her hand to her cheek. "I can't let you go without the doctor releasing you—and he's indisposed at the moment."

"Well then, I'll just go in this ugly robe you've put me in." Cass swung his feet out, let them fall to the floor, and motioned to his friends to help him stand.

Curly patted the gun hanging around his waist. "And if you don't let us take him, we might just have to resort to means that could likely be unpleasant."

Cass smiled, knowing his friend was merely teasing the lady.

"Okay, okay." The nurse sighed and reluctantly pulled Cass's belongings from a closet in the room. She gave them to him, wincing slightly as she handled his gun and holster. "I suppose we can't really keep you here against your will—this is not a prison. But please, Mr. Hite, be careful. Your pneumonia is not totally cured."

Cass stood. "Where do I pay my bill?"

An hour later, Cass boarded the train to Green River. He tried to get comfortable in his seat at the back of the Pullman car, chilled though wrapped in his big wool coat. The train made a stop in Provo, then Colton, Helper, and Price. By the time the eastbound iron zephyr rolled into Green River, it was almost dark. Cass checked in at the Palmer House and went right to bed. Who'd have thought a train ride could be so exhausting?

The next morning, Cass could hardly get out of bed. He could feel fluid gathering in his lungs again. He struggled into his clothes, gathered his belongings, and crept down the stairs. His head felt so light, he was afraid he'd stumble if he wasn't careful. He caught sight of a man in a hotel uniform and figured he'd better get some help. The way he felt, he'd never make it home riding Gold Dust.

"Hey, you, porter." Cass struggled for a good breath so he could continue. "Do you know anyone who'd be willing to drive me down to Dandy Crossing?" He wasn't sure what day it was, but he knew it wasn't Thursday, and the Green River stage only ran on Thursdays. He needed the warm weather and fresh air of Hite to get feeling like his old self, and John to help patch him up.

"Let me see what I can do." The porter slipped outside.

Cass dropped into a bench at the front of the hotel, grateful the snowstorm had stayed up north.

The porter returned shortly with a teenage boy. "This young feller says he can drive you home. He's got a rented buggy and a horse tied up out front."

"So it'll cost you a dollar extra," the boy spoke up.

"Fine." Cass looked at the boy, blinking to try to steady his vision. "Don't I know you?"

"Yessir." The boy hitched a thumb beneath his overalls strap. "Sometimes I shine shoes at the railroad depot. I'm tryin' to save money to buy myself a horse so I can get outta this town."

"You gotta name?" Cass asked.

"Yeah, but I don't care for it much. Folks usually call me Chip."

"Okay, Chip, I'll give you four dollars to take me to Dandy Crossing," Cass said. "That'll help you buy that horse."

The boy scratched his head. "Dandy Crossing? Say, you're one of those Hite brothers pannin' for gold down on the Colorado, aren't you?"

"Yep." Cass's head ached, and he didn't feel much like talking.

"It's a ways to Dandy Crossing. To go down there and back'll take four, maybe five days." Chip wrinkled his brow as he looked Cass in the eye. "Make it five and I'll do it."

Cass was too sick to argue at the high price. "Done."

Within minutes, Chip had Cass and his things loaded into the buggy, along with the boy's camping supplies. On the way out of town, they stopped by the livery stable to pick up Gold Dust and tether her to the back of the buggy.

"I used to live in Hanksville, then my ma moved me up here after my pa died," Chip said as they left town. "I wanna keep heading farther north, whether Ma goes with me or not. I'm sick of small towns." He flicked the reins, and the horse pulled the buggy faster. "I wanna live where there's people . . . and plenty to do . . . and ways to make money . . ."

Chip kept on going mile after mile, yakking away about anything and nothing at the same time. After an hour or so with the boy, Cass's head spun more than ever. He clung tightly to the handrail as the buggy bounced over the rocks.

They stopped at the San Rafael River and watered the horses, then followed the rough road south along the bottom of the San Rafael Reef. Several miles down the road, near Old Woman Wash, Chip turned aside to miss a hole in the road. The wagon plowed off the trail, bumping over mounds of dirt, then burying its wheels in a sand dune and jerking to an abrupt stop.

The kid jumped out and looked at the buggy. "We'd better unload everything if we're goin' have a ghost of chance to pull ourselves out."

Cass stood carefully and stepped out of the wagon. The ground started spinning, and he felt all balance leave him. In an instant, the sand dune seemed to rise up and meet his face. Hard.

Chapter 5

Sarah rubbed her eyes. She knew she shouldn't read by lamplight for such long stretches at a time, but so far, books had proven the best way to fill her lonely evenings ever since Clara and Cleon moved out.

A knock at the door brought Sarah's attention up from the page to the clock on the fireplace mantel. *7:10*. Long past sunset, the December darkness made it feel later than it actually was. The knock came again. "Coming," she hollered, wondering who'd be visiting at this time of evening. Ten more minutes of reading and she'd have tucked her book away and donned her nightgown. Before unlatching the lock, she moved her mouth close to the door and called out, "Who's there?"

"It's Bishop Smoot and Brother Reed. We need your help."

Sarah opened the door. Enough lamplight spilled from the cabin to see her short, elderly bishop and his equally short first counselor on each side of a taller man, whose arms were slung around their shoulders. The tall man's body appeared limp, and his head drooped. It soon became obvious that the bishop and Brother Reed were totally supporting the man's body weight. "Oh, dear," she said, wondering why they were bringing her the lifeless body of a complete stranger.

"May we come in? Put him down?" Bishop Smoot pointed with his chin toward Cleon's bed still tucked in the corner.

"Of course." Sarah opened the door all the way and swept her arm toward the bed she'd never had the heart to remove, even though the extra space would be welcome. Clara's bed still remained there in the opposite corner of the front room, also with hopes that her children, on occasion, would come home for a visit.

A teenage boy followed the men into the cabin, hefting a stuffed set of saddlebags. In the dim light it was hard to tell, but she swore he was Nyda's grandson, Chip. She wasn't sure, though—she hadn't seen him for a while.

"Don't go and get all upset at me, Aunt Sarah," the boy spoke up. "But I'm the one who suggested they come here."

"What's going on?" In a dither, Sarah looked from Chip to Brother Reed to the bishop.

Bishop Smoot lowered the lifeless body onto Cleon's bed and turned to Sarah. "Young Hezekiah here brought this fellow to us about an hour ago. Said the man paid him to take him on south to Dandy Crossing."

"But over by Old Woman Wash, the man up and passed out," Chip cut in. He deposited the saddle-bags at the foot of the bed as he continued. "I brought him to the bishop and begged him to give Mr. Hite a blessing and beg the Good Lord not to let him die 'cause if I were to return him back home dead and all, his brother woulda killed me."

Sarah looked at the bishop. "So, did you give him a blessing?"

"Yeah, me and Brother Reed did about a half an hour ago."

Brother Reed remained at the man's bedside, removing the boots from the lifeless body. "He's doing a tad better since then," he said. "At least he's stirred from time to time."

"But why bring him here?" Sarah pushed strands of hair from her eyes, trying to make sense of it all as she stared at the limp figure filling her son's bed.

"The Lord has spared this man's life, but He's leaving the nursing in our hands." The bishop rubbed his forehead. "I've got no extra beds at my place—and my wives' hands are already full."

"I'm afraid I'm in the same position," Brother Reed added. "And we asked around, you know, to those women folk who have a knack for nursing. None had room either."

Sarah imagined it was less an issue of lack of room in their houses as it was a lack of room in their busy lives for a rough-looking stranger who smelled of alcohol and tobacco.

Chip stepped forward. "That's why I told 'em to

bring him here." Though shadowed, the boy's face beamed, as if his idea had been a stroke of brilliance. "I knew you was alone, had an extra bed, and time on your hands."

"How'd you—?"

"Grandma's told my ma all about you, how you're wastin' away all by yourself, holed up in your cabin, not tryin' to find yourself another husband or even comin' into town to pay her a visit."

"Oh, really now?" Sarah needed to do something to distract her so as to not get her dander up. She stepped over to the unconscious man and felt his forehead, wondering how many other people Nyda had shared her personal business with. "He's burning up," she muttered and reached in her pocket for her handkerchief. She wiped the sweat from his hot skin and then rushed to the sink to pump some water into a bowl.

"The boy seemed to think you were the perfect choice to tend to the poor fellow." Bishop Smoot moved to the bedside and stared down at the disheveled stranger. "And I have to say, I agree with him." He picked up the man's arm that had fallen over the side of the bed and tucked it back in place at his side. "And not just because you have the room and the time, but because of your kind heart."

Chip stepped out from behind Brother Reed. "Yeah, I told them you wouldn't care none that he wasn't a church-going person and was a coarse-tongued gold miner. That you wouldn't turn your nose up at him like a good lot of folks would."

Sarah scurried back to the bed, motioning the

bishop out of her way with a sloshing bowl of water. "Well, thank you, Chip. That's very kind of you to say." She dipped a rag into the cold water, wrung it out, and placed it on the man's forehead.

"You realize, Sister Hansen, that what we're asking here is just not for tonight." The bishop readjusted his hat. "This fellow is going to need tending to for quite some time—weeks, most likely. Of course we'll send a girl over in the evening, and in the day if you need, to help and . . ." He cleared his throat. "Keep things, uh, proper. Still, that's a lot to require of you. So if you don't feel comfortable accepting this task, feel free to say no. Taking on this burden is entirely your choice."

"Who would do it *if* I did decline?" Sarah felt in a quandary. She didn't like the thought of the stranger having no one to take care of him, but tending a lone man in her cabin could set tongues to wagging.

"I don't rightly know."

"I was just curious." Sarah appreciated the bishop immensely for asking her what she wanted to do, not deciding for her and telling her what she *would* be doing. She looked at the unconscious man lying there, his hair matted with the perspiration on his forehead and the only movement he made was heaving his chest. She leaned over and placed her ear against his rib cage. A crackling sound could be heard as he exhaled, confirming her fear and the bishop's words. His lungs were full of liquid, and he would need a lot of care if he was to have any hope of surviving.

"I'll do it," Sarah said with conviction, feeling a

sense of satisfaction at having decided for herself. "I'll nurse this man back to health, God willing."

"God bless you, Sister Hansen." Bishop Smoot reached out and shook Sarah's hand after she straightened back up.

Brother Reed then extended his hand. "Tell Mr. Hite when he wakes up that I've got his horse in my corral, and I'll take care of the animal until he's well enough to ride back home."

"What about tonight?" she asked, latching onto a kitchen chair. "Have you arranged for someone to come and be with the two of us?" She indicated herself and her patient with a sweep of her hand as she carried the chair over to the bedside, where she'd likely be spending the remainder of the night.

"Uh . . . no." The bishop looked at the floor.

"I'll be glad to stay here tonight." Chip plopped onto Clara's old bed. "But tomorrow I'd better head down to Dandy Crossin' and tell Mr. Hite's brother that it'll be some time before Cass'll be able to come back down there. One of Ma's sisters'll be glad to stay with you, I reckon."

"Thank you, son." Bishop Smoot nodded at Chip with a look of relief and headed for the door.

After the bishop and his counselor left and Chip fell asleep in Clara's bed, Sarah settled into the chair she'd placed at the bedside of the stranger. She re-wetted the rag, cooling it down, and placed it on his forehead, thinking perhaps it would be best if she quit thinking of him as a stranger, but as Mr. Hite. After all, she would be spending an awful lot of time with him over the coming weeks. Likely, he wouldn't remain as a "stranger" for long. She stared at his face, thinking there *was* something familiar about it. A fleeting idea pulled up the corners of her mouth.

Maybe this poor man was not a stranger after all. Not that meeting him two years ago and speaking with him briefly after Jacob's funeral constituted him as an acquaintance, but she swore this was the same man. The one who'd proven to be anything but the man with no manners, conscience, or respect that Edna had said he was. She'd not given him another thought since that afternoon, but she had enjoyed the moment. His eyes had pulled her in, and she couldn't deny she'd found him pleasant to gaze upon back then.

He looked much different now.

Poor fellow.

Chapter 6

Cass heard someone humming. The tune sounded pleasant, as did the voice, but unfamiliar, almost like something one would hear coming out of a church. That ruled out John. But then whose voice was he hearing? And why were his eyes shut? Was he dreaming? He struggled to open his eyes. A wave of pain hit his chest and spread throughout his body.

What in blazes!

From what he could see, he was lying on a bed tucked in the corner of a humble, yet tidy log cabin with lacy curtains covering the two front windows. *I'm definitely not in Hite.* A stove sat in the middle of the room. It held a pot on its cooktop. Steam billowed from beneath its lid, and Cass could feel a portion of the warmth wafting his way. It felt good, but he wanted more. He was cold. Freezing cold. And nauseated. And felt downright lousy, like he'd been trampled by a stampede of cattle and the dang animals hadn't had the decency to finish him off but to leave him in a mangled heap out in the cold to die a slow death.

What happened to me? Where am I?

Memories came rushing back. He recalled making the trip to Salt Lake, his short stay in the hospital, and then bits and pieces of his difficult journey back home. Getting stuck in the sand by Old Woman Wash was the last thing he remembered—oh, yeah, and getting dizzy. He'd obviously passed out. That answered the first question, but not the second one.

The pleasant humming resumed. It sounded female and seemed to be coming from an opened door that led to a second room in the cabin. Whoever was in that room, humming, he guessed to be the person taking care of him. He wanted to sit up, holler to her to come out of that room and show her face so he could thank her properly, but he had no strength to do so. He found he couldn't even form the words—or at least give them any volume. A moan was all he could manage.

The face belonging to the humming immediately poked into the main room. It belonged to a very handsome woman. *It's her.*

"You're awake!" She rushed toward Cass, her eyes heavy with exhaustion, yet bright with relief.

Cass watched in disbelief as she approached. Her fluid movements made her appear to be floating toward him, as if she were flying, like an angel. She certainly looked like an angel, with that face still as beautiful as he'd remembered—and dwelt upon during patches of loneliness. For a second, he wondered if he'd died and gone to heaven, but he knew that couldn't be the case. He felt like hell.

She sat down in a chair that had been set at the head of his bed and then placed her hand on his forehead. "Your fever's down, but you're shivering. Are you cold?"

Cass managed a nod.

She darted to another bed on the opposite wall, grabbed its blanket, and ran back. "I thought we were going to lose you there for a moment or two—or three or four."

As she spread the blanket across Cass's body, he relished its warmth. Any other day, he would have relished her attention, the way she gently pulled the blanket up and tucked it around his neck and smoothed it out to make sure every speck of his body was covered, but not today. "Thirsty," he managed to squeak out.

"Of course." She slid her arm behind his back and helped him sit slightly as she brought a cup to his lips.

Cass took a sip. It tasted of warm milk and felt good going down. He took another, longer sip.

"Good, good." She nodded at him, encouraging him to take more. "I hope you don't mind milk, but I had it handy here every day, hoping you'd drink something, and thinking I could at least get some kind of nourishment down you."

Every day? How long had he been out? He pushed the glass away, having had enough for the moment, and met her eyes with his. He mustered some strength. "How long have I been here?" he asked.

She set the glass down on a small table on the other side of her chair. "The bishop brought you here three nights ago."

"Three nights?" Cass's mind reeled. "I guess . . . I was sicker . . . than I thought."

"You were, and you still are, Mr. Hite."

"Bishop?" Cass lifted an eyebrow, hoping this angel who was taking care of him could read his confusion and he wouldn't need to express it in any more words than he had to.

"It seems my nephew, Chip, was bringing you down to your place on the Colorado, and you passed out. He thought you were near dead, so he brought you to the bishop, hoping he could call down the grace of God to help you pull through." Her lips formed a timid smile, making her face all the more enjoyable. "Apparently, the Lord heard the bishop—you're still here."

Cass managed to lift his shaky hand enough to point at her. "Yeah, but why here . . . with you?" Maybe there *was* a god in heaven. And He actually loved Cass. Because that showed a whole heap of benevolence, sparing Cass's less-than-stellar life and then giving him *her* to take care of him.

"Bishop Smoot knew I had the room and the time to nurse you back to health." She picked the glass of milk back up and encouraged Cass to take another sip.

After dabbing his moustache with a cloth and then fluffing his pillow, she went on to tell him about how her two children had recently moved out and so she did have the time and space, as the bishop had indicated. Cass only half listened. He could feel his brain growing foggy once again. As his mind drifted from her story to the discomfort of his pain to a desire to let go of consciousness, it touched on the matter of his near demise. If it hadn't been for the graciousness of these Mormons, he'd surely be dead by now. Maybe he'd better think twice before he ever bad-mouthed them again.

***

Sarah poured a cup of oatmeal into the boiling water. The day before, Mr. Hite had eaten a full bowl of mush for breakfast, and she hoped he felt up to the same amount today. She also hoped he'd be up for some sort of bath. It'd been nearly two weeks since the bishop had brought Mr. Hite for her to tend, and she had yet to change his clothes. She kept hoping he'd gain enough strength to do it himself, but he was still not to that point.

Once it was done cooking, she dished up a bowl of oatmeal, added a drizzle of honey and cream, and took it over to Mr. Hite's bedside. "Time for your breakfast." She set it on the table momentarily while she helped him sit up.

He eyed the bowl. "Is that some of that mush you made yesterday?"

"Yes, it is." Sarah picked up the bowl of oatmeal.

"I don't think I've ever eaten anything tastier."

She wagged the spoon loaded with mush at him. "I can't imagine what kind of gruel you call food down there at Dandy Crossing if that's truly the case." She placed the spoon in his mouth and fed him its contents. Most likely he was up to feeding himself now, but she quite enjoyed the task. She pointed the emptied spoon at his stomach. "Or maybe having gone so long without keeping anything down, anything tastes good that stays there. I could probably feed you wallpaper paste and you'd say the same thing."

"Oh, isn't that what this is?" A twinkle lit his eyes. "I thought maybe you were fixing to put up some flowery paper to brighten up my day—help me heal faster and thus be shed of me faster—and you happened to spill a little honey and cream in there, so you decided to pawn it off on me."

Sarah pulled her face into a stern expression, though she felt quite the opposite. "Now you quit your teasing and let me feed you breakfast." Honestly, she wasn't that anxious to "be shed" of her patient. True, the past two weeks had been extremely difficult, both day and night applying poultices to break up the mucous in his lungs so he could breathe, constantly cooling his skin with cold rags to keep his reoccurring fever at bay, trying to keep food down him. But they had been some of the more rewarding days she'd ever had.

As Mr. Hite took his second bite, Sarah dozed off momentarily, then jerked herself back awake, dribbling oatmeal down his chin. She hurried and scraped off the spill with the spoon.

"I don't believe I've had food scraped from my chin since I was a babe on my ma's knee. What you trying to do, woman? Drum up memories to make me miss my departed mother and add to my pain?" he said with a wink.

His teasing always seemed to prompt a smile from her lips, and this moment was no different. "No, I'd never be so cruel. But now that you mention it, perhaps subconsciously I did spill your breakfast on purpose." She pointed to a splotch of mush that had dribbled down to his chest and onto the pair of filthy faded red underwear he'd been wearing since he'd arrived. "That's the final straw. Those long johns of yours have got to go."

"Oh, really now?" Merriment danced in his eyes, and his voice took on a heighten tone of teasing. "You want me to take them off, do you?" he asked, then broke into a fit of coughing.

"Uh . . . no, well . . . yes, but—oh, dear me." Sarah could feel heat flush her face. "What I meant was you need a bath awfully bad." She chewed on her lip. "This might prove somewhat difficult, and . . ."

Mr. Hite controlled his coughing and said, "Embarrassing?"

She nodded. Though flustered, she was amazed at how much easier she could speak with Mr. Hite about such delicate matters when with her own husband, such awkward situations had overwhelmed her with embarrassment. "Nevertheless, Mr. Hite, it's got to be done. It's not healthy for you to wear those any longer."

"I can't finish my breakfast first?" His mouth puckered into what appeared to be a forced pout.

Sarah couldn't tell for sure because his moustache hid a good portion of his mouth. "I meant after breakfast," she responded, holding back an urge to chuckle. "And I do believe that as long as I'll be assisting you with a sponge bath—mind you, I said *assisting* because I certainly can't do the whole thing—I might as well trim that rug you've grown on your upper lip."

Mr. Hite twirled one end of his moustache "What, you don't like it? I've worked long and hard to get this thing as big and bushy and annoying as it is."

She moved his hand out of the way and shoveled another bite into his mouth. "If you've got so much spunk today, I say it's time you start feeding yourself." She stuck the spoon in his hand.

While Mr. Hite fed himself, taking a break and a breather between every other bite, she warmed some water on the stove and sorted through his saddlebags to find him a clean pair of long johns. She would have liked to dress him in a full set of clothes, but she doubted that with all the recuperation he still required, they'd be comfortable enough. Plus, there was the issue of the bedpan. She pulled out a clean pair of the long underwear. As she did so, his wallet tumbled to the floor. When she reached down and picked it up, it fell open, revealing a wad of bills bigger than she'd ever seen together all at one time. She stifled a gasp and tucked the wallet back in the bags.

With the clean long johns draped over her shoulder, she collected the hot water and carried it over to his bedside. The impropriety of this all left Sarah very uncomfortable, and she wished Chip's sister Mary stayed during the day. She agreed only to spend the nights at Sarah's place once Chip had gone on his way. But seventeen-year-old Mary was soon to be married and she had a wedding dress to sew and a host of preparations to work on back at the big house during the day.

Mr. Hite struggled to lift the last spoon of mush into his mouth, making her feel bad. Perhaps he wasn't ready yet to feed himself. She moistened the rag and wiped off his mouth first. "All right, now on to the more difficult stuff." She set down the rag and began unbuttoning the top of his long johns. "Do you think you're up for this?"

He gave her a weary nod.

She peeled the filthy underwear from his upper body. As she helped him pull out of the sleeves, her hands touched his bare arms. They felt thick, well-muscled, obviously accustomed to a lot of hard work. Her fingers lingered on his skin momentarily. She jerked them away, as she did her eyes from his bare chest. She'd never seen a man without his shirt before now. Even Jacob's. The few times she'd shared his bed, it had been dark and he'd removed, or loosened, only what clothing was absolutely necessary to accomplish what was needed.

She concentrated on dipping her rag into the warm water and then wringing it out. And then wringing it out once again. Why had she found it pleasing to look at Mr. Hite's bare skin? This was all so wrong. She shouldn't be having such feelings churning around inside her chest and jumbling her mind.

Taking a deep breath, she set her mind on the task at hand. She'd given plenty of sponge baths when her young children had fallen ill and were unable to crawl into the tin tub by the stove. The process was the same, and there was work to be done. After she'd finished with his upper body, she moved to his feet.

"I feel as helpless as a two-legged dog," he said as she pulled the smelly socks from his feet.

It was the first he had spoken since she'd begun the washing process, and she wondered if he was growing exhausted. "Sorry, but you're going to have to become a little less helpless after I'm done down here." She gave his toes one last rub, a quick buff of the towel, and then set his clean underwear on the blanket still covering his legs. "Here you go. I'm going to step into my bedroom while you bathe the rest of yourself and then pull on your long johns as far as you can." *For sure at least as far as they are now.* "Holler when you're done—or you need me."

"Will do," he said with a tad more energy.

As she slipped into the bedroom, she hoped he would do all right without her. It was as clear as the cloudless but chilly blue sky out the front windows that he still needed her. She hesitated for a second in the doorway—was there enough wood in the stove? Did she need to stoke the fire so he wouldn't get cold? "Hold on, let me throw another log on the fire."

"Thank you," he said as she opened the door to the stove.

Yes, he needed her. Jacob had never needed her when he'd gotten sick. Nyda had always been his nurse. Her children, of course, had needed her when they fell ill. But that was so long ago.

Chapter 7

Cass settled onto the sofa as Mrs. Hansen washed up their breakfast dishes. It felt so nice to get out of that blasted bed and sit someplace else for a change. Just last week, he'd finally been able to put on a pair of trousers and a shirt. He had yet to put on his boots. That was okay—he didn't need them. His thick wool socks worked fine for the few times he'd crossed the hard-packed dirt floor. And he was in no hurry to put the boots on. That only meant he'd be going outside, and there were only two reasons he'd need to do that. First one would be to use the outdoor privy—which might be nice. He felt bad for Mrs. Hansen still having to empty his pot. The second reason—because he'd be heading for home.

He wasn't ready to go home. Granted, he'd taken advantage of Mrs. Hansen's hospitality and nursing for nigh onto four weeks now. But he also knew his strength still wasn't where it ought to be. Plus, and this was the bigger reason, he'd have to say goodbye to the woman who warmed his heart with her goodness and filled that lonely ache inside him each time she fluffed his pillow or made him breakfast. He wasn't ready to go back down to his empty, dirty, one-room cabin and never see her again, or hear that melodic humming or her laughter, or have her beautiful smile greet him each morning. In his younger days, he'd figured remaining single fit him best. That gray hair he'd pulled out of his head last month reminded him that old age approached. His fortieth birthday was around the corner. He didn't want to live alone anymore.

A knock sounded through the front door. Cass turned, ready to rise.

"Oh, no you don't, Mr. Hite." She pushed him back down into the cushions. "You're supposed to be resting. Do I need to put you back into that bed?"

"No, ma'am!" Cass smiled, gave her a mock salute, reveled in her concern, and settled back into the space he'd already warmed. "Whatever you say, Mrs. Hansen." He'd much prefer calling her by her given name. *Sarah.* Such a fitting name. *Lovely.* It's a shame he didn't dare use it. At least not out loud—she was much more refined than any woman he'd known, and he intended on treating her as such.

Another knock came and she hurried to the door. Cass leaned to one side to get a look at the person being ushered in out of the cold. An older woman dressed in black stood there with what appeared to be a loaf of bread in her hand. He took a deep breath and surmised it was bread—freshly baked bread that would taste so good. "Do the women around here ever wear anything besides black or gray?" he said to himself, wishing. By the palsy evident in her drooping eye, he assumed this woman must be Edna, the one who'd been with Sarah that day in the cemetery when he'd first seen her.

"Oh, Mr. Hite, this is Edna. I've mentioned her to you before." Sarah took the woman by the elbow and ushered her Cass's way. "She's brought us a loaf of fresh bread. Isn't that sweet of her?"

"Yes, it is." Cass looked at Edna and smiled. "Thank you, ma'am."

Edna set the bread on the table. "Well, I figure it's the least I can do, seeing that Sarah's done all the hard work. I mean, taking in a complete stranger and nursing him day and night for a month, investing all that time when she knows she'll never see hide nor hair of you once you return to . . . whatever it is you do down there on the Colorado."

"Who says she'll never see me again?" Cass came back a little too quickly. He couldn't help himself. It felt like a knife to his gut when she had spoken the words, even though they were most likely true.

"Of course she won't." Edna placed a limp hand on Sarah's wrist. "You two are from completely different worlds, worlds that don't mix."

Sarah seemed to bristle at her sister wife's words. She didn't say anything—only chewed on her lip.

"Really now," Cass said, struggling to maintain an even tone, unsure how to take the woman's comments.

"Well, I best be going, dear Sarah." Edna gave

Sarah a quick hug—one that held about as much affection as a lizard hugging a rock. She turned to Cass. "And it was nice meeting you, Mr. Hite. I hope you heal quickly."

So I can be on the road as soon as possible? He was certain that was what she really wanted to say.

Cass gave Edna a nod. "Thank you, ma'am," he said.

He wondered what Edna might think if she knew how Sarah had opened up to him over the last day or two. He thought back on how they carried on conversations late into the evening after her housework was done. She'd told him about her children, then about her sister wives and the husband they'd shared. He swore he'd detected a touch of sadness in her voice when she'd spoken of her marriage. Or was it loneliness? Or something else? His chest tightened into an uncomfortable knot—and not because of his passing illness. He wished he could hold her in his arms and give her the affection she deserved.

After Edna left, he looked up at Sarah. "I don't think your sister—whatever she is to you—likes me. But I'm mighty grateful to you for the way you've treated me." He patted the cushion next to him. "Sit down, take a load off. Now, please tell me the rest of the town don't feel the same way as her."

Sarah lowered herself onto the couch, seemingly glad for the chance to rest. "That's not true. I think she likes you just fine. And the rest of the town does too." She dipped her chin firmly. "You've been asleep most of the times they've come by. Folks have dropped in every other day or so to see how you're fairing, or to bring me a bottle of peaches or a slice or two of cake to help me out. The bishop's told them how you were nigh onto death. Of course they care. They're thrilled about your recovery. Edna's just being overprotective of me. That's all."

"Protecting you, eh? From what? The coyotes that howl in the distance at night?" he said in a joking tone, but he knew exactly what Edna was afraid of. The very same thing that'd been on Cass's mind not a minute or two earlier—wanting to take Sarah away from here.

"You know what I think?" Sarah turned and looked Cass in the eye.

Cass returned the gaze. *Good blazes, her eyes are beautiful.* "No, what do you think?" He leaned toward her. "That we should quit calling each other Mrs. Hansen and Mr. Hite?"

She smiled. "I think that before you head back to Dandy Crossing, after you're better, of course, you should come to church with me and thank the good people of Hanksville for their generosity. It would do you good."

Blast it all! He was finally getting close to her. She hadn't even shied away when he'd patted the couch for her to sit by him, or when he'd leaned into her a second ago. Now she had to go and bring up something he swore he'd never do—set foot in a church, a Mormon church at that.

Cass swallowed his pride. "I'll think about it." He leaned closer to her. He wasn't about to let this moment slip from him. "But for sure I'm wanting to thank the person who's done the most for me. The wonderful woman who did all the work, who saved me from dying."

He slipped his arm around her shoulders and pulled her close.

And kissed her full on the mouth.

She didn't resist, adding even more to the pleasure that erupted inside him, and if he had to guess, he would say she rather enjoyed it too. Her lips were soft and willing, stimulating emotions he never knew existed. He felt accepted, even admired and respected. The purest kiss he'd ever tasted. He'd had his share of women by the hour. They only filled one need and then left him feeling empty mere hours later. This was different. This was heaven. This was what he wanted.

Too soon, she pulled away and stared off to one side at the floor. "If you wish to call me Sarah, I'm all right with that."

***

Sarah jumped to her feet. Staring at the floor was not enough. She needed to be busy, to move away from Mr. Hite before she was tempted to let him kiss her again. Or should she say, Cass? Yes, she much preferred that to Mr. Hite. But to call him by his given name might not be wise for her. She could grow very accustomed to its sound, and want to use it more and more, and not want to let him go when he became well. "How about I slice us each a piece of this bread?" She carried the loaf over to where she kept her knives, basking in the heavenly feelings that coursed through her. She moved a dish rag aside to make room for the bread, reminding herself that the sink needed a scrubbing after they ate their bread.

She grabbed the rag. *No, I'll scrub it now.* If she were to sit back down next to him to eat, she'd most certainly think about that kiss once again. How wonderful it'd been—the feel of his lips against hers, and that of his hand pulling their bodies close, the excitement that pulsed through her veins with a wonderful feeling she'd never experienced before.

Chapter 8

Sarah pinned her hair in place on top of her head. With trembling hands, she smoothed out her dress while looking in the small mirror attached to the dresser in her bedroom. Cass had told her to wear her light gray dress, that it was his favorite. She couldn't believe he was actually coming to church with her that day. Surely a good many of the town would be shocked to see him there. Especially after he'd told Bishop Smoot in the early days of his recovery that he'd "never step foot inside a Mormon church."

But something about Cass had changed. He seemed a bit of a different man than he'd been two weeks ago.

Since he had first kissed her.

Had it been that kiss—and the four other kisses—that triggered the change? She allowed herself a moment to envision his affection for her and experience the warm feelings that daydream and his kisses always evoked.

"Are you almost ready?" she hollered through the closed door to her room.

"Almost. Blasted tie! Where'd you get this thing?"

"It was Jacob's."

"Figures. Okay, you can come out here now."

When Sarah stepped out of her room and saw Cass, she caught her breath. Dressed in the business clothes she'd washed and pressed, and with the haircut and moustache trim she'd given him, he gave her eyes reason to stare and her heart to beat faster. "You look very fine, Mr. Cass Hite."

"Cass," he corrected.

"Today you look like you deserve the respect of your full name."

"I just hope others will feel the same as you." He opened the door for her to leave. Once outside, he offered her his elbow. Together they walked toward town. January had a few days more before it slipped into February, and the air held the usual chill it did this time of year. Thankfully, the ground was dry, and Sarah didn't have to lift her skirt to keep it from the mud. She could keep both of her hands latched to Cass's arm. She much preferred that.

Sarah could hear the organ playing a half a block away from the church. Someone must be holding the door open to let the congregation in. She hoped they planned on closing it as soon as the meeting started. She didn't want to take a chance of Cass getting chilled once he sat down and quit moving. She'd hate for him to have a relapse. "Doesn't it sound lovely, the organ?" She gave Cass's arm the slightest bit of a squeeze.

"I like your humming better."

Sarah looked away, not wanting him to see her blush. Then again, was it so wrong to let him know that she loved the way he made her feel, like "she was worth her weight in gold dust," as he often said?

She let go of Cass's arm before they walked up the front steps of the tiny whitewashed chapel. She wasn't quite ready to let people know how she felt about Cass. There would be those who would frown on her being courted by a man outside the faith. She herself didn't feel comfortable with the idea. That was why her heart had practically danced a jig when he announced yesterday that he wanted to come to church with her before he headed back to Dandy Crossing and the town that bore his name. Also that he planned on taking several trips up to Green River in the coming months, and he'd for sure stop by to visit. He'd even spoke of building himself a cabin there in Hanksville so he'd not have to camp out by Muddy Creek and get himself sick again.

Yes, that sounded like he planned on courting her. And she planned on getting him to church, and eventually becoming a Mormon. The church had done away with polygamy, so what possible reason could he have against joining now?

Bishop Smoot met them on the doorstep and shook Cass's hand. "Well, well, if it isn't our friend Cass Hite. Decided to retract your words and come our way?"

Cass inclined his head toward Sarah. "She's to blame."

"So glad to see you up and about." The bishop motioned for them to step inside. "You're finally feeling better, then?"

"He has for almost a week now." Sarah followed Cass and the bishop inside. "But I made him stay around just to be sure he'd be up to traveling."

"So you're leaving us soon, I take it?" The bishop ushered him down the aisle between the pews.

"Yep, heading out tomorrow." Cass pointed to an empty pew near the back and leaned toward Sarah. "Let's take this one. You got me here, but that don't mean I want to sit up front."

The bishop slapped Cass on the back. "By the way, today's testimony meeting. I'd like to invite you to stand and share your experience, if you're feeling up to it. It's a moving story. After all, you came as near to death without stepping through the veil as a man can get." He smiled at Cass and headed up to the podium.

Cass slid into the pew after Sarah. "What's he mean? I didn't step on no veil."

"Shhh." Sarah lifted her hand to quiet Cass down—the bishop now stood at the pulpit. She blew out a breath, realizing she'd have her hands full in converting Cass over to a churchgoing man. But if she could bring him back from near death, she could do this. He'd already taken the first step. He was here in church, after all. She touched his arm briefly and gave it a squeeze. *Why should I care if Nyda or Edna see me? We are courting.*

"What's 'testimony meeting'?" Cass whispered this time.

"Once a month, members of the congregation

stand and share spiritual experiences, or testify of their belief in Jesus. Like the bishop said, I think the congregation would appreciate hearing your experience."

"I think I'll hold off until I hear a few others go first, if you don't mind."

"Not at all." Sarah scooted a tad closer to Cass to make room for Sister Reed and her children, who squeezed into the pew.

She quite enjoyed having to sit so close to Cass. She liked to think this would be how it'd be if they got married. It certainly hadn't been like this with Jacob. She'd rarely sat with him at church, only with Clara and Cleon. With that thought, she looked around at the congregation, hoping to see Clara so she could introduce Cass to her. Clara was nowhere to be seen. Sarah sighed away her disappointment, knowing her daughter lived too far from town to make it into church very often.

Sarah's heart sank. Is that what would happen to her if she and Cass were to move down to Hite if and when they were wed? *He said he was going to build a cabin in Hanksville. Why else would he do that if he wasn't planning on moving here?*

After the hymn, prayer, and sacrament, the bishop spoke for a few minutes, then turned the time over to the congregation to share their testimonies. Sister Brown number two stood and rambled on about her trip to visit her sister up in Price. Sarah cringed. This was not the kind of example Cass needed to see for his first testimony meeting. A few other people stood after Sister Brown.

Their experiences were heartfelt, and Sarah was touched by them. She hoped Cass was too.

When she saw Bishop Smoot reach into his vest for his pocket watch, she knew the meeting only had about ten minutes left—that's how it usually worked. She looked at Cass, urging him up with her eyes.

He wrinkled his brow in an expression of reluctance and then stood. "Howdy, all." His voice carried through the chapel with no problem. "To those of you who know me, I want to say thanks for all the help you gave to Mrs. Hansen, and thanks for all the prayers you sent skyward on my behalf. Those of you who don't know me, my name is Cass Hite. I have a mining company down on the Colorado at Dandy Crossing, and I often stop over in your good city on my way to and from the train station in Green River. About six weeks ago on my way home, I got awfully sick. Nearly died. If it wasn't for the help of your good bishop and Mrs. Hansen here," Cass pointed down at Sarah, "who your bishop asked to take care of me, I would have died. I'm beholden to both of them. And to God, I suppose. I have to say, there was a time when I didn't cotton much to Mormons. But now, if you're anything like the bishop or Mrs. Hansen, I hold you folks in high esteem, up there right below the Indians."

A few murmurs rose from the congregation and Sarah couldn't tell if they were for Cass or against him.

"I sure as shooting would never become one of you Mormons," Cass continued. "But I will always respect you. Thanks. That's all I've got to say." He plopped back onto the bench.

Sarah stiffened. She barely noticed the bishop

approach the pulpit or announce the closing hymn. Or heard the organ play, or the people sing. All she could think about were Cass's words, "never become one of you Mormons." Disappointment pulled her into a shell and she barely said a word as she and Cass walked home, her eyes focused on the ground.

Cass, however, seemed in a good mood. He wore a smile that stretched out from beneath his moustache. "I've got something I want to talk to you about tonight. Or maybe this afternoon. I don't know if it can wait that long."

"Oh, really now?" Sarah responded, catching a bit of his excitement. Cass, after all, was still a friend, one who made her feel of worth. She would always have that. She'd been foolish to have hoped for more. Hoped for him to be someone he wasn't. "How about you tell me before I even make us dinner?"

"Deal."

The minute they stepped into her cabin, he pulled her over to the sofa and made her sit down. Then he knelt down on one knee. "Sarah, I love you. If I had more time to show you that and court you before having to leave, I woulda. It being that I'm leaving tomorrow, I need to hurry things up a bit. Marry me. Move away from this place full of bad memories and come down to Hite with me to live."

Sarah felt as though her world had tipped upside down. An hour ago, these were exactly the words she'd longed to hear. But not now.

"My dear Cass." She gathered his hands into hers and bid him to rise. "You yourself said you could never become a Mormon, and I would never expect you to do something against your will. But neither could I live so far away from church and amongst those vulgar men you call friends." It just wasn't how a respectable Mormon woman would live, and she wouldn't disown her faith. She let go of his hands and wiped a tear from her eye. "I'm sorry, but I must decline your offer at this time."

"At this time?" Cass sat down on the sofa next to her. His eyes shone with hurt, yet a flicker of hope danced deep inside them. "Does that mean that sometime down the road, you might reconsider?"

"Perhaps," she said to sound agreeable and thus move on from this painful topic. She didn't want to dwell on the "if onlys"—if only he went to church; if only he didn't live in Hite; if only he would stop his cussing; if only he . . . She swept those thoughts from her mind and stood. "I best get dinner on to cook. I want to make you a nice one, seeing that it'll be the last nice one before you head home in the morning. Supper will just be bread and milk."

Neither said a word as Sarah prepared dinner. She peeled two potatoes, knowing that from now on, she'd only need to peel one to make mashed potatoes. What was she thinking? She wouldn't bother with making mashed potatoes for herself. She'd just boil the poor thing, sprinkle it with a little salt, and eat it plain.

After their dinner of fried chicken and mashed potatoes, Sarah set to the task of cleaning up the dishes. She noticed that Cass had lain down on his bed and fallen asleep. She felt bad. His last day in her company, and she couldn't muster anything more than trite conversations about the weather and pruning fruit trees.

By suppertime, she'd barely said a dozen more words to him. She poked at the pieces of bread floating in her bowl of milk and sugar. He did the same.

After they'd finished eating and the dishes were done, Sarah rubbed her arms and turned to the stove. It needed another log or two. A knock came at the door. Sarah glanced at the clock on the mantel. "That'll be Mary," she said, glad to have something to say. She grabbed one of the two lamps, figuring she'd stoke the fire later, and scurried to the door. She opened it to see Mary's little brother standing in a light pattering of rain.

"Mary sent me to tell you she won't be able to make it tonight." The boy shivered and shuffled closer to the doorstep. "She's caught something and ain't feeling too good."

"Thank you for the message." Sarah opened the door a tad wider. "Would you like to come in and warm up before you head back?"

"No, thanks, Aunt Sarah. Ma's expecting me to come straight back." He tipped his hat. "Bye now." He ran out into the darkness.

Sarah shut the door and stood there for a while, staring at the door. What would they do now? It was much too late to go into town and find someone to take Mary's place. "I guess we've lost our chaperone for the night," she said, not really caring at this point. It was only for one night. Tomorrow, her male patient would be gone. She turned to see that Cass no longer sat at the table. He'd slipped out of his clothes and into his bed. His faded red long johns poked ever so slightly past the covers.

"Good. I won't have to hear her snore," he said with a wink.

Sarah smiled at his comment. It felt good. More like how her day had started instead of the somber feeling of the last several hours.

"Now that's more like it." Cass reached out and grabbed her hand as she walked past him on her way to feed the stove.

"More like what?" She liked the feel of his hand around hers.

"More like the cheerful woman I've grown to love." He pulled her down to sit on the side of his bed. "I swear someone'd come in, cut out your tongue, and painted a scowl on your face the minute I asked you to marry me." A pained expression showed on his face. "That's not how I'd wanted it to be. I'd hoped you'd be as happy as me."

Sarah's heart hurt from hurting him. Her eyes watered up. "I'm so sorry." With arms outstretched, she leaned down to hug him, comfort him—she'd been so thoughtless.

His arms came out from beneath the covers and returned the hug. "It's me who should do the apologizing. I've rushed things. I should have known a fine woman like you needs more time to be courted properly." He pulled her closer, lifting the blankets so she could crawl under their cover of warmth. "It's just that it's so lonely down there in Hite. And I'm not getting any younger. I'm afeared my selfishness has gone and scared you away."

She basked in the warmth of his body, yet she knew she shouldn't be there. *But the room is so cold.* "You're not selfish," she murmured. "That's not why I said no."

"It wasn't?"

As Sarah shook her head in response, Cass leaned his face into hers and brushed her lips with a kiss. Her heart sped and her mouth instinctively pushed her lips against his, where they lingered. Cradled in his arms beneath the blankets, she felt all remnants of her lonesomeness slip away. Lost in the kiss, she lay by his side, engulfed in a wonderful feeling. She felt as one with him, a feeling she'd never had before, yet one she'd always longed for.

With how much Cass had come to mean to her and ...perhaps they could work things out in time.

Chapter 9

Cass stuffed his belongings into his saddlebags. He punched down his spare long johns to make room for his shirt, punching his fist into the bag to vent his anger. How could he have been so thoughtless? Sarah's silence was nothing yesterday, not compared to the cold, mute wall that stood between them this morning. He didn't blame her for putting up that wall—only himself.

"I won't be needing a hot breakfast this morning," he said as Sarah stood at the sink. "The dried fruit you packed for me yesterday will do me fine." He put on his hat and walked over to the door. "Goodbye, Sarah. I don't suppose it would do any good to tell you I'm sorry for letting things get out of hand."

Her back remained turned to him. She trembled, and what sounded like muffled sobs garbled her words. "Goodbye, Mr. Hite."

Cass cringed—would he ever hear her call him

Cass again? He stepped outside and closed the door to his happiness. He trudged down the road toward Mr. Reed's house, anxious to collect Gold Dust and be on his way and put the most bittersweet night of his life behind him. How could she be so tender with him and then so ashamed? Was it only because of her religious upbringing, or was there something else amiss?

Once in the saddle and miles south of Hanksville, he patted his horse's neck, seeking the animal's comfort. "I missed ya, Goldie. I'm guessing you missed me too. Six weeks is a long time. Sorry." The pain of his mistake jabbed at his heart once again. "I've got lots to be sorry for, Goldie. I've done made the biggest mistake of my life." *Not staking a second claim five miles upriver was nothing compared to this.* He breathed deep to calm himself as he replayed the events of last night in his mind, trying to figure out how he could have sunk so low.

It hadn't felt low at the time. Quite the opposite. With her lying there by his side, cradled in his arms, their collective warmth heating each other's blood, he'd never felt so wonderful in all his days. He wanted her. Not just for the moment, but for the rest of his life. Perhaps if he kept her there wrapped in his arms, he could sway her, persuade her to marry him. By the time the flaw in his thinking connected with his brain, it was too late. His passion for her trumped all reason. When she reciprocated with seeming hunger, he begged her to let him love her intimately. She whispered "yes," his emotions exploded, and there was no going back.

"And when the fireworks finally ended, you know what happened, Goldie?" Cass's heart throbbed with pain at the very thought. "She cried. Goldie, she cried!" A tear of his own ran down his cheek. He wiped it away with the back of his sleeve. "She's not that kind of a woman, Goldie. I knew that! In fact, that's what made me love her so." Tears now streamed down his face.

Cass dug his heels into Gold Dust and sent her galloping down the rutted trail. He let the wind beat at his face and grit sting his eyes, retribution for the pain he'd caused her. It wasn't enough.

***

Sarah clung to the sink for support, letting her sobbing flow as freely as her tears. Cass had surely claimed his horse and was on his way out of town by now. She hoped. He'd better not swing around and try to say goodbye once more. She didn't know if she could bear to look upon his face ever again without breaking into tears. She was a ruined woman, despite that he was now and forever her Cass and not Mr. Hite. But she couldn't think of him like that. Her shame was too great.

She peeled her clenched hands free from the edges of the sink, dragged her feet across the floor, and dropped onto the sofa.

How could he have done this to me?

The sobs and tears resumed. "No one ever need know," she muttered and stared out the front window. The thought brought a small measure of comfort. For a moment. "But I'll always know. And so will God." She reached in her pocket and pulled out her handkerchief to blow her nose. It reminded her of wiping the sweat from Cass's brow when he'd first arrived. A hundred memories rose to the surface of her thoughts, and she realized Cass was not the villain she was making him out to be.

And neither was Nyda, or Edna. Or her cousin Evelyn, who'd convinced Sarah to marry Jacob Hansen when she'd become orphaned at age fifteen. For more than half her life, she'd succumbed to other people's wishes, and then she'd put the blame on them for her misery. She'd been wrong.

A picture of Cass formed in her thoughts, with his goodness, his wit, and the way he made her feel valued, adding layers to the image that made her heart ache with pressure. When he'd pulled her into his bed, she hadn't fought. When he begged her to continue down the path they both knew they were headed, she hadn't refused. Ultimately, she knew it was her decision to bend to his will.

Cass didn't do this to me. I did it to myself.

Sarah was tempted to run into town to see if by chance Cass hadn't left yet. He deserved an apology. She'd treated him with coldness that morning—a time when they should have exchanged heartfelt goodbyes. Even if they most likely would never see each other again. She jumped out of the chair and ran for her coat. She couldn't leave him thinking she despised him.

Halfway across the room, she stopped—maybe it would be best to leave things as they were. She didn't want to give him a false glimmer of hope that a marriage could work between the two of them. A false hope might tear each of their hearts in two.

The next morning, Sarah arose early, finished her chores in quick fashion, and then packed her traveling bag. A visit with Clara was just what she needed to channel her thoughts and energy away from her sin. Dark clouds billowed in the west, giving her second thoughts about making the six-mile walk to Clara and James's ranch. "I need this," she whispered to the wind that kicked up. She plowed onward. When she made it to town and saw the corral and horses belonging to the big house, she decided to stop and pay a quick visit to Nyda.

"Sarah, my girl," Nyda exclaimed when she answered the door. "It's good to see you—it's about time you dropped in." She wrapped an arm around Sarah's shoulders and herded her toward the sofa. "Come, sit, stay a spell and tell me all about what it was like nursing that wretched man back to health."

"Cass Hite is not a wretched man." Sarah succumbed to Nyda's pull and plopped onto the sofa next to her sister wife. "And I can't stay long. I was really hoping to borrow one of your sons or grandsons to take me out to visit Clara."

"Oh, Clara can wait." Nyda wagged a hand at Sarah. "I want to hear your story—and I've been meaning to talk with you."

The front door swung open, and Edna walked in. "Sarah! What are you doing here?"

Nyda waved Edna over. "Come, she's just getting ready to tell me about her experience taking care of the gold miner. I know you'd love to hear this."

Edna hurried over and lowered onto the sofa, sandwiching Sarah in the middle. "Did it scare you, having to share your cabin with him?"

Sarah straightened her back. *No more of this. No more giving in to others!* "No, Edna, it did not scare me." She stood up. "And I didn't come here to discuss Cass Hite. I came here to see if I could get a ride out to Clara's."

"Was it that horrible—that you don't want to discuss it with your sister wives?" Nyda tugged on Sarah's elbow. "Sit back down. If you can't discuss personal matters with us, who can you confide in?"

"Exactly," Edna chimed in.

"I don't want to discuss it." Sarah jerked her elbow away from Nyda. "Now, if you'll excuse me, I'll go find Robbie and see if he can take me." She'd thrown out the name of the first boy who came to mind.

A gust of wind rattled the window behind the sofa. Nyda turned and looked outside. "I don't want you dragging Robbie out in this weather."

"Yes, you'd best just stay here," Edna said.

"If a storm is rolling in, I'd *best* head home." Sarah turned toward the door.

"But Sarah, dear, I haven't even had a chance to talk to you about what I'd been meaning to tell you."

"Maybe next time." Sarah inched away.

"No, it can't wait." Nyda's lips disappeared as she pinched them together. "It shall only take a second." She rose and draped her arm around Sarah. "I've often thought of you as one of my girls, so I feel it's my duty to give you a piece of motherly advice. I saw the way you and

Mr. Hite were sitting all cozy and close-like during church yesterday. Word of warning—stay away from men like him. They have no morals. Don't let yourself fall in love with the likes of him. He'll only disappoint you and then break your heart."

Too late. Sarah ducked out from beneath Nyda's arm. "I'll keep that in mind. Thank you," she muttered and walked to the door.

***

Sarah had tried for the last three weeks to visit Clara, but the weather always seemed to get in the way. Finally, a sky filled with blue and sunshine! She wrapped her shawl around her shoulders and headed down the road, figuring it would take her about two hours to walk to Clara's. Signs that spring lay just around the corner showed up everywhere—the budding leaves of the occasional cottonwood, the tufts of green grass dotting the roadside, and the gentle breeze that was neither warm nor cold. Perhaps it was best that she'd been delayed from traveling to Clara's until now. If she'd come the day after Cass left, as she'd first planned, the pain of her transgression would have been too raw. Clara would surely have sensed something was amiss and then probed.

Sarah could tell no one about what she'd done, not even her own daughter. Especially not her own daughter.

"They say time heals all wounds," Sarah said to a jack rabbit hopping across her path. She had healed somewhat over the past three weeks—or at least gotten on with her life. She doubted she could ever heal fully, perhaps just become accustomed to the pain. She'd committed a grievous sin in God's eyes. And her own eyes. Carrying around that constant pain was her way of taking responsibility for her mistake.

About a mile outside of town, a wave of nausea hit Sarah. She stopped for a minute and drank from her canteen of water. It didn't help. She nibbled on some dried apples she'd slipped in her pocket before she'd left. That helped a little.

Less than a half an hour later, the nausea returned. It grew worse. The apples didn't help—neither did a drink of water. Bent over in discomfort, she shuffled off to one side of the trail and sat down on a boulder. Sitting eased the nausea slightly. Then a big wave hit. She leaned forward and threw up.

Having lost her breakfast seemed to bring a bit of relief. Now she was faced with a decision. Continue on to Clara's, like she'd been trying for a good three weeks, or return home? Home lay closer than Clara's at this point, and if she had something contagious, it would be best not to expose her daughter or son-in-law to her illness. She stood slowly from the boulder and just as slowly trudged toward home.

By evening, Sarah was feeling better. A good supper seemed to help.

The next morning, before she'd even gotten dressed for the day, she threw up.

And then she cried.

She looked at the calendar and counted back to the

last day she'd bled. That confirmed her fear, and she cried again. She'd been through this before. There was no denying the signs. She was pregnant.

Chapter 10

Cass secured his bags to the saddle and led Gold Dust over to John's. He wanted to check to see if he had any mail before he left for Green River. It'd been three weeks since he'd left Hanksville. And Sarah. A corner of his heart still clung to the hope that she might write, and for some miraculous reason, tell him she'd forgiven him.

John gave a questioning glance as Cass stepped into his brother's store. "Your razor get lost? You look like you haven't shaved for a couple of weeks."

"Three weeks, to be exact. I haven't been in the mood," Cass said. "Got any mail for me?"

John sorted through a pile of three or four envelopes. "Nope. You just got a letter yesterday. Wasn't that enough? You expectin' something else?"

"Not really. Just checking."

"Well, if'n you get any more letters, I'll make sure I tuck 'em up here." John patted the top shelf of his "post office." "You can come help yourself to them when you stop in." He eyed Cass from top to toe. "You headed somewhere?"

"Green River, then to Grand Junction and on into Denver. That letter I got . . . it was from a bigshot investor in Colorado. He told me Kohler was out in Grand Junction last week, selling stock in the Colorado River Placer Mining Company."

"He's selling stock in our company?" John's face twisted with confusion.

"Not hardly!" Cass could feel his blood boil. "It's just as I'd feared. He's riding on our good name, drumming up all sorts of new investors for *his* company. Then when they go to pay him their money and he slips the copy of their sales agreement under their hand to sign, they see the words 'Colorado River' and 'Placer' there in the name, and they don't give it much thought. The man's as crooked as the day is long, and I aim to go do something about it."

"You be careful, Cass. I done held down the fort here in Hite while you were lollygagging up north for a month and a half. I don't want to go and do that again."

"I wasn't lollygagging. I damn near died. That's what I was doing."

"Exactly. Don't go out and damn near die again, or anything else of the sort that'll keep you away for so long. The men don't listen to me like they do you."

"I'll be careful." Cass gave his brother a slap on the back and half a hug. "Promise." He didn't want to come close to death again either. Once was enough. "And I plan on drumming us up some more investors while I'm out there, so don't worry." He walked out of the store and into the crisp February morning, a perfect day to travel. The last few weeks had been stormy. He had no desire to camp out at Muddy Creek in a storm ever again. The very thought made him shudder as he mounted Gold Dust and headed east for Dandy Crossing.

The sun had set by the time he made it to Hanksville. Sufficient twilight lingered in the sky for him to set up camp down at Muddy Creek. He'd be at the creek in a few minutes' time. However, the thought of staying the night there set him ill at ease. Sarah's cabin lay only a hundred yards farther up the trail, and then a stone's throw off to the west. If only he could knock on her door and ask to borrow her son's bed for the night. The idea sounded like heaven for more reasons than one. He slowed Gold Dust to a near crawl as he passed the log cabin that had been his haven for six weeks. A fleeting hope teased his heart. *Maybe she'll look out the window as I pass by and then run out and invite me in. Or at least say hello.*

"And why on earth would she do that, Goldie?" Cass spurred Gold Dust into a gallop. "I'm not to be trusted."

He set up camp at Muddy Creek, cursing his tent and telling Gold Dust every other minute, "The day we get back, I'm going to buy myself a cabin in this blasted Mormon town." When sleep failed to come, he pushed away the bad memories by thinking of Sarah and the wonderful last night they spent together—before she cried.

***

Sarah didn't leave the cabin for days, except to dart out to the privy and run back. Her fruit trees required attention, but she feared if she spent the time needed to prune them, surely someone would see her, read the guilt on her face, and know she was carrying Cass Hite's illegitimate child.

After a week of such nonsense and staring through the window at the blossoms loading her trees' branches, she forced herself outside to tend to them. With pruning shears in hand, she crept around to the side of her cabin where her trees grew.

"Hello, Aunt Sarah."

The greeting prompted Sarah to hide herself behind the limbs of her yet-unpruned apple tree.

"I said, hello, Aunt Sarah." The voice grew louder, and a second later, Nyda's grandson rounded the side of the apple tree and stood next to her.

"Hello, Robbie. Can I help you with something?" Sarah asked, not daring to look him in the face.

"A while ago, Grandma said you were looking for a ride over to Clara and James's. I'm headed over there this afternoon with a wagon to fetch some hay, and I thought I'd check to see if you were still needin' a lift over there."

"No, I don't. But thanks anyway."

"Pretty day, isn't it?" Robbie gazed around at the trees filled with blossoms with their backdrop of red rock hills and blue sky.

"Yes, it is," Sarah responded, ashamed for not taking notice herself.

"You're looking mighty pretty today, too, Aunt Sarah." He lifted his hat and set it back down on his head. "Bye now," he said before darting off.

"Bye." Sarah waved and then took a deep breath. Robbie hadn't noticed a thing. Her face obviously hadn't given her secret away. She looked down at her flat stomach, knowing it offered no hints either. For now. But what about three or four months from now? Robbie—and others—would certainly suspect something by then. What would she do? She didn't know, and that fact tied her stomach in knots.

Sarah got right to work thinning and shaping her trees, all the while shaping any and every idea she could so as to deal with the upcoming birth of her child—and the time leading up to the event. By the time she'd finished her fourth and final tree, and running through myriad possibilities ranging from confiding in Edna to running away from Hanksville and finding a childless couple to adopt her baby, she knew the best answer was to contact Cass.

If he could look past her cold-hearted rejection, perhaps they could wed soon enough to avoid the wagging tongues that were sure to come about the baby. They'd need to come to a compromise as to where they would raise the child. She kind of liked the idea of being married to Cass. He'd been so tender with her. She could imagine he'd do things like coo at their baby and tickle the child under the chin. Cass would also be different with her than Jacob had been. There would be a different kind of love in their marriage, warm and mutual. She realized now that even if Cass never set foot inside a church, she still loved him.

She tucked her tools away in the lean-to on the other side of cabin and ran inside to pen a letter.

She folded the tablecloth back and placed a clean sheet of stationery on the hard wooden surface. A quick dab of her pen into the well of ink, and she began her letter.

Dear Cass,
I have bad news.

She wadded the paper into a ball, not liking that beginning at all. She placed a clean sheet of paper before her and tried again.

Dear Cass,
I hope this letter finds you well. I am writing it for various reasons. First of all, I want to apologize to you for my discourteous actions the morning you left my cabin and headed back to your home. Please forgive me.

Now I must discuss with you a certain problem I have that directly affects you. It appears you have left me with child. Though I have the means to raise this child myself, I feel it would be unfair to the poor thing to be raised without a father. I wish to inquire if your offer of marriage is still open. I realize you do not wish to adopt my faith and the lifestyle I wish to live. Unfortunately, I cannot raise our child in the town of Hite. The child would lack for playmates and I for female companionship, not to mention the less-than-desirable environment in which to raise a child. I'm not sure I care to raise the child in Hanksville, either. I'm hoping we can come to some kind of

compromise if you are still willing to take me as your wife.
Sincerely,
Sarah Hansen
P.S. I still love you. I have not yet fully forgiven you, nor have I forgiven myself, but in time, that will come.

Sarah blotted the letter dry and then read over it. Perhaps she should rewrite it again and this time leave off the P.S. She peered into the box of stationery and saw she had so very few pages left. Hating to waste another piece of paper, she opted to send it as it was. She folded it in thirds, placed it in an envelope, and addressed the front.

Cass Hite
Dandy Crossing/Hite, Utah Territory

She donned her shawl, tucked the letter in her pocket, and headed to the Hanksville store so she could mail it immediately. The longer she waited to marry, the more embarrassing things could become for her child later on in its life. And awkward for her.

***

Cass hated Grand Junction. It was a dirty railroad town with lots of saloons and a lack of good lodging. He headed for the train station, anxious to be shed of the place. He only wished he'd been able to get his hands on Kohler and stop the madness. He'd spent the last two weeks trying to right the wrong that had been dealt the Colorado River Placer Mining Company only to find out the maggot had spread lies about his and John's company on top of all the deception. Cass had spent most of his time in Denver convincing his bigshot investors that Kohler's lies were just that—lies. When Cass had told them they'd been hoodwinked into investing into Kohler's ramshackle operation whose name sounded nearly the same, but the quality of the stock was nearly worthless, the investors became livid. Some went and got drunk. He'd heard that others sent telegraphs trying to locate Kohler and demand their money back.

On the platform, Cass swore he saw his brother, John, climb off a train that had just arrived from Green River. He walked faster, approaching the man with caution before calling out his name.

Good. It is him. "John!" Cass called out. "What in blazes are you doing here?"

"We've gotta talk," John said the moment he reached Cass. "Kohler's in Green River and he's been makin' threats. He's packing a Winchester, and people say he's sworn to get even. He's mad as hell about what you told those bankers in Denver."

"How'd he get wind of that? I just barely got back myself." Cass had wanted to come home sooner, but fixing Kohler's mess took time. He only wished he could fix the mess he'd caused with Sarah in the same amount of time.

"You've been gone a good couple of weeks, Cass. Anyway, I caught the ten thirty eastbound to head you off and give you warnin'. I don't know if he would really follow through on his threats, but I thought you ought to know before you got to Green River."

"Thanks." Cass pointed to a bench tucked in a

corner of the rail station away from the crowds. "Let's sit over there where we can talk in private."

"The problems don't stop there," John continued as they sat down. "Some of our boys have come up to Green River for a break—and to find you, Cass. They wanna get paid. Kohler's somehow got a hold of them. He's been tellin' them you've spent the company's money on gamblin' and women, and that's why they're not getting paid."

"Are all the men in Green River?"

"Homer and his crew are still at Dandy Crossing," John said. "But the rest—all twelve of them—are waitin' for you in Green River. We were expecting you last week."

Cass glanced at the small traveling bag John held. "You're not planning on staying long in Grand Junction?"

"Hell, no. Just came to warn you."

"Well, let's head back to Green River right now."

It was early evening by the time Cass and John stepped off the train in Green River. "Let's head over to the Red Rock Saloon," John said. "That's where I left most of the boys this mornin'. My guess

is they're still there and they'll be wantin' to see you. And that money belt you hopefully filled up in Denver."

The smell of whiskey and sweat filled Cass's nose before he even swung open the door of the saloon. He spotted a handful of his men seated around a table in the middle of the place, playing poker. He strolled over and pulled up a chair. "Hey, boys. Good to see you."

"'Bout time ya got here," George spoke up. He was the scrawniest of Cass's men, but always seemed to have the biggest mouth. "I wanna get paid."

"Sorry," Cass offered. "I didn't intend to be late paying you all. I got hung up in Denver with a couple of bigshot investors. They kept begging me to tell them more Indian stories, so it took a long time." Cass didn't want to tell them the details of the mess with Kohler. He patted his money belt. "Don't worry. I got your money. Let me have a drink first, and I'll divvy it out."

"Only if ya tell us which of yer Indian stories ya done told them." George downed his glass and wiped his mouth with his sleeve.

"Yeah," agreed a handful of his men in unison. For some reason, his men liked to hear his stories. It was as if they found it hard to believe that Cass could be such friends with the Indians.

After one glass of whiskey, Cass leaned across the table to get his men's attention. "What do you say we go over to the Palmer Hotel after I pay you and get us something decent to eat? It's on me." Cass knew the company didn't really have the money for such extravagance, but he needed to keep up appearances that the company was doing well. He also needed to keep his workers happy.

He shelled out crisp, new dollar bills to each of his men and then they left the bar. On the way to the hotel, they passed Grammage's boarding house.

Joe, the biggest and most reliable of his men, pointed to the place. "I hear that's where Kohler and a couple of his men are staying."

"You don't say." Cass stopped in his tracks. His blood was still boiling from all the extra work he'd had to do in Denver. "You boys go on without me. I'll be to the Palmer House shortly."

John latched on to Cass's arm. "You're not thinkin' of confrontin' Kohler, are you?"

"That's exactly what I'm doing." Cass didn't want to miss this chance to talk to the maggot if he was indeed so close. Maybe if they could discuss things out in the open, all civil like, he could talk some sense into the man and convince him that lying to those investors was against the law—and he had no plans on turning a blind eye to the problem.

"But he's totin' a rifle," Joe said.

Cass patted the gun in his holster. "I'll be fine."

Joe reached down and touched his own gun as if confirming it was still there. "I'll come with you."

"Suit yourself," Cass said.

Mrs. Grammage, the lady who owned the place, was out in her yard and looked up as Cass and Joe approached. "Get out of here, Cass Hite," she hissed, pointing down the road. "You've come to cause trouble, and I ain't putting up with it here. I don't want no fight on my property."

Cass gently but firmly pushed her aside. Obviously, she'd been tainted by Kohler's gossip. Joe took her by the arm and led her back into her kitchen, talking quietly to her to calm her down. Cass stepped up to a bowery that acted as a front porch for The Grammage

House.

Frank Drake, Kohler's right-hand man, stood there, leaning on a post. He motioned for Cass to have a seat. "What you doing here?"

"I come to see Kohler," Cass said as he sat down.

The screen door creaked open. "What the hell you want?" Kohler stepped from inside the house and remained in the doorway. His face looked flushed with high emotion. He cradled a Winchester over his arm, the barrel pointed downward toward Cass.

"Put the blasted gun down and let's talk," Cass said

Kohler lowered the gun. "What do you got to say, ya filthy, lying son of bitch?

Cass struggled to contain his anger. That rifle was a blasted nuisance. This here squabble of theirs was a clear-cut case of what was right and wrong. They ought to be able to take care of this problem like intelligent men— talk it out, not shoot it out. He leaned toward Kohler. "I'd say any man who totes around a Winchester looking for trouble is a coward. That's what I'd say. Now, put that thing down and let's—"

"Coward? You good for nothing—" Kohler jerked the rifle up.

Cass ducked.

Kohler pulled the trigger.

The bullet went over Cass's head. Kohler jacked another shell in the rifle and fired, grazing Cass's arm. "Hold on, now!" Cass yelled. "I ain't here to shoot more than my mouth off."

Another shot whizzed past Cass's ear.

Cass gained his feet, and with gun in hand, he darted off the porch, shooting three bullets in rapid succession behind him in self-defense as he ran away. He heard someone fall to the ground. Was it Kohler? Still running, he turned his head. Drake lay lifeless on the porch

Kohler jumped off the porch and raised his rifle toward Cass. "This time, I'll aim to kill."

Cass ran toward the backyard. A third bullet from Kohler's rifle sent splinters flying. It'd hit the clapboards on the corner of the house. On the side yard, Case whirled to face his opponent, gun ready. Kohler came around the building in hot pursuit. Cass fired a shot. Kohler fired too. Both men turned to run. Cass headed for cover at the back of the house. When he heard no more bullets being fired, he peered around the corner. Kohler crumpled to the ground. A red stain blossomed through his shirt. Cass's bullet must have hit him.

Knees shaking and arm hurting, Cass headed for the Palmer House. Not to eat, but to check in to the hotel. He'd better patch up his arm before meeting up with his men for supper. On second thought, he'd best send someone down to the dining room with some cash and a message that he wouldn't be able to join them for the meal. He didn't feel like eating. Shooting a man—make it two men—churned his insides as with a whisk made of barbed wire. Even if it was clearly self-defense.

As he hurried down the street holding his arm, blood oozing through his fingers, he noticed that people had come out on their porches and into the street, obviously pulled toward the sounds of the gunfight. He tipped his hat to the few who glowered with disdain, trying to appear normal despite feeling sick at what just happened. To those who gave him a nod, he nodded back, appreciating their understanding.

***

The next morning, Cass awoke to a knock at his door. He pulled his head off the pillow and noticed that the light streaming through the window shone with the brilliance of midday. "I'm coming," he bellowed as he swung his feet around to climb out of bed.

The door flew open. A man barged in. He wore a badge on his chest.

The hotel's clerk, holding a ring of keys in his hand, cowered behind a portion of the doorframe. "Sorry, Mr. Hite. This here's the county sheriff—came down all the way from Price. He dragged me up here and made me open your door."

"Come on." The sheriff grabbed Cass by the arm.

Cass jerked his arm away, remaining seated on the edge of the bed. "Careful!" He pulled up the sleeve of the newly donned pair of underwear, revealing the bandage he wrapped around his wound the night before. It held traces of blood that had soaked through the muslin rags. Thankfully, the bleeding had stopped soon after he'd bound his wound.

"Sorry." The sheriff let go and grabbed his other arm.

"What's going on?" Cass asked, feeling lousy enough as it was. He didn't need this.

"We're going over to the jail," the sheriff said, pulling Cass up from the bed. "We gotta hold an inquest to decide guilt, justice, and the probable cause of last night's incident." He produced a set of handcuffs.

"What's to decide?" Cass didn't like how he was being treated like a common outlaw. "It was a clear-cut case of self-defense. Kohler shot at me first. I was simply there to talk to the man."

"Save it for the inquest." The sheriff tried to clamp the cuffs around Cass's wrists.

Cass pushed them away. "Blast it all! At least let me to put on a pair of trousers."

Cass took his time getting dressed. His arm hurt from the bullet. His gut hurt from shooting two men. And his heart hurt even worse—what would Sarah think of him now? Finally, he allowed the sheriff to drag him out of the Palmer House and then walk him over to the jail. Cass kept his head held high.

Once inside the stone building that housed the town hall and jail, the sheriff handed Cass off to an older fellow. This man's gray hair looked to be near white when he walked past the sunshine pouring through the window. "This is the justice of the peace from here in Green River," said the sheriff.

The old man pulled Cass into a cell. "You'll have to hang out here for a while until we're ready for you."

"Ready for me? What's that supposed to mean?"

Cass plopped down on the bunk, not liking this one bit. He needed to get back to Dandy Crossing and see to operations. He'd been gone long enough. He didn't have time for this nonsense.

"It means just what he said—you gotta stay here 'til we're ready for you." The sheriff stepped away from the cell as the justice of the peace turned the key, locking Cass in.

Lying on the lumpy mattress, with nothing to do, his thoughts turned to Sarah and how he'd made a mountain-sized mess of everything. Not only had his lack of refinement robbed her of her virtue, his rough lifestyle had led him to shoot two men. He and Sarah came from two different worlds. He doubted he could step up to her level, though he was willing to give it a try. Sure as shootin,' he didn't want her to step down to his.

Late in the afternoon, after a measly dinner of watered-down soup and a crust of bread—made extra lousy by having to eat it with handcuffs on—the sheriff returned. He let Cass out of the cell and then led him into a room.

The white-haired justice of the peace sat in a chair and looked up at Cass when he walked in. Next to him sat a younger man dressed in an expensive suit and a bowler hat. The old man pointed to the younger one. "This is the county's district attorney. He and the sheriff took the first train down from Price once they heard the news of the killin'."

"So you fellows are the extent of my 'inquest,' as you put it, sir?" Cass narrowed his eyes at the attorney as the sheriff guided him into a chair set in the middle of the room. Why did he even need an inquest? It was clearly a case of self-defense.

"Yep," the sheriff responded and settled into a chair next to the white-haired man. All three of the men now faced Cass.

The man in the expensive suit removed his hat and rested it on his knee. "There's no need to pull in a jury and make this a full-fledged trial. We've been interviewing witnesses all day, as well as investigating the evidence—"

"I tried to tell them most of the physical evidence had been erased by the time they got here." The justice of the peace scratched his gray-white moustache. "Mrs. Grammage, being a stickler for keeping her house and yard tidy, had the mess all cleaned up by morning."

The sheriff eyed the old man. "But we still had to look anyway."

"Now, Mr. Hite." The young district attorney turned his attention to Cass. "Tell us your version of the story.

As Cass retold the events of the previous night, all three men moved to the edges of their chairs and focused on Cass in earnest. If their eyes weren't lying, Cass held some hope that they accepted his description of the events as accurate. If their eyes were lying—well, he didn't want to think along those lines.

The three men then discussed how each of the witnesses had twenty-four hours to discuss the event and come to an agreement on what they saw and what they thought they saw. Of course, there were conflicting accounts of the incident between Cass's people and Kohler's people, but in time, the lawmen made a decision.

After an hour of discussion, the district attorney stood. "Well, gentlemen, I think we can all agree that this was obviously a case of self-defense."

The sheriff stood, and then the justice of the peace somewhat slowly, rubbing his back as he rose. The sheriff unlocked Cass's cuffs. "Well, Mr. Hite, I believe you are free to go." He gathered the cuffs into one hand and shoved them in his pocket. "And I'm catching the next train to Price." He looked at the attorney as the young man placed his fancy hat on his head. "Do you care to join me?"

"Most certainly."

Cass rubbed his wrists and dashed out of the jail. He wanted a drink—a good, strong one. That had been too close for comfort. What if they *had* found him guilty? That meant murder. That could have destroyed everything—his reputation, his mining company, and what miniscule chance he had left to change his life around for Sarah.

***

Cass worked alongside his men, shoveling his share of dirt into the placer. Some of his men had quit because of Kohler's lies. One had even gone to work for Kohler's company that was still in operation upstream. Cass pitched in. He had to admit, he enjoyed getting his feet and hands wet again, actually searching for gold rather than being off in the big city searching for investors. But he'd had little time to do much else since he'd returned from Green River a month ago. In a way, it was a blessing. It helped keep his mind off that gunfight with Kohler. The awful memory had faded to where it was manageable now, and he hoped to put the whole incident behind him soon.

If only his memory of parting ways with Sarah had managed to fade as well.

He shoveled another load of dirt into the placer and looked up. A stranger walked onto the site. Cass noticed the badge of a federal marshal pinned to his chest. "Who you looking for?" Cass asked in a lighthearted voice. "Did one of my men forget to pay a saloon bill up in Green River?"

"I'm looking for a man by the name of Cass Hite."

"Why?" Cass's tone lost its humor.

"I have a warrant for his arrest. He's wanted for murder."

Chapter 11

The first day of March, a healthy wind stirred up the dust on the road as Sarah walked into town. So far, the month proved to come in like a lion. That meant March would go out like a lamb. She couldn't muster a smile at that prospect. She'd be three months along with her pregnancy at that point, and likely still unmarried. Another month after that, she'd have to wear looser-fitting dresses, of which she had none. She'd loaned out her maternity clothes a year after she'd had Cleon when it had become apparent that Jacob no longer planned to share her bed on his every-other-week visits. Even though she'd been somewhat relieved when she'd discovered her husband's only motivation for being intimate with her had been to give her a child, it had hurt. It had left her feeling unlovable. Her guess was that Jacob felt he had done his job—he'd given her both a son and a daughter and figured his duty had been fulfilled. Thus, Sarah could feel fulfilled.

Sarah fought the urge to tear up. Cass had found her loveable; he'd told her so. He'd made her feel like she was more important to him than all the gold he'd ever pulled out of the river. But he had yet to respond to her letter. She could only hope a letter awaited her in the post office. If not, she'd be forced to follow through on one of her other plans. The thought made her shudder.

"Good morning, Brother Brown." Sarah offered him a smile that was merely a movement of her lips as she approached her short, stout friend standing behind the counter. "Do you have any mail for me today?"

"You were just in here two days ago, Sister Hansen. The mail's only delivered twice a week."

Sarah's heart sank. "Sorry. I was just checking—just in case."

"You expecting an important letter, I take it?"

"Not really expecting. Just hoping."

"Who from?" Brother Brown peered at Sarah over the tops of his spectacles. "I can keep an extra eye out for it, if you can tell me."

"Never mind. Don't worry about it." Sarah walked back outside.

She turned toward Edna's house, dreading the implementation of her first alternate plan. As she plodded down the dusty road, she gazed at the children playing in the yards. She knew every one of those children by name. She knew each of their parents. And they knew Sarah, knew she'd been widowed for two years. Knew she was yet unmarried. For her to give birth to a baby out of wedlock in this community would be condemning the child to a lifetime of ridicule and misery. She couldn't do that to her child.

Sarah spun on her heel to return to her cabin and pursue her other alternate plan. She'd need to write another letter and come right back to put it in the outgoing mail. Time was not on Sarah's side.

Once in the privacy of her cabin, she placed another sheet of paper on top of the table, remembering her kindly cousin, who was her last hope, and began writing.

Dear Evelyn,

I realize it has been some time since I have written to you. I apologize for my thoughtlessness. I apologize also for the favor which I am about to ask. To come to you only in a time of need shows a horrible lack of manners on my part, but I have nowhere else to turn. You were so helpful after the death of my parents, the way you arranged my marriage to Jacob Hansen. I will forever be in your debt for that assistance.

Because of a lack of good judgment on my part, I have found myself in a most unfitting situation for a woman of my upbringing. I am in the family way. Unfortunately, the father of the child cannot be found and thus I will be unable to marry him. Could I possibly impose upon your charity and stay with you until the baby is born, and then impose further and ask for your assistance in finding a good home for the child? You've always seemed to have a bounty of connections to people throughout the territory.

Please, help me. I don't know what else to do.

Sincerely,

Your cousin, Sarah Jones Hansen

Sarah blotted the letter and then left it on the table

to dry a little longer. The thought of giving her baby away tore at her heart with razor-sharp claws. She already wanted to hold the wee babe in her arms, take care of it, and let it fill the hours of her lonely days.

Folding that paper into thirds and placing it inside the addressed envelope took great strength on Sarah's part. With quivering chin, she licked and sealed it shut, reminding herself that *she* had brought this tragedy into her life, *she* was to blame, and so it was fitting that *she* was going through this firestorm of suffering. The important thing now was to see that her child did not suffer. She stepped outside, and a whirlwind of hope and fear tore at her emotions. She forced herself forward and plodded toward Brother Brown's store to mail her letter.

***

Sarah knelt in her garden spot, clearing the young weeds from the soil in preparation for planting. A week ago, when she'd mailed her letter to Evelyn, she'd decided there would be no sense in her planting a garden, for she would be moving to Price very shortly. That morning when she'd awakened, a horrible thought had lodged itself in her head.

What if Evelyn was unable or unwilling to take her in?

Life had to go on. If Sarah was sentenced to live out her life with her illegitimate child here in Hanksville, she'd need her garden to help her survive.

Boots clomping in the distance tore Sarah's attention from the weeds and turned her eyes toward town. Brother Brown strolled down one of the ruts of the road, quickly closing the distance between him and her cabin. An envelope poked out of his shirt pocket. Was it for her? From Evelyn already? Or had Cass finally written?

She jumped to her feet, ready to run, and then held herself still, merely gazing at Brother Brown as he approached. He didn't deliver mail. It was the townspeople's duty to come into his tiny post office and collect their own. Why else was he out here, then?

"Hello, Brother Brown," Sarah said with reserve.

"Good morning, Sister Hansen. Beautiful day, isn't it?" He looked around. He focused on Sarah as he made it to the edge of her garden spot. "I thought I'd just take myself on a little walk this morning, it being so pretty."

"Well, thank you for stopping by my place." Sarah wanted to ask about the envelope in his pocket.

He pulled it out and waved it in the air. "This came this morning. You seemed a little upset when I had nothing for you the other day, so I thought I'd bring it to you. Hopefully it's the one you were looking for."

Sarah took it as he offered it to her. "Thank you very much." She glanced at the return address. *Evelyn Bigler, Price, UT Territory.* It wasn't from Cass. Disappointment squeezed her chest. At the same time, there was some relief at having such a timely response from her cousin. She held up the envelope and headed toward the door of her cabin. "I'll take this inside."

He seemed planted in that spot, not wanting to move, as if he'd expected Sarah to share the reason for the letter.

"It's from my cousin. Thanks again and good day, Brother Brown," she said and slipped inside the privacy of her cabin, unwilling to share anything this letter contained.

She sat at the table and tore open the envelope. Her hands trembled as she unfolded the single sheet of paper. Fear gripped her as she glanced at the first line.

Dearest Sarah,

I am so sorry to tell you that I am unable to take you in during this difficult time in your life. My dear, sweet husband passed away a month ago, and my daughter has insisted that I come live with her. Thus I shall be moving to Provo next week and be sharing a house with my daughter, her husband, and their four little children. I would love to take you with me, but there is barely enough room for me in their tiny house.

Sarah set down the letter and took a deep breath, trying to calm the sinking feeling that begged to overtake her body. She refused to cry. Recovering from mistakes like hers was never meant to be easy. She glared at the letter, feeling like tossing it into the stove that very minute. Then she realized a paragraph of the letter remained unread. She picked it back up.

I do, however, have another possibility that might work out for you. My neighbor, Wayne Barker, lost his wife shortly before I lost my dear Henry. He's not that old, maybe a year or two younger than you. He's been left with two little girls under the age of three, one still in diapers. He's beside himself, unable to take care of the girls, his job, and his church responsibilities. I mentioned your predicament to him. Don't worry—I didn't tell him the nature of your pregnancy, only that you are recently widowed and you are with child and in need of support. He said he'd be more than happy to marry you and help you raise your child, and in turn you would help him raise his girls. He's anxious to marry right away.

I must warn you, however, that he was desperately in love with his wife, so I'm afraid this would be a marriage of convenience for the both of you. But love could come later. If this is amenable to you, please write me back as soon as you can so I can arrange things before I move. He suggests that the two of you be wed by the justice of the peace. Hopefully, you are amenable to that as well.

Sincerely,

Your cousin Evelyn

Sarah leaned back in her chair. Her mind spun with this new possibility. It was definitely not the marriage she'd dreamed of, but she could keep her child. That alone was worth further consideration of the matter. As far as being one of convenience and not one of love, she was used to that. It would be much, much better for her unborn child than staying in Hanksville and being raised by an unwed mother. One other thing, and it gave Sarah a bit of satisfaction—something woefully missing in her life at the moment—was that if she decided to marry Wayne Barker, it would be her decision. No one else made it for her.

Chapter 12

Cass stuffed another shirt into his trunk without folding it. The marshal waited right outside his cabin, probably tapping his foot on the ground right about now.

John paced the cabin's floor. "Of course you know I'm comin' with you."

"I appreciate the offer, John, but it's really not necessary." Cass knew he was taking longer than he should to pack, but he wanted to talk to his brother and make sure everything would be taken care of down here while he was gone. "It's already been proven that I shot Kohler in self-defense. And Drake survived the crossfire, so they can't hang me for that. I'm sure this is just some kind of formality. I'll get it cleared up and be back in a week or so."

"You're probably right." John gave Cass's arm a friendly punch. "You take care." He opened the door, and the marshal poked his head into the cabin.

"You done?" he asked. "Daylight's burning. We need to get on the road."

"Yeah, I'm coming." Cass didn't bother to hide the annoyance in his voice. He closed the latch on his trunk, having filled it good and full. The lawman had told him to pack in case he was gone for a very long time. So Cass did, on purpose, so as to weigh down the marshal's wagon—though he thought it a blasted waste of time. He just wanted this ridiculous interruption in his schedule to get over with as soon as possible, so he'd complied.

"Oh, Cass," John spoke up. "I forgot to tell you that there's a letter sittin' over on the post office shelf for you. It's been there a few weeks already, what with you spendin' that time in Denver and all. It didn't look like anything business related when I looked at it, so I didn't open it. You might want to stop by and pick it up on your way out." He tipped his hat and slipped out the door past the marshal.

"Thanks, I will," Cass said to his brother's back.

The marshal grabbed Cass by the elbow and pulled him toward the cabin's door. "My wagon's waiting on the other side of the river. Let's get a move on if we're going to make it Provo before I grow old."

"I'm coming, but I need my stuff." Cass jerked his arm away and hefted his steamer trunk with both hands from off the floor. "And I'm not fixing to run away, so there's no need to treat me like a hardened criminal." He paused, letting the marshal's words sink in. "Provo? Why Provo?"

Once outside, the marshal grabbed Cass by the elbow again. "That's what they told me, so that's where

I'm taking you."

Cass pulled away. "I can carry this infernal trunk down this slope a hell of a lot better without you hanging on to me." He spouted off a rant of cursing at the rocks cluttering the path and then at nothing in particular. Grunting extra loud, he loaded the trunk into the marshal's wagon. "I loaded it good—like you told me." He growled and climbed aboard. How could such an asinine thing be happening to him?

He and the marshal hardly said a word to each other for the first hour or so. Cass finally had enough of the silence. "So, do you have a name?" he asked the big man, whose bent knees reached nearly to his chest with his feet propped up on the front of the wagon like they were. "Or do you want me to continue calling you 'marshal' for the rest of the trip? It's a long ways to Provo, I'll warn ya."

"I'm fully aware of the journey, seeing that I've already made the trip coming down." The marshal lifted his hat. "The name's Walters. Rex Walters. Marshal Walters to you."

"Fine." Cass tipped his hat. "My name's Hite, Cass Hite. Prisoner Hite to you." If he was going to have to make this trip with a blasted stiff shirt, he'd likely go crazy. Maybe the guy just needed a little loosening up. "You live in Provo?"

"Mm-huh. Moved there a few months ago when I took the job of marshal."

"Got a family, wife, kids?" The moment Cass said that, he remembered he'd forgotten to pick up his letter.

What if it was from Sarah? "Blast it all! I forgot something."

"I have a wife and children, and I want to get back to them as fast as I can. Sorry, we're not turning back now. Whatever you forgot, you'll have to make do without." Walters flicked the reins, and the horse picked up speed. After a minute, he said, "I hope it wasn't anything important."

"So you *do* have a heart," Cass said out of the corner of his mouth. "I thought maybe you were an emotionless mute the government sent down to fetch me 'cause they figured if you were a personable fellow, I'd try to warm you up and talk you into leaving me alone."

"Sorry, Mr. Hite." Walters glanced at Cass with a set of tired-looking eyes. "I guess I no more wanted to make this trip down to Dandy Crossing than you want to go to Provo." He focused his attention back on the trail. "It's me and my wife's wedding anniversary tomorrow. We've been married ten years. I'd kind of hoped to spend the day with her. Not you, Mr. Hite. No offense meant."

"None taken."

"You may not believe this, but I think this whole new trial is a waste of time. It's already been proven that you acted in self-defense. I've read the reports, gone over the witness statements, and I see you as an innocent man."

"Wait a minute!" Cass held out his hand to stop the marshal from rambling. *Good gracious. With this man, it's either one or the other.* "Did you say *trial?*"

"Yep. That's why I told you to pack heavy. I hope that's not the case, but sometimes these federal trials can take some time. I've known some to last nigh onto a year."

"But I've already been declared innocent. What the blazes is going on?"

"It appears that Mr. Adolf Kohler's friends and/or associates have appealed the original ruling."

"Sons of bit—"

"But don't worry," Walters cut in. "You'll be okay. This is the West. People have to carry a gun, and use it sometimes, if they want to feel safe. The general population believes this. You'll be fine, Mr. Hite. It'll just take some time and patience to work this ridiculous mess out."

"Please, call me Cass. And I hope you're right." For the first time since the marshal showed up on the dig a couple of hours ago, Cass felt a bit of worry niggle at his gut. "Say, where you from, Walters?"

"Price. Lived there all my life 'til I move"

"Price, huh? I'd of thought that's where I'd be tried—if there *was* a reason to try me. Why's that blasted trial going to be held farther up north in Provo?"

"Kohler's associates requested it."

Cass's niggle got worse. He surveyed Walters as the wagon rolled along the bumpy trail. The marshal's eyes, though kind, were deep set in his weathered face above a crooked nose that had seen its share of fist fights. He was Cass's peer, hailing from a rough-and-tumble mining town, a man who understood gunfights and self-defense. Cass felt a wave of outrage wash through him as he thought about Provo, how it was far away from Green River. He knew exactly why Kohler's men pushed for the re-trial to be in that city. In Provo, he would not have a jury of his peers. It would take place in the heart of Zion, the center of Mormonism. Before he'd met Sarah and had been the beneficiary of Hanksville's compassion, he'd said some pretty nasty things about Mormons. Many of them had made it into newspaper articles. So his bias against that group of people was no secret in this territory.

A few miles before they reached Hanksville, Cass said, "I know of a fair-to-middling place along Muddy Creek where we can set up camp for the night."

"Thanks for the tip, but we're not going to be camping out." Walters wore a smile of pride that appeared almost sinister in the orange glow of the setting sun. "On my way down, I ran into a fellow who has an empty cabin on the south of town. He let it out to me for two bits for the night I spent there. I told him I wanted to rent it again on my way back up. He said he'd meet me there at sunset to unlock it for me. Another reason I wanted to hurry you up this morning."

***

The cabin ended up being more on the southeast end of town. It was just off the trail, and Cass could see the chimney of Sarah's cabin peeking over the tops of a stand of junipers as he stood by the front door waiting for the owner to unlock the place. Cass walked in behind Walters and scanned the interior. It held a single room, a sink in one corner, a bed in the other, and a stove in the middle. It wasn't much, but a whole lot better than his tent pitched at Muddy Creek. "Have you ever thought about selling the place?" Cass asked the owner, an older man with a ratty salt-and-pepper beard in need of a trim.

"All the time. But there's not much call for such a small cabin in a town whose people generally have big families—and very little money."

"I'll give you twenty-five bucks for it." Cass pulled out his wallet and extracted the right amount. "I've been wanting a place to tide me over on my trips up to Green River. This is perfect."

"I'll take it." The man took the money, stashed it in his pocket, and then pulled out a key. He dropped it into Cass's outstretched hand. "She's all yours."

"So, who gets the bed?" Walters asked the second the door shut behind the man.

"I own the place, so I say me." Cass plopped onto his back and tried out the springs. "Not too bad." He shifted onto his side and pointed to the hard-packed dirt below him. "You can have the floor, no extra charge."

"Gee, thanks."

"Hey, I swore I saw a bedroll packed out in the wagon. You'll be fine, a young buck like you. Me, well, I'm nearly forty—getting up in years. That's why I bought myself a bed and a roof to cover the blasted bed."

The mention of getting up in years drew Cass's eyes to the cabin's lone window. He peered out and saw smoke billowing from the chimney belonging to Sarah's cabin. She was so close. In less than five minutes, he could be over there, standing at her doorstep, watching with anticipation as she opened the door—before she slammed it in his face. At least he'd get to catch a glimpse of her eyes. It might tide him over a little longer. His memories of her had already faded around the edges. The letter sitting on John's shelf came to mind. Could it possibly be from her? Who else would send him a letter besides an investor or a creditor?

"Hey, Walters, since you're such an understanding fellow," Cass spoke up as the marshal pulled some beef jerky and dried fruit from his pack, "how about you let me pay a quick visit to my new neighbor to the north before we head out tomorrow?"

"You are technically under arrest, Cass. This is no time to be neighborly."

"Actually, I already know the woman who lives there." Cass's throat tightened as he tried to form his words. "Me and her were really close once. Then I went and did something in really bad taste and I burnt my bridge with her. But I'm thinking that letter that got left behind back there in Hite could be from her. And if it is, and she's giving me another chance, I sure as blazes don't want to blow it. If you could just let me drop by for a minute or two tomorrow and ask her if that letter was hers, I'd be much obliged."

Walters rubbed his clean-shaven chin and gazed at Cass with a look of empathy. "Sure, I guess I can let you do that."

Cass struggled to fall asleep that night. He tossed from his back onto his side, then onto his back again, trying to get more comfortable than his thoughts would allow. How would Sarah react when she saw him? If she slammed the door in his face, could he take that rejection again? He deserved every bit of it if she did. But was there not one moment of their tenderness that she cherished? What if she invited him in? And forgave him? And allowed him to court her once more?

The next morning after a breakfast of coffee and dry biscuits, they packed up the wagon. Before climbing aboard, Cass hid the key to his new cabin under a hefty rock behind the place. As he walked around to the front where the wagon sat and Walters stood ready to go, he gazed in the direction of Sarah's cabin. "Can I head on over there?" Cass pointed to the chimney still billowing smoke.

Walters lifted an eyebrow.

"You know, like you said I could . . . to see if she's willing to give me another chance."

"Oh, yeah, your girl." Walters said. Then he shook his head. "Heck if I'm going to let you go by yourself, though. I can't see the front door to her place from here. How do I know that you won't take off and hightail it to Mexico?"

"Seriously, Walters?" Cass swept his arm toward Sarah's cabin. "Come on. Put handcuffs on me if you want. Walk me over there if'n you need to. But just let me go—and at least take them off while I talk to her in case she lets me give her a hug. I'm sure as hell not going to pass up that moment 'cause you've got me tied up."

"I haven't used handcuffs on you yet." Walters started walking and motioned for Cass to fall in step alongside him.

"I know," Cass said. He quickened his pace and could see her front door now. "Let's keep it that way. But I do have another big favor to ask of you."

"Uh-huh?" Walters sounded skeptical.

"Can you at least stand around the corner of the house? And take off that blasted badge in case she does catch sight of you. The last thing I need is for her to know I'm heading off to jail. Even if it *is* temporary."

"Fine."

Once they made it to Sarah's, Walters motioned Cass toward her door. He lagged behind, walked over, and leaned against the side of the cabin.

Cass crept up to the doorstep. He took in a deep breath, released it, and knocked on the door.

It creaked open, and a young woman, about twenty-ish, stuck her head around the door and stared at Cass. "Yes? May I help you?"

"Is Mrs. Hansen here?" Cass croaked out his words. He craned his neck to one side, peering into the cabin to see if Sarah was sitting at the table or something and had merely sent this visitor of hers to open the door.

"Oh, I'm so sorry, you just missed my aunt. She moved out yesterday. But she's graciously letting me and my new husband live here in exchange for keeping up her garden."

Cass then recognized the girl. It was Mary, the gal who played chaperone for him and Sarah. She didn't seem to recognize Cass—most likely from the beard and long hair he'd grown since his last trip to Hanksville. It was probably for the best. Though his gut wrenched at Mary's news, he couldn't let go. "Where did she move to?"

"Price."

"Price! Great. I'll be passing through there tomorrow. Do you know where in Price I might find her?"

"No. I only know that she's getting married tomorrow to a grieving widower she just barely met. It was all pretty fast, but he's a good man."

"Tomorrow?" Cass felt numb.

"Yeah. Sarah is likely to have her hands full with two little girls and a new husband, so I don't know if she'd have much time to visit. Should I tell her you stopped by if she happens to come back for a visit soon? What was your name? You look vaguely familiar."

"No, don't bother to tell her. And I probably won't stop by her new place." A pain swelled in the back of Cass's throat. "Like you said, she won't have much time for me. Thanks, miss." He crammed his hat onto his head and beelined it around the cabin to where Walters stood.

"Let's get out of here," he said to the marshal.

"What happened? Your girl still mad at you?"

"I don't want to talk about it."

While riding on the train all the way up to Green River, Cass thought about Sarah and what Mary had told him. There could be only one possible reason why Sarah would be getting married so quickly—to a man she barely knew. She was with child. *My child.* It was as if a thousand anvils piled upon his shoulders, weighing him down and pressing against his heart till it felt ready to burst. Had he not caused her enough pain by robbing her virtue? Now this? Sentenced to marry a widower she obviously didn't love so she could raise his children, all so she wouldn't have to suffer the ridicule of bearing a baby out of wedlock?

Was that what was written in that letter sitting in John's post office?

Maybe he could convince Walters to let him stop in Price, find Sarah, and stop the wedding.

And then what? Convince Sarah to marry him? And then tell her she'd have to wait until after he went to trial for murder, and that he might be gone for a year?

No, he couldn't do that. He *deserved* to be thrown in jail, for her sake, once he and Walters made it to Provo. And the key thrown away. Unfortunately, that wouldn't solve her problems.

Chapter 13

S arah hadn't been on a train or to Price since just after her father had died. This trip proved to be a little less unnerving. Her age and determination saw to that. She was going to make the best of things—for her unborn child's sake. She moved to the edge of her seat, too fidgety to lean back. The idea of marrying a man she didn't know—or love—didn't appeal to her any more than it had twenty years earlier, though both marriages served to remedy her unfortunate circumstance at the time.

When the train finally slowed to a stop, she leaned past the woman sitting next to her and looked out the window. In the letter Wayne Barker had sent her, he said he'd pick her up at the station and to look for a man with red hair wearing a gray suit and carrying a yellow rose. It had been their only communication. She'd been unable to gather even a hint of his personality from that letter. It felt more like a business correspondence. *What if that* is *his personality?*

The very idea made her want to cry. Would she never have a husband she could laugh with, cry with, or discuss things like beautiful sunsets? Her heart drifted lower as she longed for Cass.

She cleared her throat, reminding herself that she needed to stop fretting and look for her husband-to-be. True, there were no feelings of affection between her and Mr. Barker now, but surely that would change over time.

The train jerked forward and then came to a complete stop. Sarah gave up looking out the window for Mr. Barker, stood, and followed the crowd of people disembarking. She collected her bags with the help of the porter and moved off to one side of the platform so she could gain a better view of the station.

There he was, standing on the stairs at the end of the platform, well apart from the mass of people scurrying to and fro next to the train. It *had* to be him, with that sandy-red, but full head of hair and a limp yellow rose clasped in hand. He appeared several inches taller than Sarah. Good—she preferred to look up into her husband's eyes rather than down. His slight build looked as though it could use lots of heavy cream and home cooking. Was the slump in his shoulders due to poor posture or severe sadness? In either case, he wasn't what she'd expected, or rather, hoped for. She took a deep breath, picked up her bags, and walked over to him.

"Excuse me," Sarah said. "Are you Mr. Wayne Barker?"

"Yes." His face lit up ever so slightly. "And you must be Sarah Hansen."

"I am." Sarah hoped that tiny spark in his eyes meant he found her appealing, or at least amenable.

"Shall we be going, then?" He motioned with the hand holding the rose for her to lead the way down the remaining steps. "Oh, so sorry." As if he'd barely noticed the limp flower, he extended his hand toward Sarah. "Take this—it's for you. I'll grab your luggage."

"Thank you." Sarah accepted the flower, touched by his gesture and pleased at the prospect of a yard filled with rose bushes for her to tend and enjoy. She also wondered if her new home had a big garden with grapevines and fruit trees like those she'd left behind. The prospect lifted her spirits. She followed Mr. Barker away from the platform and gazed past the station, taking in the sights and sounds of the town she would now call home.

As they left the train station behind, she saw an occasional tree growing along the dusty streets that divided the small city into a handful of blocks. As they walked down the sidewalk, she noticed that a couple of houses stood out from the others on the foothills of the mining town. Their red-orange brick and two-story Victorian architecture told her they were homes of the mining executives, no doubt. The remainder of the homes they walked past appeared mostly to be tiny framed homes made of clapboard, some whitewashed and some not. In the distance, what looked to be a large manmade pile of earth sat next to a hole cut into the hillside. She assumed that must be the entrance to the coal mine that gave this town life.

"Sorry, I don't have a horse and buggy." Wayne Barker hefted the larger of her two bags onto one shoulder and kept walking.

Sarah helped him situate the bag so as to distribute its contents evenly. His wiry frame gave her cause for concern. "Do be careful with that one. I have a glass jar of honey in there I would hate to have break."

"No, we wouldn't want that."

"No." She mustered a smile. "And no need to apologize about the buggy."

"I'm afraid the mine doesn't pay their bookkeepers enough to buy and keep a horse. But the town is small, and I find walking much easier than having to worry about hitching up a wagon."

"I don't mind walking." Sarah easily kept pace beside him. "I didn't have a horse back in Hanksville, either."

"I take it you weren't accustomed to many other luxuries, then?" His voice held what sounded like hope.

"No, not really." Sarah thought about her garden. Maybe that could be deemed a luxury—not everyone had a garden as nice as hers back home. *Stop thinking of Hanksville as home. This is your home now.*

They walked in silence down a street she surmised to be the town's main street, it being dotted with places of business. She breathed in the fragrance of her withered rose, wishing to mask a fermented smell that tainted the air. Surveying the buildings a little closer, she noticed three saloons on this one block alone.

At the end of the second block, Wayne Barker spoke up. "I hope you don't mind if we stop by the justice of the peace before I take you to my house."

"No," Sarah said quietly, trying to calm the wave of disappointment swelling inside her. The justice of the peace had little to do with her tender emotions. It was the fact that she was getting married yet again to a man not of her choosing.

But this is your choice, remember?

"It's on the way, right there." Mr. Barker lowered her bag from his shoulder and pointed to a building on the corner of the next block. He had yet to look at her as he spoke. "I apologize for the civil marriage, but under the circumstances . . ." His words trailed off, and he kept walking. "It'll save us time," he continued after several steps. "I'm sorry, but I have to get right back to the office as soon as I bring you home."

Sarah stared at him, trying to get his eyes to meet hers. "Your boss couldn't even give you a half day off for your wedding? What kind of man is he?"

"A horribly callous one." His eyes remained focus on the road ahead, yet he appeared thinking on something miles away. "He has made the past four months since Genevieve passed even more unbearable. He cares not one whit that I have no one to look after my children. The Relief Society sisters, bless their hearts, have all taken turns while I'm at work, but I can't impose upon them indefinitely."

At least this man was Mormon. *Why should that matter to me now? I don't go to church anymore, not after . . . my mistake.*

Mere minutes later, Sarah stood in front of the justice of the peace in the borrowed white blouse and golden brown skirt Edna had lent her for the occasion. She held the limp yellow rose as her bouquet, thinking about how she'd have to send the clothes back to Hanksville by way of mail if she couldn't find someone soon who was heading that way. Her thoughts were pulled back to the matter at hand by the words, "Do you take this man to be your lawfully wedded husband?"

"I do." Her mouth formed the words without emotion, neither good nor bad.

"I now pronounce you husband and wife." The justice of the peace looked to Wayne. "You may kiss the bride."

Wayne stiffened. A look of fear flashed in his eyes as he turned to face Sarah. He hesitated, leaned slightly, and kissed Sarah on the cheek. He then gathered the marriage license and Sarah's bags and ushered her to the door of the courthouse. Once outside, he finally looked at her for more than a fleeting moment. "I'm sorry . . . about the kiss. But being widowed yourself, I'm sure you understand. This is going to take some time for us—for me, at least. Genevieve was my world. I can't let go of my memories overnight."

"Nor should you." Sarah gave his arm a tender pat, which seemed to calm him slightly. She held on to that bit of satisfaction, for his statement had done little to calm *her* nerves.

They turned off the main street, passing home after home, each built in the same fashion out of white-washed clapboard. They all had small yards, apparently so as to fit more of them into a city block. She hoped at least that his yard would have tidy little patches of garden bordering a white picket fence like a handful of the other yards they'd passed. Perhaps even a fruit tree or two . . . along with a bed of flowers.

Wayne Barker slowed his pace in front of a house that looked as though it had been abandoned. The picket fence surrounding the yard had never met with a brushstroke of whitewash. Its waist-high gray slats were overgrown with what had to be years of dead bindweed. The green of new growth could be seen weaving its layer atop the old. A mass of new weeds sprang up in what looked at one time to be a small garden plot, and what appeared to have once been a patch of lawn was brown, even though it was April and the spring rain had been plentiful this year. "Here we are." He opened a rickety gate in the gray picket fence with his foot and bid Sarah to enter before him.

Sarah walked toward the house, dragging her steps. What had she gotten herself into? The wood-framed home had received at least one more coat of whitewash than its fence. A window sat on each side of a front door that appeared to have met with some paint. Though it flaked off in spots, the blue paint on the door added enough color to the house to help Sarah imagine she could, in time, make this house a home.

Off to the side, at one corner of the house, grew a rose bush of enormous size, obviously untouched by pruning shears for several seasons. However, not a single vine of bindweed touched it. A few yellow flower buds stood out amidst the green foliage. "What a striking rose bush," Sarah said, trying to dwell on the positive.

"That was Genevieve's pride and joy." Wayne stepped onto the small covered porch while his eyes stared at the rose bush. "I gave it to her when we first moved here five years ago. Before that, we lived in Thistle. That's where we met and fell in love. But there's no way to make a living in Thistle unless you own land. That's why I moved her here—I found a job working for the mines." He ducked his head as he set down one of her bags momentarily and turned the doorknob. "But I fear the coal dust in the air only made her health worse." He pushed the door open, grabbed the bag, and stepped inside before Sarah.

It didn't bother her so much that he'd forgotten his manners. The most likely reason behind his forgetfulness, however, gave her cause for concern: Genevieve.

The minute Sarah walked in the door, an older woman with a crying babe in arms rushed toward her with a look of relief on her face. "Oh, wonderful! Is this your new wife?" she said to Wayne and shoved the baby into Sarah's arms. Her eyes met Sarah's. "And your name is . . .?"

"Sarah."

Wayne set Sarah's things by a narrow bed tucked in the corner of the living room. "This is Sister Wilkes, our Relief Society president."

"Nice to meet you." The woman pointed to one of two doors on the wall opposite the front door. "The three-year-old is in on her father's bed, napping. Her name's Beth. She's had a spot of dinner, but Julia here hasn't. I was just trying to feed her when you got here. The poor thing doesn't cotton much to cow's milk."

Sarah laid Julia against her shoulder, swearing the baby felt close to the weight of a newborn, but her wail sounded older. "How old is she?"

"Near four months old now," Sister Wilkes said, and looked to Mr. Barker. "Does she not know?"

"Know what?" Sarah asked.

"Genevieve died giving birth," he said and then motioned to the baby with an incline of his head.

"I did not know that," Sarah responded, aching for the entire Barker family, living and/or deceased.

"Does that change things?" Wayne Barker sounded worried.

"No, no, it doesn't," Sarah responded honestly.

Sister Wilkes spoke up. "Maybe you can do something to help her keep the milk down." She gave the crying baby a pat on the skinny leg poking out of the blanket. "I've got to go now. I suppose I'll see you at church. If you need any more fillin' in, I'll talk to you then." She grabbed her bonnet, tied it around her neck, and hurried out the front door.

Sarah gulped. She hadn't set foot in church since the day she went with Cass.

"Sorry to leave you like this." Wayne swept his arm to indicate the disheveled furniture, unfolded laundry, and toys cluttering the room. "But I must get back to work before one o'clock. It would be best, too, if I were to leave before Beth awakes. If she sees me, she won't let me leave without a fit of tears. She misses her mother so— almost as much as I do." He lifted his hat and raked his fingers through his hair before putting it back on. He looked at Sarah. A smile that appeared to take effort formed on his clean-shaven face. "Good-bye, Sarah. I'll see you at suppertime."

"Goodbye." Her half-hearted farewell was surely drowned out by the wail of the baby in her arms.

Patting little Julia's back while bouncing her up and down, Sarah looked around the cluttered front room for the bottle Sister Wilkes had been using to feed the poor thing. She spotted it atop a small table shoved next to the arm of the sofa. She grabbed hold of it and sat down, immediately inserting the nipple into the baby's mouth. Julia took a few sucks and pulled her mouth away. The crying resumed. Then she threw up and quieted down.

Curdled milk drenched the front of Sarah's borrowed blouse. The sour smell churned Sarah's stomach. With babe in arms, she rushed out the front door and threw up on the weeds. She walked back inside, laid Julia on the sofa, tucking a pillow next to her to secure her in place, and ran over to where Wayne had left her bags. She dug through them to find a clean dress, wishing she could hang the rest of her clothes up and put her things away. But where? She'd been given no such instructions. She felt like a weekend guest, not the woman of this house. But how could she? It was obvious the woman of this house—at least in everyone's hearts—was still Genevieve.

Standing next to her bags in the corner of the front room, she held her breath and peeled off her soiled clothes. She hurriedly slipped on her work dress, grabbed Julia's bottle, and ran toward the door she assumed led to a kitchen. A sink full of dirty dishes met her eyes first, then the opened cupboard doors off to the left, revealing not much more than empty shelves. A round table with three chairs sat in the middle of the room, and against the wall opposite the cupboard was the stove. She glanced again at the dishes, overwhelmed with the mess needing to be tackled while the screams of the baby demanded she let the housework go.

A pitcher of milk caught her eye. It sat in the window sill above the sink, obviously someone's attempt at keeping it cool. She scurried over, pulled it down, and braved a whiff. *Thank heavens.* It smelled fresh enough. She then washed out a small pot, poured in a cup or so of milk, and set it on the stove to scald. The stove felt stone cold. *How had they cooked breakfast?* Maybe they hadn't.

The baby continued to cry. Sarah used the last of the wood that sat next to the stove and got a fire going, thinking she'd better ask Mr. Barker that night where the wood pile might be—she couldn't see one outside. She stuck a finger in the milk to check its temperature and then did a quick search of the kitchen to see what kind of food she'd have to work with for supper. A pound or two of flour and a small tub of lard, along with salt and baking powder and a few other spices, was all she could find. She rushed back to the front room to find her smallest bag.

Before she'd left Hanksville, she'd filled it with the dried apricots and apples leftover from last year's harvest—along with her quart jar nearly full of honey. Last fall, she'd traded a full bushel of apples for the honey. She hadn't wanted to leave that behind. She'd already left a good number of bottled peaches and other food for Nyda's daughter, along with her dishes, furniture, and bedding. Sarah grabbed hold of the honey in one hand and the screaming baby in the other, and headed back into the kitchen.

"I can't pine over all that food I left behind, now can I?" she said to the baby, but was speaking to herself. "Or we'll have even more crying in this kitchen." With the baby on one hip, Sarah carefully poured the scalded milk into Julia's bottle and added a bit of honey like she used to do for Cleon after her milk dried up early. She then placed it in one of the sink's numerous dirty bowls and dowsed it with water from the pump, testing the bottle from time to time. When the droplets she squirted on her wrist no longer felt hot, but comfortably warm, she inserted the bottle in the baby's wailing mouth. The infant took to the milk much more aggressively than before.

Exhausted, still holding the baby and the bottle, Sarah lumbered into the living room and dropped onto the sofa. Before she had even finished the milk, the baby fell asleep. With the utmost care, Sarah placed her into a basinet that sat next to the bed in the front room.

The silence sounded wonderful. Sarah looked around the cluttered front room, then in the kitchen at the pile of dirty dishes. Where should she start? She peered out the window at the mass of weeds overtaking what looked to be a possible garden plot. For some reason, Sarah had a sneaking hunch that she'd need to grow her own vegetables if she, and the rest of this family, were to survive.

Turning a blind eye to the dishes and the clutter, ignoring her nausea, and refusing to give in to her desire to lie down for a nap of her own, she opened the front door.

"Mama!" The terrified cry came from the bedroom.

Sarah gripped the doorknob, wanting so badly to continue pushing it open and then run outside and flee far away. Slowly, she pulled the door shut instead and headed for the bedroom. A tiny wisp of a girl sat up in the bed, winding her strawberry blond curls around the fingers of one hand while the other hand rubbed at her eye. "Your mother's not here, sweetie." She sat on the bed and pulled the child into a hug.

The little girl resisted, pushing Sarah away. "I want Mama. When's she comin' home?"

"I'm sorry, but she's up in heaven and won't be coming home." Surely three-year-old Beth would realize her mother was gone by now. Then she thought of the girl's father, Wayne Barker, her new husband. She imagined he'd likely done little to help the child let go and move on, seeing that he'd not been able to do the same. Sarah tried to gather Beth back into her arms. "I'm your new mama."

"Uh-uh," Beth wailed.

"Can I at least be your friend?"

Sarah ran into the front room and grabbed a handful of dried apricots from her supply and hurried back. She held them out for the whimpering child. "How about a treat?"

Beth nodded and snatched them up. She immediately stuck one of them in her mouth.

"Would you like to help your papa smile?"

Beth nodded again.

"I have an idea. How would you like to help me make a garden for your papa? I'll even give you some more apricots if you come outside with me and help."

Beth crawled off the bed and took hold of Sarah's extended hand.

By the time Mr. Barker walked in the door that evening, Sarah had cleared a spot in the yard and gotten it ready to plant. She'd also washed and put away all the dishes, and prepared a supper of biscuits and apricot sauce. The cluttered front room would have to wait for another day.

"Supper is almost ready," she said as he hung his hat on the hook by the front door. She placed the baby into his arms. He resisted for a second, but she persisted. "Hold her, please. I've got to take the biscuits out of the oven."

"Smells good." Wayne followed her into the kitchen and dropped into a chair at the table. "I'm hungry." He glanced around the near-spotless kitchen, but said nothing more.

She pulled the biscuits out of the oven, placed them on the table, and sat Beth atop a box on one of the chairs. Sarah stared at her new husband, waiting for him to pray or ask her to pray. He sat just sat there as if in a daze. "Would you offer a blessing?" she said, too tired to wait any longer, and dropped into the remaining chair.

He handed her the baby, prayed, and dug into the food without another word.

Sarah had hoped he'd keep hold of Julia and give her arms a break. She'd hoped he would have acknowledged the clean kitchen. She'd hoped he would have noticed the cleared garden space at the side and rear of the house.

"This is tasty," he finally said.

"Thank you." Sarah didn't know this man well enough to determine if she should be flattered or upset with this meager expression of gratitude. For now, she'd take it as a compliment and not let it weigh her down— there were plenty of other things to do that already. She squared her shoulders, ready to take on those things for the remainder of the evening and on into tomorrow, and the next day . . . and the next. She deserved nothing better.

But these children did! "I'm glad you like it. But I'm afraid, Mr. Barker," Sarah spoke in a firm voice, trying hard to control her anger, "that I'll be unable to put anything else on the supper table tomorrow night unless you put some food in the cupboards and replenish the woodpile. I'll be happy to go and purchase the supplies I need tomorrow if you will but give me some money, point me to the general store and where you get your milk, and tend the children while I do so."

Mr. Barker stared at her with his mouth slightly agape. "I won't be able to give you anything until tomorrow evening." His gaze shifted to the floor. "Sorry."

"Why?" And had she heard him correctly? "Tomorrow is Saturday. I had hoped to have your help with the children. And we desperately need to get a garden in before spring is completely gone. Does your employer always require you work on Saturday?"

"Only when I need to make up for time I've had to take off when I couldn't find someone to watch the children. Which has been often as of late. The service offered by the Relief Society sisters has dwindled. They're worn out. I've had to dip into my reserves to pay a lady to tend the children a few days a week, and another one to bring in supper from time to time. That's why I've no money right now. But I'll be getting a paycheck at the end of my shift tomorrow."

Sarah's heart sank. That would be much too late to go to the store. "Do you not have any credit at the general store?"

"Not anymore."

"Can you at least get me some more milk for the baby?" Sarah thought about the near-empty pitcher of milk sitting on the window sill.

His eyes finally met hers. "One of the brethren from the ward has a farm just outside of town, and he brings me fresh milk every morning. And another one brings eggs from time to time."

"Thank heavens," Sarah said as her mind struggled to come up with a way to make that little bit of milk, eggs, flour and lard, and her dried apricots last this family until

Monday. "It appears our meals from now until Monday will be rather sparse. Little Beth will most likely become cranky, and I shall have to lie down from time to time during the day, so I think it will be best if the children and I don't go to church on Sunday." Sarah had hoped to start anew in this town with no expectations from neighbors for her to go to church. She was the worst kind of sinner and wasn't worthy to step inside a chapel. Her new husband would be hard-pressed to get her to church the following week as well. She only hoped Wayne was not a stickler on such matters, that he wouldn't mind spending his Sabbath—his only day off, it sounded like—at home. After all, it was he who insisted on being wed by the justice of the peace—not a bishop.

"I presume that would be admissible this one time." Mr. Barker's forehead wrinkled with noticeable angst. "The ward members should understand."

What's for them to understand?

"Perhaps you should stay home with us," Sarah said. "You look as though you could use a rest." His wiry frame and gaunt face gave her reason for concern.

"I'm afraid that is out of the question."

"Why?"

He looked at her like she should already know this. "I'm the bishop."

Chapter 14

S arah took a deep breath of the autumn air and stepped inside the chapel with her usual anxiety. She struggled to bring her feelings under control, determined to maintain a measure of happiness. Or at least contentment. Julia wiggled in one arm as Beth tugged on Sarah's other while leading them into their usual pew at the very back. Except for her first Sunday in Price nearly six months ago, she hadn't missed a week of church. It seemed so very important to Wayne that she and the children come to church and she had not the heart to disappoint him—he already had enough disappointments in his life.

Thankfully, the members of the Price ward had made the task a tad easier by their unspoken rule of leaving the last two benches in the chapel open for those with babies. As usual, she slipped into the chapel during the opening hymn and prompted Beth to give a quick wave to her father up on the podium so he knew they were there. Again, she decided the moment she heard the amen of the closing prayer, she'd take the children and rush out the door. She didn't want to give people opportunity to talk with her—and probe further into her life.

As their bishop, Wayne had told the congregation that he had married a widowed woman he'd been introduced to from Hanksville. He'd then had Sarah stand for everyone to see and welcome into the ward. That was enough—that was all these people needed to know about her. Not that she carried a bastard child inside her womb, or that she squeezed in next to a three-year-old on a cot in the living room rather than share her new husband's bed.

Beth began to fidget even before the opening song finished. Sarah blew out a breath—this was going to be a long meeting. She sat ten-month-old Julia on the bench in between her and Beth and took a handkerchief out of her pocket. She folded it into a doll-in-a-cradle and showed Beth how to swing it to make the cradle rock.

In time, Sarah looked up from the handkerchief toy and her efforts to calm the two children and noticed the deacons coming down the aisle carrying the sacrament trays. *Oh, no.* This was the hardest part of being at church. If only Julia was fussy. Perhaps it wasn't too late to ask Beth if she needed to visit the privy—another excuse she relied on to step outside until this part of the service was over.

A deacon moved into place at the side of Sarah's bench, blocking her exit. He held out a tray holding the broken bread. She hesitated. He moved it closer. She grabbed hold of the tray, picked up a piece of bread, held the tray out for Beth to take a piece, and then passed it on to a young boy belonging to the family sharing her bench. After the boy passed the tray back and she handed it to the deacon, she glanced around to make sure no one was watching and popped the small piece of bread into Julia's mouth. "It's time I get you used to taking the sacrament anyway," she whispered into the baby's ear as she picked her back up and set her on her lap.

After the sacrament, the first speaker rose and came to the pulpit. "My talk is on honesty," he began. His eyes focused on the back of the chapel.

Sarah cringed. It was as if the man at the pulpit knew her secret and was delivering his sermon just for her. As if her infidelity wasn't enough, she was deceiving her husband, her bishop, still leading him to believe the child she carried inside her was Jacob's child. She picked up Julia and latched onto Beth's hand, ready to run from this holy house of God where she didn't belong.

Her unborn child kicked with such force, Sarah let out a gasp and rushed her hand to her stomach.

Sarah couldn't leave early, not today. The strong movements of her unborn child reminded her that she needed to talk with someone. Soon. This child was due to come into this world any day now and she had yet to find a midwife. Unfortunately, she knew Sister Wilkes, the Relief Society president, would be the best person to ask to help her find one. That meant she'd have to stay after church. Or worse—go to a Relief Society meeting on Wednesday morning, where all the women of the ward could easily talk to her and ask her why she hadn't been to any of their other meetings. Then they would look at her, scrutinize her, and see through her to all the unseemly secrets she tried so hard to keep hidden.

Remaining in her seat, Sarah tuned her ear to the painful words delivered from the pulpit. For Wayne's sake, she was trying to make the best of her new marriage. The poor man always seemed in a somber mood. She didn't want to be dishonest and add to his sadness. Her deceit wore on her conscience and weighed her down with unpleasant feelings. But she didn't know how to avoid the lie, given her situation. She had nowhere else to go if Wayne turned her out. Maybe if she listened hard, it would help sooth her guilt.

It didn't.

The second speaker talked about the Savior, and how Jesus paid the price for mankind's sins. Sarah barely listened, choosing instead to look around the chapel, trying to spot Sister Wilkes. When she'd spotted her three pews up, she then made Beth another handkerchief dolly, this time swinging it back and forth herself for the girls to watch. She didn't need to hear about Christ's sacrifice—it didn't apply to her. She'd knowingly sinned. It was her mess to deal with on her own.

When the meeting finally ended, Sarah stood, let the family next to her exit the pew, and then waited. She watched as the Relief Society president made her way to the back of the chapel.

"Excuse me." She reached out and touched Sister Wilkes's arm. "I need to talk to you, if that's all right. Do you have a minute?"

"Certainly." Sister Wilkes motioned for Sarah to sit back down with the girls and scoot down the bench to make room. "What can I do for you?" She held up her hand to stop Sarah before she could answer. "First, I want to tell you how glad I am that you've bid me to come speak with you. I've wanted to visit with you for some time, but you never felt up to it when I've stopped by. Other sisters in the ward have tried to visit you too, but they've been unable as well." Sister Wilkes took Sarah's hands in hers. "Is everything all right?"

"Everything is fine," Sarah responded, wearing the usual smile she forced upon her face. "I've truly been too busy or too tired to talk. Plus, I hate to take other people's time. But today I was hoping you could help me find a midwife."

"So the happy rumors are true?" Sister Wilkes's mouth curved up in a sweet smile. "You and the bishop are expecting a child?"

Sarah chose her words carefully. "I am with child, yes."

"Certainly I have the name of a good midwife. A lot of the sisters in the ward have used her." Sister Wilkes batted a hand at Sarah. "But that's down the road a piece. Right now, can the sisters make you a new baby quilt, or bring you in a meal or two when you're feeling nauseated?"

Sarah smoothed the smock over her rounded belly. Like Clara and Cleon, she carried this child high and deep, but surely this woman could see she was past that point in her pregnancy. "I'm well beyond the nausea, thank you. In fact, I could give birth any day now." The moment Sarah said that, she realized the mistake she'd made.

Sister Wilkes raised an eyebrow. "But you and the bishop were barely wed five and a half months ago." She stared at Sarah, and it was obvious she struggled not to look at Sarah's belly. "So, this is not Bishop Barker's . . .?"

"Child." Sarah finished the sentence for her. "No."

"But . . ." Both of Sister Wilkes's eyebrows raised now.

"Do you not remember when Wayne introduced me back in April? He said that I was recently widowed."

"Ah." Sister Wilkes's face relaxed. "So this child is from your previous husband?"

It pained Sarah to do so, especially after that guilt-generating message delivered over the pulpit less than half an hour ago, but she gave a slight nod.

"Everything makes sense now." Sister Wilkes patted Sarah's hand. "You've been dealing with the loss of a husband, a pregnancy, and taking on the hefty task of those two little girls. No wonder you haven't felt very sociable. And the bishop . . ." She inclined her chin toward the podium, where Wayne moved down the steps at its side. His arm wrapped around a coarsely dressed fellow while his other hand locked with the man's in a handshake. "What a good-hearted man to take on another man's child and raise it as his own."

"Yes, my new husband is a good man, that is for sure." Sarah's stomach twisted. Wayne *was* a good man. She wished she could be of the caliber he deserved. "Now, as for the matter of the midwife?"

"Her name is Anna Campbell, and she lives three blocks north of you on First Street in the house with yellow planter boxes on the windows. Just so you know, she's not Mormon. I hope that's not a problem for you."

"Not at all."

"Good. There are some very lovely people out there who are not of our faith," Sister Wilkes said. "Anna being one of them."

"Yes, there are." Sarah nodded in agreement as her mind ventured to where it often wandered. *Cass.* She wondered how he was doing. Had the pain her rejection inflicted upon him healed at all? It must have affected him sorely for him to disregard her letter as he had. She sniffed away an impending urge to cry.

Later that evening, after Wayne finally made it home from church, she cooked a modest supper, fed the family, and tucked the children in bed. He approached her as she tidied up the kitchen. He carried a small package wrapped in newspaper in his hands. "This came for you yesterday while you were out back in the garden. Sorry I forgot to give it to you then." He held it out for her to take and then offered her a timid smile. "By the way, thank you again for that wonderful garden. I've always seemed to kill plants easier than grow them."

Sarah took the package and turned her face away from him, unaccustomed to his personalized attention. She also felt uncomfortable with him thanking her for an activity she engaged in as an escape. "Growing a little extra food is the least I could do to repay you for taking on me and my unborn child."

"You make it sound like it's been a chore for me." He latched onto her arm and pulled her around to face him. "You're the one who's been inundated with chores." His timid smile returned, and his hand moved down her arm and intertwined its fingers with her free hand. "Thank you for taking on me and my two children. I know it hasn't been easy."

Sarah felt inclined to pull her hand away. Until now, he'd rarely touched her, and she'd preferred it that way, preferred that he clung to the memory of Genevieve. It made it easier to cling to memories of Cass.

She gave his hand a little squeeze because *he* deserved it, and pulled free so she could open the package. "I wonder what it is."

"Who's it from?"

Sarah looked at the return address. It was difficult to read, having been written over the printing of the newspaper that had been used to wrap the package. "It appears to be from my cousin Evelyn."

"Ah, Evelyn. Such a good neighbor," Wayne said. "How's she doing?"

"I don't know. This is the first thing I've received from her since she moved up north." Sarah took a butcher knife and cut the string that bound the package. "And then for it to be a package . . . What on earth would she be sending me?" She pulled the string away carefully, treasuring that bit of newspaper and wanting to save it for later. It not only would come in handy to build fires in the stove, but a quick glance below the main headline told her it was a recent copy and could make for some interesting reading for those rare times when she had a minute or two to herself. She peeled away the newsprint to reveal two books and a short note.

Dear Sarah,

You have been in my thoughts and prayers often. I hope this letter finds you healthy, you are settled in your new marriage, and that the birth of your baby has gone or does go smoothly. I wish I could have had the means to send you something of more use for a mother with a newborn child, but things are tight. Including our living space.

I have to admit, I am sending you these two books not so much as a gift, but because I am trying to find good homes for all of my novels—there just isn't enough room here for them. I know you love to read, and hopefully on those late nights when the wee babe insists on staying up, you might indulge yourself in reading one or both of them.

Love,

Cousin Evelyn

Sarah looked up. "She's sent me a couple of her books. She doesn't have room for them, and she knows I like to read."

Wayne reached for the books. "That's awfully thoughtful of her."

"Yes, it was." Sarah's eyes watered. "She didn't have to do that." True, it was but a small gesture, but it meant a lot to her. It communicated that Evelyn didn't love her any less because of her mistake.

Wayne held up the books and read their covers. "*Uncle Tom's Cabin? Little Women?* Have you read either of these?"

"No, but I've wanted to." Sarah teared up further at her cousin's thoughtfulness.

Wayne handed her the books, turned her around, and pointed her toward the front room. "Treat yourself to a break for a change. Go curl up in the overstuffed chair and start reading one of them tonight. I'll finish cleaning in here."

"Are you sure?" Sarah resisted only slightly as he nudged her into the front room. She clutched the books to her chest, along with their newspaper wrapping. Escaping into another world through a book sounded heavenly.

"Absolutely." Wayne guided her into the chair. "With a new baby on its way, I doubt you'll get many more quiet evenings like this for some time."

"You're probably correct." She glanced up at Wayne. "Thank you," she said with sincerity.

As Wayne walked back into the kitchen, Sarah placed the newspaper and *Little Women* on the round table next to her chair, ready to delve into the first page of *Uncle Tom's Cabin*. The headline of an article at the bottom of the newspaper's front page caught her eye.

Cass Hite Petitions for Change of Venue for Murder Trial

Uncle Tom's Cabin fell from her hands. *Little Women* immediately joined it on the floor as she whisked the newspaper off the table. *No, that can't be! Cass is not a murderer!* The newspaper shaking in her hands, she read on.

Gold mining legend, Cass Hite, who will shortly go on trial for a second time in district court in Provo for the murder of Adolf Kohler, is petitioning for a change of venue. He is convinced that the prejudices of the predominantly Mormon courtroom were the cause of the hung jury. "Had I faced a jury of hardy outdoorsmen, a true jury of my peers," Hite claimed, "I would have surely won an acquittal."

Hite has always maintained that he shot Kohler in self-defense. The case against Hite was tried initially in the Emery County court where he was pronounced innocent of murder at that time. However, friends and colleagues of the deceased had appealed the verdict and pushed for the case to be tried again. They succeeded and pushed further to have the case tried in Provo.

Numb, Sarah set the paper down. Though she'd read very little of the circumstances that led to the demise of this man named Kohler, she knew Cass enough to know he was telling the truth; he'd acted in self-defense. But now he was being tried for murder.

Her woes suddenly paled immensely compared to this man whose life had once been so closely connected to hers.

Oh, poor Cass.

Her mind raced, scrambling for ideas of how she might help him. Nothing came. Only silent tears. She was in no position to help anyone.

Chapter 15

Cass sat on his bunk. The smell of mildew wafted up from the straw mattress as he struggled to ignore the anxiety spreading out from his sour stomach. He leaned back against the stone wall and waited for the jailor to come fetch him. His attorney claimed this would be the last day of the trial, saying, "Come hell or high water, they're going to reach a verdict." After months of a seeming lifetime spent inside courtrooms, it looked like Cass was going to get his tongue-in-cheek wish of being locked up and the key thrown away. Only it wasn't for robbing Sarah of her virtue. If he was still a betting man, that's where he'd put his money—on being sentenced to prison.

The jingle of keys brought Cass to his feet. He rushed to the door of his cell, anxious to get this day over with.

"You got a visitor," the jailor said as he inserted the key. With an incline of his head, he pointed to a man coming up behind him.

"John!" Cass's upset stomach found a moment of calm. "What in blazes are you doing here?"

John stepped inside the cell and gave Cass a hug. "I would have been here sooner, but I kept thinkin' the damn trial would be over by the time I made it to Provo and we'd just cross paths on your way back down to Dandy Crossing. But when I received word that it kept draggin' on, I figured I'd better hightail it up here and give my big brother some moral support."

"Thanks a heap." Cass motioned for John to take a seat on his bunk. "I could use all I can get right about now." He plopped down on the mattress and let its sour smell unsettle his gut once again.

"Don't ya go frettin' like an old woman fallin' through an old outhouse floor. You're gonna pull through this, we'll have a whole passel of drinks to wash away the bad memories, and then you'll come out smellin' like the Colorado in springtime."

"I hope you're right, little brother. I hope you're right."

"'Course I am. Everyone loves ya, Cass. Back home, the boys are all askin' when you're comin' back—I make for a lousy foreman. They've even pitched in one week's salary each to help with your legal fees. And when I stopped in Green River on my way up, I swear every person in town was buzzin' about the trial, hoping you'd come away from it a free man. They're all on your side, Cass."

"Yeah, well, that's the problem, ain't it, John. This blasted year's worth of trials isn't being held down there.

Provo is Utah's second largest city and is a long way from Green River. Here, I could never hope to have them rustle up a jury of men who understand gunfights and self-defense. What do these men know about a man's honor and his right to settle a score?"

"Whoa, settle down, Cass. You're right." John's cheery expression fell away. "Unfortunately, it ain't no secret that you've bad-mouthed Mormons since the day you arrived in this territory. I'm sure that little fact has made its way up here. Hopefully it doesn't come back to ya, Cass, and bite ya in the butt."

Cass pushed out his chest. "But I don't do it no more!"

"Really." John raised an eyebrow. "Why not? That don't sound like you."

"Let's just say I met a few—one in particular—who changed my view."

"Maybe you should bring that up in your trial today. It could help you. Or better yet, get some of them Mormons who like you and have them testify on your behalf."

"I don't get to bring nothing up—just answer their blasted questions." Cass crossed his arms tight against his chest. He seriously doubted bringing Sarah into the courtroom would help his cause—only bring the judge's gavel down with a shout of "guilty" a little faster.

Footsteps approached in the outside corridor, followed by the jingle of keys. The jailor approached. "Sorry to interrupt you boys, but the bailiff's here to take the prisoner over to the courthouse."

Cass stood. "Thanks for coming, John. It means a lot." He pulled his brother up and gave him another hug.

"It was the least I could do." John gave him a friendly punch in the arm. He opened his eyes wide, like he forgot something. "Oh." He pulled an envelope from his jacket pocket. "I brought your mail. The ones that looked like business stuff, I opened myself, but this here letter's been collectin' dust on the self since the day after you left for Denver nearly eight months ago."

"Thanks, John." Cass reached for the letter.

"Hold on." The bailiff snatched the envelope from John's outstretched hand. "I need to check that before you give it to the prisoner and make sure it don't got a file or no knife in it," he said with a laugh. He tore off the end, peered inside, and then pulled out and unfolded a single sheet of paper. "It appears to be safe enough—just a letter. Nice handwriting, I must say."

Cass reached for the letter again with hopes that it came from Sarah.

The bailiff turned away. "I'll just put this this away for safe keeping until we get into the courtroom. I can't have you reading it while we walk across the street to the courthouse, now can I?" Sporting a smirk, he tucked the letter into his vest pocket and clamped a pair of handcuffs onto Cass's wrists.

"That stinks." John fell in step with the bailiff as he pulled Cass out of the cell. "This whole place stinks." He spread his arms, indicating the jail. "But it'll be over with soon, big brother. Tonight, we'll get good and drunk, celebrate real big."

"Yeah," Cass responded as the jailer pulled him up a set of stone steps. He hoped his brother was right.

Cass and the bailiff headed toward the rear of the courthouse while John went toward the front. The fall air smelled of dust and harvested alfalfa, fresh compared to Cass's stuffy cell. He took in a deep breath, looking forward to taking an even deeper one come the end of the day—hopefully. Anticipation quickened his step, and that prompted the bailiff to walk faster. Cass not only wanted this day to hurry and get over with, but he wanted to read that letter sitting in the man's pocket. The glimpse he caught of the handwriting, with its neatly flourished letters and distinctive feminine flair, gave him hope. Since his ma was dead, he could think of only one other woman he knew well enough that could possibly have a reason to write to him. *Sarah*.

Inside the building, the hard wooden floor amplified their footsteps. There was not a soul to be seen in the back hallway. Cass knew that was because they were all inside the courtroom waiting for him to arrive.

"Produce the accused," a deep voice came through the slightly ajar door.

The bailiff pulled him by the elbow. "That means you."

"I know, I know." Cass went willingly into the courtroom alongside the bailiff.

The courtroom brimmed with people, almost double the number of yesterday or any previous day. Many sat on the edges of their hard wooden seats, leaning their elbows on the back of the benches in front of them, wearing expectant expressions in their eyes. Were these men colleagues, investors and fellow frontiersmen, anxious to see him acquitted? Or those who only knew of Cass's cursing tongue and other weaknesses, not the real Cass Hite, and were anxious to see him convicted? The bailiff guided Cass to the first row of benches, pulled the envelope from his pocket and handed it to Cass, then retired to his spot guarding the side door. Cass slid in next to his attorney, immediately opened the letter, and read it as the judge moved the court into session.

His throat tightened as he read Sarah's plea to forgive her for her discourteous actions the morning he left. He focused on the next line.

It appears you have left me with child.

He suppressed a gasp. It was as he'd feared.

"Is everything all right?" his attorney whispered and motioned to the letter.

Cass nodded, though it was a lie. He read on.

Though I have the means to raise this child myself, I feel that would be unfair to the poor thing to be raised without a father. I wish to inquire if your offer of marriage is still open. I realize you do not wish to adopt my faith and the lifestyle I wish to live. Unfortunately, I cannot raise our child in the town of Hite. I'm hoping we can come to some kind of compromise if you are still willing to take me as your wife.

Sincerely

Sarah Hansen

P.S. I still love you. I have not yet fully forgiven you, nor have I forgiven myself, but in time, that will come.

Yes, it would! He could give it time—as much time

as she needed. And a compromise? Yes, he was more than willing. His heart might leap out of his chest at a chance to make it all up to her. He wanted to stand up right then and there, throw his hat into the air, and shout, "Yippee!"

Cass tucked the letter away and concentrated on the witness the prosecution questioned, hoping his heart rate would settle. He willed the man being questioned to say the right things, to strengthen Cass's cause—he wanted this blasted trial to end, and end good. The second it did, he'd be on the first train to Green River, and then the stagecoach to Hanksville. As soon as absolutely possible, Sarah needed to know he'd accept her on whatever terms she asked.

"I'd like to call another witness," said the prosecuting attorney. "Could Mr. Johnson from Price please take the stand?"

Price! The mere mention of that town's name brought Cass's euphoric moment crashing down like a mine shaft set off with dynamite. He couldn't marry Sarah. She was already married. *Dang! Dang! Dang!* If only he'd read this letter in time!

Frustration, regret, and anger boiled inside him to where he felt he'd burst. His cheeks puffed with air until he realized the need to breathe.

"Mr. Hite." His attorney nudged Cass in the arm. "They called your name. You need to take the stand."

"Oh, sorry." Cass scrambled to pull his mind together.

"The prosecution wants to question you again.

Remember what we went over, and you'll do fine."

Cass dragged his feet up to the witness stand, not remembering anything at the moment—except that he hadn't responded to Sarah in time.

Some man in a tweed suit held out a Bible for Cass to rest his hand upon. Cass didn't know who or what the man was, nor did he care at the moment.

"Do you swear to tell the truth, the whole truth, and nothing but the truth, so help you God?"

"Yes," Cass said in a near whisper.

"So, Mr. Hite," the prosecution began. "It has been established that you visited the Grammage Boarding house on the evening of January tenth of this year. Is that correct?"

"Yes, sir," Cass answered, his mind in a fog.

"And that it was your intent to speak with Mr. Adolf Kohler, correct?"

"Yes."

"And is it correct that you went there with your pistol strapped to your waist?"

"Yes, but I always carry my gun with me."

"Always?"

"Yes, always."

"You didn't don your gun purposely to have it handy when you found Mr. Kohler?"

"Hell, no!" Cass was losing patience with these asinine questions. "Like I said, I always carry my gun with me."

"You may step down, Mr. Hite." The prosecution looked at the judge. "I'd like to call another witness."

Cass didn't pay attention to the name that was

called. He just noticed an overly prim and proper, yet familiar-looking gentleman take the stand. The man lacked any sort of facial hair, and what little remained on his head appeared the same color as his buttoned-up suit and judgmental eyes—gray.

"Mr. O'Brian," the prosecution said, "are you acquainted with Mr. Cass Hite?"

"Yes, I am, though not personally. He does business with our bank in Salt Lake City."

"How often does he come into your bank, Mr. O'Brian?"

"I'd say at least three or four times a year."

"How many times have you seen him carry a gun?"

"Not once have I seen him wear one into our bank."

Cass's blood boiled. He set his stance to rise to his feet, but his attorney pulled him back down. After a string of curse words, he whispered to his lawyer, "Of course I don't wear my gun into that big city bank. I'd cause a scene. No one carries guns there—they don't need 'em. But Green River ain't Salt Lake!"

The prosecution looked at the judge. "So, given what Mr. O'Brian has told us, and what Mr. Hite just told us, who is to be believed?" He glanced at Cass. "Mr. Hite has yet to produce a viable character witness." Then back to the judge. "Yet in yesterday's session, I produced numerous witness who not only testified of Mr. Hite's foul mouth, lack of respect of his Mormon neighbors, and his obsession with gold, but of his indulgence in liquor and ladies of," he cleared his throat, "ill repute. Mr. O'Brian, on the other hand, is an upstanding citizen, a member of the chamber of commerce, and a churchgoing family man. I daresay the jury would have cause to believe Mr. O'Brian's statement over Mr. Hite's. And thus, if Mr. Hite doesn't always wear his gun, it is reasonable to conclude that he purposely wore his gun the night of the tenth of January for the express purpose of settling the quarrel—that we've already established existed between the two men over their respective mining businesses—by means of taking the law into his own hands."

Finally, the prosecution sat down.

Cass's attorney stood and took his turn.

"This trial is clearly in violation of Mr. Hite's constitutional rights. He has already been tried and acquitted . . ."

Cass's thoughts churned on matters outside the courtroom as his attorney rambled on about the Fifth Amendment and various legal terms, during which Cass lost focus. He was doing math in his head instead. It had been just over nine months since that night with Sarah. He most likely had a son now. Or a daughter. In either case, he was sure the child was beautiful. How could his child not be, with a mother like Sarah? But he would never know, never see that sweet infant, never have a chance to hold his own child—or its mother.

He turned his attention back to the proceedings when his thoughts became too painful.

The court dragged on into the afternoon with more distorted accounts that made Cass look bad and claims that his trial in Green River had not been carried out properly and thus held no credibility.

At four o'clock, the jury foreman stood and pronounced, "We the jury find the defendant, Cass Hite, guilty of murder in the second degree with recommendation of mercy from the court."

The judge looked at Cass and dropped his gavel. "I sentence Mr. Cass Hite to twelve years in the territorial prison."

Chapter 16

Sarah sifted some flour into a bowl, relishing the quiet moment of both Julia and baby Maggie napping at the same time. Maggie was nearly nine months old now, and this blessed occurrence rarely happened. Sarah turned to four-year-old Beth, who stood on a chair peering into the mixing bowl that sat on the kitchen table. "Would you like to add the sugar?"

"Oh, yes." Beth accepted the half cup of sugar with noticeable delight. She dumped it in and looked up at Sarah with her big blue eyes brimming with a question. "What we makin', Nana?"

"Sweet muffins."

Beth pulled a face.

"What's wrong?"

"Dat's what Papa calls Mama." Beth wrinkled her forehead and then looked at the floor and sniffled. "Why did Mama go away?"

"I'm sorry, sweetie." Sarah didn't like to see Beth hurting. She gathered the child into her arms, wishing like always that she had more of an answer for the little girl. "I don't know. But I do know your mama's with Heavenly Father now."

"But I wanna see her."

"You will someday . . . when you go to heaven too."

Beth puckered her lips into a pout and peered back into the mixing bowl.

"Do you want to crack the eggs?" Sarah would much rather do that herself, but Beth deserved the diversion.

Beth nodded. "Um-huh. I like to cwack eggs."

The first egg, Beth cracked with no problem. With her second one, a large piece of shell fell into the batter. As Sarah fished it out, the screen door opened, and Wayne stepped in from the backyard. Startled, she dropped the eggshell back into the bowl. "What are you doing home in the middle of the day?"

Wayne cocked his head to one side, and with an amused smile, said, "Sarah, it's Saturday."

"Oh, yes, but of course." She knew he'd been working half days on the weekend ever since Christmas to try to help make ends meet. "Sorry. I guess one day just feels like the next lately. Except for Sundays, of course," she added quickly for his sake.

"No need to apologize." Wayne stepped over to the table and kissed Beth on the cheek. "How is my big girl doing today?"

"Fine, Papa." Beth stuck the mixing spoon in the

bowl. "I'm helping Nana make sweet muffins."

Wayne's face blanched.

"I apologize, Wayne. I didn't know that was your pet name for her." Sarah purposely avoided saying "Genevieve." For the past fifteen months, since their marriage, she'd learned it was best not to remind Wayne of his departed wife.

"How could you? I've never mentioned that." He gazed out the window like he was staring at something far away.

After a minute of his silence, Sarah resumed the task of making muffins. "What if in this house, we just call them cupcakes?"

He didn't respond, but continued staring.

Sarah took the spoon from Beth and stirred the batter, thinking about how sometimes he would mope for days thereafter when she'd brought up Genevieve. Lately, however, he'd warmed up to Sarah. Somewhat. She didn't want to ruin that. She'd enjoyed the attention. "Or perhaps it would be best if I don't make them at all."

"No, you go ahead and make them. Like you said, we'll call them cupcakes." He leaned and kissed her on the lips. That surprised her, yet she enjoyed the warmth she felt. Every other day after work, he'd greeted her with a peck on the forehead or the cheek. She'd contented herself with his kindness in lieu of physical affection and hoped that would come in time.

Though unspoken, she knew Wayne, like herself, recognized that their marriage was one of convenience, one of utility, one of necessity. But deep in Sarah's heart, there lay the yearning to someday have their marriage grow into one of mutual love—like the marriage she'd always dreamed of.

A thought unsettled her. Was she possibly the one to blame for the lack of progression in their relationship? Could she, realistically, ever feel more than human kindness and gratitude toward this man who was six years her junior? Perhaps her heartache over Cass held her back much the same as Wayne's loss of Genevieve did.

"The backyard looks nice," Wayne said, pulling Sarah out of her contemplations. He leaned back away from her and returned his gaze out the window. "It appears the peas will be ready to pick any day now. You certainly have a way with soil and seeds."

"Thank you." Sarah appreciated the compliment. He seemed to be saying more nice things to her as of late. She should try harder to praise his good points as well.

"You are welcome. And I am going to help you pick those peas when they're ready. I need to help out more around here."

"But you're tired when you come home from work. You deserve to put your feet up and relax for a while." She worried about him; he always appeared tired.

He looked at her. "And you don't?"

"Well, yes, but I don't have another job after my duties are completed here in the house." Sympathy pulled her lips into that smile she usually offered him after he'd spent long hours at the church.

"I still could make time to help you here and there." He pulled the spoon from her hand, set it on the table, and gathered her hands into his.

Though cold, his slender fingers felt good. They brought a measure of comfort to that lonely space in her heart. "That would be very kind of you," she said softly.

"You are so exhausted at the end of the day." He squeezed her hands. "I swear you're half asleep before your head even hits the pillow. That's not good. For either of us. We rarely say a word to each other once the children are asleep."

"True." *Even though I no longer sleep in the front room, and you're there beside me in bed.*

"Like I said, I'm going to help you more, and hopefully you'll not be so tired at night, and we can. . . well . . . I think you know what I'm referring to."

Had she heard him correctly? She believed she did.

Was she ready? Her mind spun, grappling for an answer. *Yes.*

He had waited an admirable amount of time, first with her being pregnant, and then her recovery after giving birth. He'd hinted as much, those being the reasons for keeping his distance, but she'd been reluctant to believe them fully. Genevieve always seemed the more accurate reason. Perhaps she'd been wrong.

Sarah looked at her feet and nodded in response to his hint.

A quiet cry came from the front room.

"Julia." Sarah focused on the door into the other room. "Hurry, Wayne. Could you get her before she wakes the baby?"

"Yes, of course. No time like the present to start helping." He offered Sarah a smile as he darted from the room.

Sarah spooned batter into the baking cups, thinking back to how he'd given up his bed and bedroom for her when Maggie was born. He'd slept on the overstuffed chair for a month, Julia having taken Sarah's spot on the cot next to Beth when the cradle was needed for new baby Margaret. When she'd recovered from her delivery, she told him she would take the chair and for him to sleep in his own bed. "We are married, Sarah," he'd said as if reminding her. "As husband and wife, it is okay for us to share a bed." So she did, willingly—it being much more comfortable. For the last eight months, they slept together on the double-sized mattress in the home's single bedroom. Wayne never touched her, except for a bump from his elbow or a nudge from his leg as he rolled over. Part of Sarah had felt relieved, yet part of her ached with lonesomeness—and wanted to be loved.

It appeared he was ready to love her. As his wife. His new wife. *Finally*.

A swell of angst spread through her. Was that other part of her ready? The attraction she wanted to feel for Wayne wasn't there yet. It had nothing to do with his red hair and freckled face, or his overly skinny frame—he offered his own unique flavor of appeal. His sincere appreciation of her stepping into the role of mother to his children was enough to endear him to her for a lifetime. But she wanted to feel the kind of attraction that pulled her to him with inner desires and outward excitement, with constant longing to be next to him.

Like it was with Cass.

She shook her head to dislodge the unrealistic ideas. Her previous marriage held no such charm. What made her think her second marriage would be any different?

Maybe with time.

Wayne came back into the kitchen with Julia in his arms. "Beth, do you want to come out into the garden with me and your little sister? We're going to pull weeds."

Beth clapped her hands and climbed down off the chair.

Wayne smiled at Sarah with a rather pleasant grin. "I promise, I know the difference between a weed and a vegetable," he said before scurrying out the back door behind Beth. The screen door slammed behind them.

Immediately, a wail came from the other room, telling Sarah that Maggie had heard the screen door and now she was hungry. Sarah shoved the pan of "cupcakes" in the oven and walked into the front room.

"There, there, I'm coming." She scooped up the infant from the bassinet, admiring the child's thick locks of dark hair that almost from day one Sarah could twist into curls with her fingers and a little water. Sarah settled into the overstuffed chair and fed Maggie. She found it rather a treat to be able to nurse the baby without another baby and a four-year-old hanging on the chair or demanding her attention.

Once Maggie was fed, burped, and her diaper changed, Sarah sat her upright on the kitchen floor at her feet with a doll and started to make the rest of supper. Filling a pot with water to begin her soup, she looked out the window at Wayne playing with the older girls. She sighed. *This is nice. I could easily become accustomed to Wayne's help with the children—including baby Maggie.* The other day, she'd caught him cooing at Maggie and tickling her under her chin as he did with Julia when she was that age.

She sighed again. Yes, maybe happiness was possible. But just as she'd found she couldn't let others determine what was best for her, something inside her said neither could she let others determine her happiness. She should continue to work at this marriage. And learn to love Wayne so that one day, those inner desires and outward excitement would come together.

Right now, however, she would enjoy Wayne's help.

Supper proved to be delightful, with Wayne spoon-feeding Julia her soup for his first time. She blew her last bit back into his face and then tipped the near-empty bowl of creamed potatoes into his lap. All the girls laughed.

"Go ahead, laugh at your father. I suppose he deserves it." Wayne wiped a potato off the side of his nose. "Now, hurry and finish your supper, Beth, and it's off to bed for you."

"I don't wanna go to bed." Beth twisted her mouth.

"You are going, and so is Julia," he said in a firm voice, and then glanced at Sarah. "Nurse Maggie in the kitchen while I put the girls down. The dishes can wait."

While Wayne told the girls a bedtime story in the

front room, Sarah nursed the baby while sitting in a kitchen chair. It wasn't nearly as comfortable as the overstuffed chair, but she felt flattered, and that made it worth the lack of comfort. Wayne was obviously working hard to make this the night they consummated their marriage. At least, she assumed that was his intention.

Maggie's eyes fluttered closed, and she fell asleep while nursing. "Thank you, little one," Sarah whispered to her baby, hoping the remainder of her evening went as smoothly. She stood up ever so carefully and tiptoed into the front room carrying Maggie. Beth still fidgeted as Wayne rubbed her back. Sarah laid the baby in the bassinet and crept back into the kitchen to get a start on the dishes.

Not more than a minute later, Wayne walked softly into the kitchen wearing his nightclothes. He pulled Sarah's hand from the dishwater and tugged it away from the sink. "Leave them. It's my turn for your attention. I've waited long enough." He led her to the bedroom. "Change for bed," he whispered, "and then open the door when you're ready."

Sarah felt a slight rush of embarrassment. Why had he only kissed her once if he felt so strongly for her? And how long had he wanted to be intimate? A mixture of excitement and apprehension churned inside her as she removed her dress and corset, and then pulled on her nicest nightgown. She padded across the floor, barely cracked the door open, and whispered, "I'm ready."

He stepped in and carefully closed the door behind him. Taking Sarah by the hand, he led her to the bed. "I have been trying to be thoughtful of your situation . . . and wait to . . . impose myself upon you. I expect I've given you enough time. I am a man, after all, and I hope you understand that men have certain needs. Thank you beforehand for helping me take care of these needs." He lay down and bid Sarah to lie next to him as he turned down the lamp.

She complied, though his words bothered her somewhat. Was this all their interaction was meant to be, a task she would perform for him like scrubbing his floors or taking care of his children? Surely she had misunderstood him.

He took her into his arms and kissed her lips with energy. His hand raked through her hair, then down her body as his lips crept toward her ear. "Sweet muffin," he murmured in wispy tones.

Was this use of Genevieve's pet name a sign that he was starting to love her in the same way? She could only hope.

Or was he imagining he held Genevieve in his arms? The thought whisked Sarah away to that place she would visit the times she and Jacob became intimate. A slight, silent laugh swelled inside her as her thoughts ventured further. At least in the future, she would be forewarned when her husband needed her wifely services.

She stiffened. A whirlwind of hurt swept her thoughts back to that spot she'd go with Jacob. That place held no comfort and her mind begged to move on to somewhere more soothing. It ventured into a corner of banished memories and delved into the most bittersweet experience of her life. The moment she envisioned Cass holding her rather than Wayne, she knew it was a mistake. But it was too late to go back.

Chapter 17

The morning's sunshine spilled onto the cot where Beth and Julia wiggled about as Sarah dressed them for church. The rays of light did little to dispel the dark clouds gathering inside her. How could she possibly step inside that chapel today and pretend once again that she belonged there? Last night, treading on memories she had no right to revisit, she'd let herself relive each and every moment of her indiscretion with Cass.

As if that wasn't bad enough, the truth hit her full force and amplified her guilt tenfold. She still loved Cass Hite. And the fact that she had enjoyed her intimacy with him, beyond anything she could have ever imagined, tore at her conscience with razor-edged shame.

Sarah ran the brush through the tangles in Beth's long red hair. The child squirmed such that Sarah struggled with the simple task. She grabbed the child's arm and willed her not to move. "Hold still!"

Beth's lower lip jutted out, and she appeared as though she'd burst into tears.

Sarah hugged her. "Sorry, sweetie." *I'm sorry about a lot of other things, too.* "Forgive me."

"It's okay, Nana." Beth hugged her back.

If only Sarah could be forgiven of the *other things* so easily. She was sincerely trying to be happy, but the burden of infidelity weighed heavier than her determination had the strength for at times.

"I'll try to be more careful." Sarah resumed brushing Beth's hair, attempting to brush aside her despair as well. "Just because I am out of sorts this morning, it gives me no call to be rough on you."

Beth looked up at Sarah, her forehead wrinkled with confusion. "What's outtasorts?"

"Never mind. It's a big person's word you need not bother yourself with."

Sarah tied a ribbon in Beth's hair and latched onto Julia as the toddler tried to crawl off the cot, obviously bored with sitting there waiting her turn. Three quick strokes of the brush took care of Julia's short strawberry-blonde strands. She gathered Maggie from the bassinet, hating to disrupt the baby's nap, wishing she could use that as an excuse to stay home this Sunday in particular. However, the children's father expected his family to be there unless on their sick beds.

I don't feel well.

Spiritual sickness doesn't count.

At least Wayne seemed to be in good spirits that morning before he'd left for church. Apparently he'd not been upset by last night; he was getting what he needed from their marriage.

Her heart sank. She was getting what she needed too—a roof over her head and the last name of Barker for Maggie. What she ultimately wanted didn't matter. The price of sin was high.

She propped Maggie on one hip, led Julia by the hand while bidding Beth to take her sister's other hand, and headed toward the chapel three blocks away.

Once there, Sarah corralled the girls into their usual spot on the back pews, grateful to have the bench to themselves. The luxury was short-lived. During the sacrament hymn, some late arrivals—a man, woman, and three young school-aged children—squeezed onto her bench.

The mother sat down next to her. Sarah hardly knew the woman, only vaguely remembering her name to be Sister Anderson. But then again, Sarah had not made much effort to get to know any of the sisters in the ward—a sore spot with Wayne, she imagined. If only they spoke more of deeper matters, she would know for sure.

Sister Anderson leaned toward Sarah and whispered, "Could you please move in a tad so we can all fit?"

Sarah scooted the girls toward the wall, resenting this woman who was breaking the unwritten law of the back pew. She was not a mother of fussy youngsters or infant in arms.

When the sacrament was passed down the row,

she placed Julia and Maggie between her and Sister Anderson to help disguise the fact that she didn't partake of the bread and water, but only gave it to her children. Between wrestling with three small children by herself, and wrestling with her guilt, Sarah had grown to hate church. With sadness, she remembered the time when she used to love attending worship services. Now she rarely listened to the words coming from the pulpit. They always made her feel poorly. This day was no exception. In fact, it was worse. Guilt rode heavy on her shoulders, what with being in love with a man other than the one she was married to. As things appeared, that wasn't about to change anytime soon. How could she sit here in church like a hypocrite? For that matter, how could she pretend at home, either?

When the postlude music finally piped from the organ, Sarah stood, anxious to exit the building before anyone else.

Sister Anderson seemed in no hurry to leave. She didn't budge from her seat. Instead, she picked up Julia and stroked the child's thin hair. "This girl's a darling, that's for sure." Patting the bench next to her, she said, "Sit for a while. There's no need to rush off. Besides, I feel I hardly know you, yet you're the bishop's wife. I've been meaning to come visit you."

Sarah gave a feeble smile.

"And offer to help." Sister Anderson now patted Sarah's knee. "After all, I'm sure it's a challenge, raising three little girls so close to the same age, basically by yourself, what with your husband's responsibilities as bishop."

That's the least of my struggles. "I am doing fine." Sarah glanced around the chapel. The congregation filed outside, but most lingered, meeting with friends and chatting. She didn't want to stay and take the chance of someone else wanting to talk to her. It hurt to remember how she used to enjoy getting to know new people and chatting about the things they liked to do or what they learned that day. She pushed old memories aside and breathed deep. "Yes, things are going well, but thank you for your thoughtfulness." Sarah picked up Maggie, hoping that would give the signal that she wanted to leave.

Sister Anderson reached over and wrapped one of Maggie's dark curls around her finger. "What beautiful hair this little one has—and so much of it." She stroked Julia's head. "The bishop's little girls are as different as night and day." Her eyes gravitated to Sarah's hair. "It's hard to imagine a child with such dark features having parents as fair as you and Bishop Barker."

Sarah's insides tightened. "Oh, have you not heard?" She cradled Maggie close. "This child is not Wayne's; she's from my first husband. I was widowed shortly after I conceived."

Lies and more lies!

"No, I hadn't heard." Sister Anderson's eye's widened. "I'm so sorry. Yes, everything makes more sense now."

How many other people had noticed Maggie's coloring and made speculations?

Was she going to have to lie to them, too, in order to cover up her immorality? Was that single sinful act not enough? How could adding deceit to her already insurmountable load of guilt ever help her pull out of the deep gulf she'd fallen into?

It couldn't.

Yet she could see no other way around it.

Maggie cried, and Sarah shot up from off the bench. "Excuse me, Sister Anderson, but it's Maggie's dinnertime." Dragging Julia behind her and motioning with her chin for Beth to follow, she side-stepped past the woman, her family having left already, and escaped into the aisle. Immediately, she darted for the exit, feeling ready to collapse.

Trudging down the street, she told herself she was stuck in this pit. And since she'd created it for herself, she figured no one else should be put upon to pull her out. *An actress on the stage. Yes, that's what I'll become.* She'd give people the lines they wanted to hear. She'd take care of her new husband's needs without letting on that it dredged up memories that added to her guilt. And she'd wear a practiced smile every day to convince others, and herself, that she was something she wasn't—happy. She would be the happiest miserable woman there ever was.

She walked faster, as if that would secure her new determination in her soul and bring her a measure of peace.

It didn't work. Everything felt wrong. Acting happy wasn't the answer. She needed to *be* happy.

But how? She'd been trying so hard already.

But had she really? Or was she merely bottling up

her feelings again and letting others decide for her?

Well, one thing was for sure. Loving her own husband would help her be happier. And only she was in control of that.

***

After supper and the children were asleep, Sarah ignored the dirty dishes piled in the sink and pulled a kitchen chair into the living room. She parked it next to the overstuffed chair where Wayne sat reading a book. When she sat down, inching the chair even closer to Wayne's, he looked up, meeting her eyes with an expression of surprise. "What are you doing?" he said with a twist to his grin.

"Getting to know my husband." Sarah closed the book in his lap and then leaned on the arm of his chair with her elbows propping her chin. "We've been married a year and a half, and I don't even know what your favorite color is."

"Blue."

"Ah, I would have guessed that," she said, remembering things he *had* managed to reveal to her. "Is that because you enjoy the brilliance of a morning sky without clouds? Or because that was the color of Genevieve's eyes?"

His eyes shot to the floor. "I'm sorry. I know I need to forget her and move on, but—"

Sarah placed her fingertips to his mouth and could feel his lips tremble. She moved her fingers to his chin and raised it to where their eyes met. "You shouldn't forget her—she was an important part of your life."

"But you deserve—"

She rushed her fingers back to his lips and felt the slightest hint of a kiss to them. "Genevieve deserves to be remembered. She deserves to be loved. The human heart isn't consigned to love only one person at a time. I know you know that. I've seen the way you love all the people at church. And I've seen you cradle little Maggie in your arms and kiss her forehead. Does that mean that you love Beth and Julia any less because you've given a portion of your love to their stepsister?"

He shook his head. "No"

"Tell me about Genevieve. She must have been a dear woman for you to love her so deeply."

"Oh, she was," he responded quickly and then sucked in his breath. "Sorry."

"No need to be sorry." Sarah placed her hand on his. She liked how it made her feel connected to him. "I truly want to hear what you have to say about her." If she could learn a few things to help her obtain even a fraction of the love those two shared, perhaps that would be enough to help her.

"Fair enough." Wayne took her hand in his. "Then you can tell me more about you. And about your departed husband."

"Okay," Sarah responded hesitantly. She longed to open up, confess all, unload the weight that sat constantly on her shoulders. "I . . . uh . . ." She'd tell Wayne about Jacob instead. She dared not say more than that. Her energies need to be spent learning to love Wayne, and hopefully he would come to love her. Tainting the process with mention of Cass would only serve to destroy either of their chances to find new love.

Chapter 18

Sarah took a break from weeding, wanting to sit in the shade of their neighbor's poplar tree and read the letter the mail carrier had delivered a moment ago. It was from Edna—only the second correspondence she'd received from her former sister wife. The first one came three years ago after Sarah had first moved to Price. She headed for the only spot of lawn left in their yard, having cultivated every other speck of ground. The garden space still proved insufficient. With the increased cost of rent, Wayne missing more and more work because of his ailing health, and three little girls ages two, three, and six now, Sarah felt the pressure to grow even more of their own food. As she lowered onto the grass, her thoughts went to the scanty sandwich she'd sent to school with Beth that day, a single slice of brown bread spread with a thin layer of strawberry jam and then folded in two.

She opened the letter and read.

Dear Sarah,

It is with sadness that I pen this letter. Our dear Nyda passed away last evening. She had been battling poor health for some time. We can, however, take comfort in knowing she is in a better place now and suffers no longer. The past few weeks, she inquired after you often, wondering if anyone had heard from you. She always worried about you. I know it would mean a lot to her children, and to her as she watches from heaven, if you could but find a way to attend the funeral. It will be held this Saturday morning, September13, at the church here in Hanksville.

I, too, would love to see you again.

Sincerely,

Your sister, Edna

Sarah folded the letter and stuffed it back into the envelope. The desire to see Edna and pay her last respects to Nyda swelled inside her chest. She wanted to go. She needed to go—to do something to relieve the emptiness that plagued her soul a little more each day. It had subsided for a while a year and a half ago when her love for Wayne had blossomed—and his love for her had done the same. At that same time, Clara and Cleon had visited her often, along Clara's new baby and Cleon's new wife. Then her grown children raised questions, dates were compared, and Sarah had to string a new set of lies to explain sweet little Maggie's birth date.

Her grown children rarely visited after that. Perhaps it had been because Sarah was too preoccupied with Wayne's health to invite them, or they had made judgements of their own that kept them away. In either case, it created yet another painful pebble in her shoe on her life's journey.

Sarah rushed into the house to change out of her work dress. Minutes later, clean and hair combed back into a proper bun at the nape of her neck, she headed toward Wayne's office. She'd taken this half-mile hike up toward the mine so rarely. A few minutes later, rundown houses with brown, week-choked yards lined the streets and the air reeking of coal dust reminded her why. She slowed her steps and thus her breathing as she approached the mine office at the top of the hill.

The metal steps rocked as she ascended them to access the side door that would take her the fastest to Wayne's office. A stout man with a bushy moustache, big cigar pouring out smoke beneath it, sat behind a desk. He looked at Sarah with scrutiny darkening his eyes as she stepped inside. "Excuse me, ma'am, you must use the front door. This one is only for employees."

Sarah did not want to go out and around the building to the front—and go past Wayne's tyrant supervisor to get back here. With the tales Wayne had told her about the man and his volatile tongue and demeaning nature, she wondered how her poor husband endured this place. "I'm coming to speak with my husband, Wayne Barker." She pointed down the narrow hallway. "His office is just right there. Please allow me to come this way—it's very important that I speak with him."

The man wagged his cigar at her. "Ah, get on yer way, then. Just hurry and don't let no one see ya."

"Thank you, sir."

Sarah hurried to the first door in the hall and

opened it.

Wayne's eyes lit up. "Sarah, what are you doing here?"

Sarah gave him a peck on the lips, then pulled Edna's letter from her pocket and waved it ever so slightly in the air. "I just received word that Nyda, my former sister wife, passed away."

"I'm sorry to hear that." Wayne motioned for her to take a seat in the extra chair tucked in the corner of his small office.

Sarah sat down. "I rarely ask you for much, Wayne, so I'm hoping this one time you'll say yes." She wrung her hands and looked at the floor. "I want to go to the funeral. Down in Hanksville."

"You're incorrect."

Sarah looked up, slightly rattled. "What?"

"You *never* ask for anything." Wayne's eyes demanded that she stay fixed to his. "Day after day, you take whatever life dishes out to you without complaint. Frankly, I'm worried about you, Sarah. I sense you're bottling it all up inside you to where happiness has no room to reside there. I never see you smile."

"I smile!" Sarah said quickly, fighting back the hurt—she made an extra effort to force a grin onto her face every day.

"Only on the outside. And only when people are watching." Wayne stood and approached her, his hand outstretched. "When is the funeral?" he asked as if purposely changing their conversation back to its original subject. He pulled Sarah to her feet and wrapped his arm around her shoulders.

She appreciated his touch. "Saturday," she responded to his question as her back relaxed against his arm. "The day after tomorrow."

He gave her a quick hug. "Go home and get our things packed. We'll leave first thing in the morning."

"Oh." She was caught off guard—she'd expected to go by herself. But the thought of Wayne and the girls accompanying her prompted a tingle of excitement inside her. It had been ages since she'd felt anything like it. And the girls had yet to visit Hanksville. Edna would love to see the girls. Perhaps Clara would warm up to a visit of her little sisters as well.

As quickly as it appeared, the excitement vanished. "But the cost, train tickets for five, and then the stagecoach fares. Can we afford such extravagance? And there is your time off work. And church." She buried her face in her hands. "I'm sorry, Wayne. I don't need to go."

"We'll manage." He pulled her hands away from her face and tipped her chin up to look into her eyes. "Besides, I think the five of us deserve a vacation, seeing how we've never taken one. I know I do. And I *know* you do." He wiped a tear from Sarah's cheek, one she'd done a poor job of hiding. "Yes, I do believe an outing is just what this family needs. You head on home, and I'll talk to my supervisor and try to wrangle some time off. And don't worry about church. There are plenty who can cover for me."

Sarah hurried out of Wayne's office, her steps feeling rather light, and that surprised her. Ignoring the man with the cigar, she rushed to the side door and stepped outside into the sunshine. She hoped Wayne was right, that this trip to Hanksville would do her some good. And him as well—the air was so much cleaner in that little town. He had been so kind to her there in the office, yet he admitted seeing through her façade. A lump caught in her throat. She loved Wayne, and he deserved to be told the truth. She'd wanted to tell him numerous times over the last year and a half, but fear of losing him always got in the way.

At the moment, she couldn't worry about such matters. She had clothes and food to pack for the journey. A small measure of excitement fluttered inside her again.

Chapter 19

The stagecoach slowed to a near crawl as it jostled Sarah, Wayne, and the girls along Hanksville's Main Street. Luckily, they'd had the coach to themselves.

"I'm so excited, Mama." Beth bounced on the edge of the bench seat she shared with Maggie and Julia.

"Well, we're almost there. Aren't we?" Wayne asked.

Sarah nodded, thinking how for the entire coach ride from Green River, little Maggie never gave her a spot off trouble. She never grew bored with the long ride. When she wasn't napping, she toddled constantly from one bench seat to the other, entertaining her sisters with giggles and hugs. As in times past, Sarah gathered morsels of happiness as they spilled over from her two-year-old daughter's zest for life. *Maggie, my silver lining.*

The stagecoach stopped.

"Are we here?" Beth asked. She chewed on her lip and peered out the window.

"Yes, we are here. We're done traveling—for today." Wayne opened the door and stepped out. He held onto Sarah's hand as she hopped out and then helped the driver get their bags down from the top of the stage while Sarah assisted the girls.

With their belongings tucked under their arms or toted in bags, Sarah led her family down Center Street to Edna's house.

"Where we staying tonight, Papa?" Beth looked up at Wayne, clinging to one of his hands while Julia had hold of the other.

Wayne looked to Sarah.

"I'm hoping there is room at Edna's." Sarah hitched Maggie farther up on her hip. "The big house, where Nyda lived, will most likely be full with all her children coming back for the funeral."

"So, you don't know where we're staying?" Wayne's voice held noticeable concern.

"Not really, but don't worry," Sarah said, hoping to comfort both Wayne and the girls. "I've got plenty of family here. Everyone knows me. There'll be no problem finding a place to bed down."

They walked the next block in relative silence. A yawn or two from the littlest girls accompanied the chorus of crickets in the background. The smell of fresh-cut hay filled the air, and Sarah relished her every breath. Edna's two-story frame house with its large front porch came into view. Light glowed from the two of the bottom windows. "We are fortunate indeed," Sarah said, quickening her pace and switching Maggie to her other hip. "It appears someone is still up in the front room. Let's hurry."

Sarah hurried toward the house, ran up the porch steps, and knocked.

Edna pushed open the screen door. "Sarah!" She pulled Sarah into a hug. "I truly hoped you would come. And you have." She let go and stepped back. "And you have brought your new family. Wonderful! Come in for a minute."

"A minute?" Sarah bit on her lip. "I had hoped we could stay here for the next two nights. We don't have the funds to stay at the boarding house."

"Don't you worry. I've got an even better place for you to stay." Edna ushered them all inside. "And I got it ready for all of you, just in case you did come."

"The big house?" Beth spoke up.

Sarah put her finger to her lips. The tiniest of grins tugged at her mouth as she looked at Beth, reminding the child to use her manners.

Edna smiled. "I see you mother has told stories of her life before she married your father."

Sarah cringed. She'd told so very few stories. "So that is where we'll be staying?" she asked Edna.

"No, you will be staying at your own cabin on the edge of town." Edna smiled like she'd delivered Sarah the best news possible during a time of mourning.

"Oh," Sarah squeaked.

"That's wonderful." Wayne looked at Sarah as if to confirm.

Sarah offered a reluctant nod. Part of her looked forward to visiting the log cabin where she raised Clara and Cleon, and once called home. But part of her dreaded what might happen if she returned there and shared a bed with her husband in the place where she had willingly sinned. She feared those banished memories would return once again and revive the painful sting of her remorse.

"What about Mary and her family?" Sarah's words rushed out. "I hardly think we could all fit in there."

Edna offered a demure smile. "Not to worry. Just a week ago, they moved into the big house so Mary could take care of Nyda. She and her family are going to live there from now on. So your cabin, dear Sarah, is vacant—and ready and waiting for you."

"Well, that answers our lodging question." Wayne hid a yawn with his hand. "And as it is late and we've had a long journey . . . Sarah, would you be so kind as to show us the way?"

"Wait just a minute." Edna held out her open arms. "I want to meet these three lovely girls first. I fear that tomorrow, with the funeral and all, things might get a mite hectic and I could miss this opportunity."

Sarah nudged Beth to step forward. "This is our oldest."

"I'm happy to meet you, Aunt Edna." Beth bent her knee in a curtsy.

"These are our other two daughters, Julia and Maggie." Sarah touched each girl on the shoulder as she said their names, and they offered a smile.

Edna brought the palms of her hands together. "Beautiful girls, all three of them." Her eyes focused on

Beth and Julia. "Now, these two girls I can definitely see that they are their papa's girls, with that red hair of theirs." She switched her attention to Maggie. "But this little one. . ." Her eyes glanced over to Wayne and then looked at Sarah. "She doesn't resemble her papa in the least."

Sarah froze. How could she have been so foolish to have let this happen? The fabricated answer as to Maggie's dark hair wouldn't work here. Everyone knew Jacob—knew he had light brown hair and a complexion as fair as Wayne's. Warmth flushed through her face as the sudden urge to flee back to Price consumed her. *Whatever was I thinking, coming down to Hanksville?* She scrambled for a way out of this.

"She takes after my mother and my grandmother," Sarah said, feeling much less confident than her smooth words. *Lies and more lies!*

Edna seemed to accept Sarah's explanation, and after some more hugs and a few goodbyes, they were on their way.

Wayne seemed extra quiet as they made it to the cabin with the help of the near-full moon and Sarah's vivid memory of the streets of Hanksville. Good memories and tender feelings flooded Sarah as she stepped inside her old cabin, distracting her from the guilt caused by her lying tongue. The memories lingered as she prepared her family for bed. How she longed for these pleasant feelings to fill her once again, for them to be with her always rather than her frequent dark clouds of remorse.

Beth and Julia claimed Clara and Cleon's old beds

in the front room, slipping beneath the covers while Wayne went outside to visit the privy.

"And where shall you sleep?" Sarah asked little Maggie with a nibble to her chubby cheek at the same time Wayne stepped inside.

"Go ahead and share the other bed with your mother." He ruffled Maggie's curls and dropped into the chair in the middle of the front room. He propped his feet atop the footstool. "I shall sleep here."

"Thank you, Wayne." Sarah kissed her husband on the forehead before leading Maggie into the bedroom. "I really appreciate it." *More than you'll ever know.*

The next morning, Sarah inched in front of Jacob's headstone as the bishop dedicated Nyda's grave. She didn't want Wayne to see it when he opened his eyes after the prayer. She'd not thought out this trip at all. Perhaps it was for the best, elsewise she might not have come. But the girls were enjoying their outing immensely—except for the funeral earlier in the day.

After the bishop finished his prayer, people filed past Nyda's grave, offering a sprinkle of dirt upon her coffin, or a tear and a thoughtful nod of their head.

Memories of standing in that exact spot five years ago filled Sarah's thoughts. Her emotions nearly mirrored those she felt at Jacob's burial—sad for the loss of this dear person who had been a part of her life, but devoid of grief. She brought her handkerchief to one eye, willing it to produce a tear or two. Why could she not cry? Why could she not feel the same as this throng of people with eyes red and brimming with tears, surrounding her and the grave that held her former sister wife? It couldn't be simply because Nyda had meddled in her life years ago. That was well behind Sarah now.

Maggie wiggled through the crowd of mourners trickling away from the cemetery and side-stepped over to Sarah. She latched onto Sarah's hand and squeezed like she often did when something didn't make sense and she wanted an explanation. With sadness in her eyes, she pointed a chubby finger at Edna. "She cwying."

"That's because your Aunt Nyda is no longer with us," Sarah whispered. "She has gone home to live in heaven with Jesus. These people are sad because things won't be the same anymore." She doubted Maggie understood, but it spawned a realization that hit hard, like an arrow hitting its mark after almost no practice. It explained her own question.

Her life wasn't the same anymore, not since that unforgiveable night. And in dealing with the pain, she'd turned off all emotion—at least, all she could. She supposed remorse, self-loathing, and guilt could be deemed emotions. Those she'd been unable to turn off.

Now a tear appeared. And then another. *She* had allowed the last three years of her life to become empty, not living life, merely existing. She might as well have thrown those years of her life away. Sadness swelled inside her, filling her nearly emotionless shell. The only emotion she had allowed was her love for Wayne and the girls. If she hadn't had that, she imagined she wouldn't have survived. As she swiped the trickle of moisture from her cheek, she felt an arm wrap around her shoulders.

"It's all right to cry." Edna's voice interrupted her trance, and her hand took the place of Maggie's. The toddler backed away from the grave to stand by Beth and Julia. "Let those tears flow, dear sister." Edna squeezed her. "I'm so glad to know you've finally learned how to grieve."

Sarah shook her head. No, she'd learned so very little.

Standing on her other side, Wayne placed his hand on her shoulder the moment Edna let go. He leaned down and spoke softly in her ear. "It's okay; crying is a good way to purge the pain."

Though Sarah could tell he'd intended to lend comfort, his words had the opposite effect, imagining he'd read her mind and now knew that their marriage had been filled with lies. *Nonsense! How could he know?* He couldn't— she'd honed her theatrical skills well. "Thank you," she responded, using them once again.

"If you are ready," Wayne continued in his soft, calming voice, "perhaps we should head to your sister's house for that meal that was mentioned. I know the girls are ready—and I think a bite to eat will do you good too."

Beth spoke up from behind. "Yes, please, can we go, Mama? Julia's hungry."

Sarah turned to view Beth standing next to Maggie and Julia. With eyes wide and pleading, they all nodded their heads. "Yes, a good meal in a less somber setting will do us all some good," she said, wanting a cheerful diversion.

Sarah led the way, holding on to the crook of

Wayne's arm while the girls followed a few steps behind. When the big house came into view, she could see swarms of people and tables filled with food in the backyard of the big house, along with a large number of children playing with each other.

Beth came up even with Sarah and Wayne. "Can I play?" she asked Sarah, her eyes begging.

"Yes, go enjoy the rest of the day." Sarah motioned Maggie and Julia forward. "Take your sisters with you."

Wayne looked at Sarah, his brow wrinkling like it often did when he felt concern. "Is that prudent, to tell them to enjoy such a solemn day?"

"They're children, Wayne. No sense burdening their lives with sorrow before it's time."

"I suppose you're right."

"Good, because I think I'm going to try to enjoy this day too—what's left of it." *And what's left of my life.* New resolve filled her. A silent prayer consumed her heart, and she hoped God was listening. *Please, Lord, help me find the courage and the right moment to tell Wayne the truth.*

She added her other hand to the one latched to Wayne's elbow and tugged him toward the front yard instead of following the girls. "Let me show you some photographs and tell you about my days spent in Hanksville." The idea appealed to her for some reason. Perhaps visiting those memories of days gone by—ones she realized now that were happier than that she'd once thought—could help her muster some courage.

Sarah knocked on the front door and then entered, figuring everyone was probably in the backyard. She turned and bid Wayne to follow, and together they stepped into the front hall. The stairs lay directly in front of them, the parlor to the right. She led Wayne to the large family photograph in the parlor that was taken a few months before Jacob died. Set in a dark wooden frame and covered with glass, it hung above the fireplace mantel with elegance.

"It's quite the family." Wayne reached up and touched the glass atop Sarah's small image. "How many are Jacob Hansen's children, and how many are his grandchildren?"

Sarah, prepared to respond with some of her fond memories, was caught off guard when someone from behind cleared their throat.

"Twenty are his children, and twelve are his grandchildren—in that picture. He now has thirty grandchildren and ten great-grandchildren."

Sarah spun around to see Nyda's daughter enter the room. "Oh, hello, Mary. I hope you don't mind, but I wanted to show Wayne some pictures of our family."

"Of course I don't mind." Mary walked toward them.

"I understand you're living here now," Sarah said.

"Yes, we moved here just a week ago, barely before Mama died." Mary sucked in a quick breath. "It's a good thing, since no one else in the family is in need of a place to live right now, and I'd hate to have the house sit vacant." She glanced at Sarah with an apologetic smile. "Sorry, but that leaves your cabin vacant. Thank you so much, by the way, for letting me and my little family live there for the past couple of years. I'm afraid if we stayed much longer, we'd soon outgrow it." She placed a hand on her round belly. "But my husband and I will continue to tend to your fruit trees. At least, as long as you need us to do so."

"Thank you," Sarah said, grateful her fruit trees need not die of neglect. Though she and Wayne would miss the few extra dollars each month Mary sent them as rent.

Mary stepped over to the adjacent wall and bid Sarah and Wayne to follow. She pointed to a couple of portraits hanging above a rolltop desk. "These two cherished photographs were taken the same day as the other one. They offer a much better view of my parents."

Wayne walked over and looked closely at the two pictures, concentrating more, it seemed, on Jacob's. Sarah had seen them plenty of times, so her eyes skirted around the room for anything else of possible interest to show her husband before they moved out to the backyard for something to eat.

"In this picture," Wayne said to Mary, "is Jacob's hair gray?"

"No, Papa never turned gray. It's light brown. His coloring was almost as fair as yours. It's hard to tell such things in a photograph, though."

Sarah quit looking around for things to show Wayne. Her husband had obviously found plenty to hold his interest—things better left alone, as far as she was concerned. "Shall we head outside and join the girls?" she asked. Her voice held more urgency than she had intended. The air in the room felt thick, uncomfortable.

"In a minute." He stared at Sarah. His eyes questioned her. She'd seen that look on the day he discovered a discrepancy in his employer's accounts. Confronting his boss the next day hadn't been easy for him, and she could tell he was going to have just as difficult a time asking her about this portrait. "We'll eat shortly, but first I want to ask your niece a question." He stared once again at Jacob's portrait. His eyes moved down to a plaque hanging beneath its frame, something that hadn't been there ten years ago.

Sarah caught her breath. At the cemetery, she'd kept Wayne from seeing Jacob's headstone. But she hadn't counted on this.

"Certainly," Mary responded. "Ask away."

"These numbers beneath his name—I presume they represent years. Jacob's birth and death dates, perhaps?"

"Yes, correct. Jacob was born in the year 1833, and passed away in 1889. Two years before you and Sarah were married."

"Thank you." Wayne inclined his head at Mary. He then took Sarah by the elbow and led her away from the portraits, toward the door. "We'll be joining the others now. It was nice meeting you."

"Thank you again for taking care of my cabin," Sarah said over her shoulder, hoping to change the subject and dissipate the stifling awkwardness that filled the air. This was not how she'd wanted the truth to come out—it was like someone else, again, was making decisions for her.

The moment they stepped out the door, Wayne whispered gruffly into her ear, "We need to talk."

Chapter 20

That afternoon, she and Wayne never had a moment alone to talk. Upon walking out of the house, Edna snagged them immediately and proceeded to drag Wayne around to every uncle, aunt, and cousin and introduce him—something Sarah should have done earlier, but didn't. Now she, Wayne, and the girls shared the comfortable, but cramped space of the cabin. Wayne's occasional glance told her they would "talk" once the girls went to bed.

"Mama, hurry out and help us pick beans. Papa's making a mess of them." Beth's voice carried in through the opened door with the kind of excitement only a child could muster.

"I'm coming," Sarah called out. She tossed another log onto the now-healthy flames and headed for the door.

Fifteen minutes or so later, after the vines had been picked clean, Sarah settled onto a stool at the side of the house and started snipping the beans. The earthy aroma of the freshly broken green beans reached her nose, but she could barely enjoy the smell. Out of the corner of her eye, she could see Wayne picking apples. Mary had told them to take anything they wanted from the garden. Sarah wanted to take all they could carry back to Price, where their tiny garden had yet to see them through the winter. He constantly glanced her way. His gaze told her he had not forgotten that they needed to talk

After a supper of fresh green beans and new potatoes, Sarah got the girls to sleep. No more delays could push aside the inevitable any longer. Wayne stood from the table and approached her. He held out his hand. "Let's go outside."

She took his hand and let him lead her, appreciating that he didn't wish to chance the girls listening in on their conversation. Once outside, he snagged the stool she'd sat on earlier and carried it to the front of the house. He lowered onto the door step as he motioned for her to sit on the stool. "I've known for some time that you've been troubled," he said.

I guess I'm not the actress I thought. "Really?" Sarah said, almost whispering.

Wayne took her hand in his. "Why didn't you tell me? Why did you lead me to believe that Maggie was Jacob Hansen's child?"

Tears swelled in Sarah's eyes. The urge to cry filled her entire body. She fought it. "Because . . . I thought . . ." Her words felt nailed to her tongue, agonizing and difficult to pry free.

"You thought what?" Wayne squeezed her hand. "That I wouldn't understand?"

Sarah nodded quickly, trying to force her words loose, to release them from their pain. "I feared you would reject me and not take me as your wife, then my unborn child and I would be on our own, left to suffer the taunts and humiliation due an unwed mother and her bastard child." Her tears broke free and escaped, along with her penned-up secrets. "I couldn't subject my baby to that—I just couldn't. I had to protect her. So one by one, the lies crept in order to cover my unforgivable mistake." She sucked in a breath between sobs. "Then came the guilt, so heavy at times that I pled with myself to give up and I curled into ball and begged God to take me home. But I soon realized the irony of my pleadings. I no more dared to face my Maker if He were to whisk me off this earth and up to heaven, for a judgment of guilt would have been pronounced without question, and I would have speedily been sent down to hell."

Wayne reached up and wiped the tears from one of her cheeks. "Is that what you think, that you are unforgivable?"

That familiar ache pressed against her heart and her chin quivered. She managed a nod. Then in a ghost of a voice, she explained, "I knew better, but I willingly sinned."

"Oh, Sarah, Sarah, Sarah." Wayne wrapped his arms around her and pulled her head against his chest. "You are human, and as such, you make mistakes. I make mistakes. We all make mistakes."

"But mine are more numerous and far worse than

yours, I am *sure.*" She was amazed, yet grateful that he didn't inquire as to whom Maggie's actual father was—she couldn't bear to have Wayne think poorly of Cass.

"That is what is so wonderful about the healing power of the Savior," Wayne continued. "He has already paid the price for any, and all, sins you have committed."

Sarah resisted his attempt to comfort her. She knew of Jesus Christ's sacrifice, but it didn't apply to her.

But he was a bishop, and had experience with confessionals. Could she dare to hope? "Even for those I willingly and wantonly committed?" she blurted out with agonizing passion.

"Yes." He pulled her face away from him and looked her in the eye. "But only if you accept His offer and allow His atonement to heal you."

"How?" Oh, she wanted so much for his words to be true, but couldn't see the way to make it happen.

His mouth lifted slightly on one side like he was telling her something she already knew. "Remember the steps of repentance from Sunday school?"

Sarah shook her head, pulling it away from his tender grasp and burying it in her hands. "No—I feel so uncomfortable at church anymore."

"Yes, this is all making more sense now." He lifted her chin with the tip of his finger and made her look at him. "You've suffered long enough for your mistake, dear Sarah. Obviously you've more than sufficiently taken care of recognizing the sin and feeling remorse. I sense this has plagued you ever since I married you. I am only glad to know now that I am not the source of your unhappiness." He offered her a crooked grin as he let his finger fall from her chin. "At least, I hope I am not."

Her aching heart melted at his kindness through all of this, especially when he had every right to be angry with her. "No, no, you were not, Wayne. You've been nothing but good to me. I am so sorry to have caused you to think otherwise." She wiped the moisture from her eyes. "Oh, dear, I don't know how to rectify my mistake—isn't that a step? I can't undo what I have done."

"In your case, you must confess to your ecclesiastical leader—your bishop. Which is me." That hint of a grin returned. "You have just done that, my dear. Now all you have left to do is to get on your knees, pray to God, promise never to commit this sin again, and ask His forgiveness." He took her hand in his and squeezed. "And He will grant it, I am confident."

Hope stirred inside Sarah. She leaned forward, her hands clasped at her bosom. This hope gave her a measure of strength, letting her see the sun peeking out from behind those dark clouds as they parted.

She moved a hand on top of his and squeezed. "Thank you, Wayne." She leaned farther and shared a sweet kiss on the lips with him, and then stood. Without another word, she stepped past him into the house. Tiptoeing past Beth and Julia, she crept into the bedroom, and then knelt in a corner where the braided rug covered the floor. Careful not to wake Maggie, she approached the Lord in a whisper.

"Dear Heavenly Father, I come before you in humble prayer to beg thy forgiveness . . ."

Her words faded into a silent prayer, not wanting to disturb Maggie with her pleadings. She repeated her words for a second time, pouring her whole heart into her prayer with more energy this time. Her body spent, she ceased kneeling and sat on the floor, pulling her knees to her chest and hugging them close, all the while willing God to soothe her soul.

A spot of warmth formed inside her guarded heart. It grew more intense in the most indescribable, wonderful sort of way, filling her chest and then reaching up to her mind. She knew in that instant that God forgave her. The liberating experience became even more sweet as she felt her Heavenly Father's unconditional love for her.

She broke down and wept.

Eight Years Later

Chapter 21

The door to Cass's cell opened for its last time—at least for him. Some other poor fool would have the dubious honor of residing in there from now on. "It's about time," Cass grumbled to the guard he knew simply as Moe. "I've been chomping at the bit all morning for you to get here with my stuff."

"Calm your horses." Moe stepped inside the cell Cass had occupied alone for the last year. He hauled in Cass his old steamer trunk. "You've been waiting nigh onto ten years to walk out of these doors on your own. What's an extra hour?"

"Everything." Cass stood up from his straw mattress and accepted the trunk he hadn't seen since he'd been locked up in this territorial prison after that hellish round of worthless trials. He shook his head to rid it of those disagreeable memories, then the trunk to determine if it still held anything. "I don't want to spend a minute longer than I have to in this blasted place." Under his breath, he muttered, "Especially since I never deserved to come here in the first place." He riffled through the trunk to discover that his tweed suit, white shirt, and cowboy boots were still there. "Could I at least have a bit of privacy this one time while I change? I am a free man now, after all."

"Yep, I suppose." Moe walked toward the cell's door. "Seeing that you got let out early for good behavior, I figure it'll be okay."

"I wouldn't call two years out of twelve early." Cass shooed him out in the corridor with a swoop of his hand. The last ten years of his life had felt like a hundred. The only thing that kept him sane was clinging to cherished memories of his past—his friendship with Hoskininni, becoming blood brothers with the chief's son, and following the old Indian's instructions so as to discover gold at Dandy Crossing. And especially the memory he gravitated to most often—Sarah.

He pulled off his "striped pajamas," as he called them. Pinching them between his thumb and pointer finger, he deposited them in the corner like they were still contaminated with lice. A hot bath would be good right about now to wash away the remnants of the past ten years. Those cold showers out in the open with a dozen other men were something else he wanted to leave behind. He put on the suit over his dirty long johns and then called out, "Okay, Moe."

Cass gathered what meager possessions he owned and followed Moe down the corridor, peering through the bars at his neighboring inmates, and then over the metal railing to the cells below, waving his goodbyes and good riddances.

After receiving his official release papers and a handshake from the warden, Moe led Cass through the main door, outside to freedom. Standing there together on the steps of the state penitentiary, the old guard turned to Cass. "Wait right here. The coach that runs from Sugar House into Salt Lake will be here soon. Once there, you can catch the train." He scratched his nose and looked at Cass. "So, what are you goin' to do now that you're out?"

"Start a new life," Cass said with an air of flippancy, but he was dead serious. Ten years had given him plenty of time to evaluate his life and determine that his time on earth held little meaning. Gold was the only thing that seemed to bring him happiness. That didn't feel right somehow, but it's what felt good at the moment. He'd figure the "new life" thing out later.

Moe slapped Cass on the back. "Good luck, old man," he said and then stepped back in the prison.

Old man? Cass would like to have punched Moe if he knew it wouldn't land him in back inside that hellhole. Okay, so he was nearly a half a century old, having turned forty-nine a month ago, but that didn't make him *old.* He still had plenty of years in him. Heading straight down to Dandy Crossing, getting his feet wet again, and helping his crew sluice a bag full of gold dust to hold in his hand was just what he needed.

When he climbed aboard the train to Green River and settled into his seat next to the window, he gazed outside. A lot had changed since the last time he'd traveled to this station. A new government building now reached farther into the desert sky than the Mormon temple, a handful of the city's major streets boasted pavement, and a wooden platform stood next to the tracks, making it a snap to climb aboard the train. Not to mention that Utah had received its statehood and a new century had arrived. Cass struggled to keep his chin up, trying not to think about all he had missed, and all he could have accomplished, had that jury been less hostile. He'd basically lost ten years of his life because of them, time wasted and gone forever, never to be reclaimed.

A young man wearing a snappy suit and a bowler hat walked down the aisle of the passenger car and sat down next to Cass. He settled into his seat, and as the train rolled out of the station, he turned to Cass. "Where are you headed?"

"Dandy Crossing."

"Never heard of it."

"It's down on the Colorado River—really out of the way."

"I didn't know the train went—"

"No trains where I'm going." Cass scratched his moustache as he peered out the window again. He was anxious to get home, take a bath, and shave. "Least wise, there didn't use to be. Who knows—" Out the window, he caught a glimpse of another one of those contraptions that didn't make sense.

"You look like you've seen a ghost." The man leaned in front of Cass toward the window. "What's out there?"

Cass had seen a similar one on his coach ride from Sugar House into Salt Lake. He'd heard about horseless carriages while in prison, but he'd not given the ridiculous notion much thought. But here they were, in real life. "People actually use those blasted things? Where's the damn horses?"

"You're talking about that?" The man pointed to the horseless carriage that caught Cass's attention. The thing spit out a trail of smoke out of its rear as it moseyed behind a wagon and a team of horses.

"Yep."

The man lifted an eyebrow. "Where you been for the last decade, mister?"

"You really care to know?"

"Sure, why not? I've got nothing to do—at least till the train stops."

Cass spent the next little while telling the man in the bowler hat about his being locked up unfairly.

Shortly after Cass finished his story, the man stood.

"Excuse me, but I need to stretch my legs." He grabbed his bag and walked into the adjoining car.

Cass doubted the man would return. *Good riddance.* Ready to delve into a string of silent cursing toward the gentleman, Cass caught himself. Perhaps this fellow in the bowler had done him a favor, showing him right away that it wouldn't be wise to share his misfortune with others. People were prone to judge without having all the facts— or *caring* to have all the facts. It would be best if he kept his experience to himself.

The remaining two hours of the train ride to Green River, Cass rode on the bench by himself. He didn't mind—he was used to being alone. Even though he'd had his share of cellmates, he was alone for most of the past ten years. Thugs and murderers made for poor companions, so he preferred to have none.

In Green River, he disembarked from the train and walked over to the front of the telegraph building where the stagecoach operated from. He dodged a puddle or two left over from the morning's spring thunderstorm, loving the squish of mud under his boots, grateful this town hadn't changed much since the last time he came through. No paved streets or horseless carriages here—just good ole-fashion dirt under his feet and the smell of quality whiskey wafting his way from the town's three saloons. He purchased his ticket and slipped next door into one of those saloons.

"Give me a bottle of your best whiskey," Cass said to the bartender.

The bartender, a middle-aged man with a small moustache and a large belly, popped off the lid of a bottle, poured part of its amber contents into the bottom of a glass, and pushed them both toward Cass. "That'll be four bits."

"With pleasure." Cass laid down the coins. "I've been waiting a long time for a decent swig of whiskey." He'd had a number of drinks while in the pen. It was mostly homemade stuff, rotgut at best, smuggled in somehow. Cass didn't know how it got in, and didn't care.

"You might be waitin' a lot longer," said the

bartender as he swept the coins into his palm. "We're plum out of the good stuff."

Cass chugged this first shot. "Tastes good to me."

"Where you been, fellow? The North Pole?"

"Close enough." Cass poured a second shot, careful to say no more.

After a second glass, he took the bottle and headed outside. Just in time. The stage sat in front of the telegraph office, ready to go. He climbed aboard, eager to be home, eager for his life to get back to the way it once was. The inside of the coach held one other passenger. He held out his hand for Cass to shake.

"The name's Williams, Seth Williams. And you are?"

"Cass Hite." Cass shook the man's hand and settled into the seat across from him.

"Where you headed?"

"Dandy Crossing." Cass could tell by the man's vacant expression that he hadn't a clue where that was located. "It's on the Colorado River near the bottom of the territory—uh, I mean state. Where you headed?"

"Santa Fe. Got business down there. I work for an explosives company in Salt Lake, and I'm headed down to wine and dine and hopefully pick up a new account—a mining company down there."

"Good luck to you."

Mr. Williams crossed his arms and looked intently at Cass. "What do *you* do?"

Cass felt trapped. If he answered truthfully, that he

owned a mining company, the man would surely try to sell him a heap of dynamite or something else he didn't need. Most people, this guy included, thought mining meant blasting holes in the ground. Very few thought of sluicing a river's sandbar as mining. Fine, he could ramble on and tell Mr. Williams the difference, but then the man would most likely inquire as to how Cass's business was doing, and improvements he'd made as chief of operations over the last several years, and Cass would either have to lie or tell him he didn't have a clue—because he'd been rotting in prison for the past ten years with little news of his mining company. John was about as good at writing letters as Goldie was at sluicing.

Goldie. It still hurt. One of the few letters he'd received was to tell him that John had put down Gold Dust—broken leg. It seemed letters only brought bad news, so it was just as well he got so very few of them.

"I said, what do you do?" Mr. Williams repeated.

"Me?" Cass responded. With a wink, he added, "Well, I do as little as possible. I'm just headed down to Dandy Crossing to visit my brother. And if you don't mind, I'm going to try to get some shut-eye. I'm a might tired."

Cass lay down on the leather-covered seat and closed his eyes. Thankfully, Mr. Williams kept to himself for the remainder of the trip.

The sun had barely slipped behind the western hills by the time the coach pulled into Hanksville. Mr. Williams bid Cass a cordial "Good night" and headed with the coach driver over to Mrs. Brown's, the town's only boarding house. Cass took off in the opposite direction, southeast of town, to the cabin he'd used only once.

Though the dusk's muted light quickly faded, he located the stone at the rear of the cabin where he'd chosen to hide the key ten years earlier. He walked around and inserted the rusted key in the lock. It took several attempts, wiggling the key inside the key hole, before the lock opened. Cobwebs and dust met Cass when he stepped inside his cabin. Dark shadows filled the one-room dwelling, impeding his attempts at locating the lamp and some matches or a flint and steel. He found a new lamp and a new box of matches on the shelf above the fireplace.

"Good ole John. He's been here and kept things up—somewhat," he said to the cabin walls.

In one of the four measly letters he'd received while locked up, John had expressed his appreciation of the cabin on his many trips up north. Some of their boys used the cabin as well when they traveled through. It'd made the purchase of the property feel worthwhile, and Cass was grateful for that. It made one less thing he regretted those long hours he spent with nothing to do but contemplating life. He had enough regret.

Cass looked out the front window toward *her* place. He knew she no longer lived there, but still, he wanted to see if a column of smoke rose from the cabin's chimney. For some stupid reason, he thought it might bring him a bit of comfort—as if it could wind back the hands of time. Twilight shrouded the rocky hills in darkness. He laughed at himself and trudged over to the cabin's single bed. "Who knows if her cabin is even still there? Maybe the current occupant tore it down and built something bigger. What the blazes—there might not even *be* any tenants, just a pack of coyotes by now." He dropped backwards onto the mattress, stirring up a cloud of dust, and tried not to think about any neighboring cabins. And Sarah.

Ten minutes later, he jumped out of bed, grateful his boots were still on, and tromped over to her cabin. Just because. Just in case.

Nothing but darkness shone through the windows. Not even the moon lit the glass with its reflection. He knocked anyway. The *rap, rap, rap* was returned with silence. He headed toward town, to Edna's house. If anyone would know about Sarah and his baby, it would be her.

Only a single lamp glowed through an upper window as he approached Edna's home. He stepped onto the porch, lifted his hand to knock, and stopped. The woman was most likely in her nightclothes. And even if she wasn't, he couldn't speak with her about Sarah's baby—which was no longer a baby, but about ten years old by now. In Edna's eyes, what good reason did he have to be inquiring about the child? Logic dictated that no one knew the truth about the child except for him and Sarah.

He turned, stepped off the porch, and plodded back to his dusty cabin.

The next morning, the stage left just after dawn. The trip to Dandy Crossing felt especially long. It didn't help that Cass continually redirected his and Mr. Williams's conversations away from Cass's life and onto other subjects—the price of beef in Wichita, the proposed new train station in Salt Lake City, the weather.

After the stage forged the river at Dandy Crossing on a new, much bigger and better ferry, Cass could barely contain his relief at pulling into Hite.

Before he climbed out of the coach, he extended his hand to his traveling companion. "Goodbye, Mr. Williams. And good luck with your dynamite sales."

Seth Williams shook Cass's hand. "Thank you. And it was a pleasure meeting you. Enjoy your visit with your brother."

"I will." Cass tipped his hat as he stepped out. *I'll go visit him right now before I head home.* He beelined it for his brother's place.

John's eyes opened wide as goose eggs when they caught sight of Cass. "Well, I'll be hog-tied. If it isn't my big brother." He stepped over and hugged Cass tight and long, blubbering something about how much he'd missed Cass. "I thought ya had two more years to go."

Cass let go of John and settled into one of the chairs around the gambling table. "Didn't you read my last letter I sent you?"

"What letter? I didn't get nothin' from you. Least not since May."

"Dang mail service down this way. I must have beat it here."

John sorted through a bundle of mail that had come on the same stage that brought Cass. He pulled out an envelope. "Here it is. I recognize your handwritin'. And the return address—State Penitentiary, Sugar House, Utah." He glanced at Cass. "That's much too nice a sounding town to have a prison located there."

"What can I say?" Cass held out his arms. "A lot of things are messed up with the judicial system." He pulled his arms in and poured himself a drink from what was left in the bottle of whiskey he'd picked up in Green River. "But that's behind me now. It's time for my life to get back to the way it was. Tell me about things. How's the company doing? Holy blazes, John, I swear, if those few letters you wrote were any more vague, I would have been reading a simple hello and goodbye in each of them."

John pulled up a chair and sat across from Cass. "I hate to tell you this, big brother, but things aren't so great."

"What do you mean by that?"

"After I put your horse down about a year after you left, things kept goin' downhill."

"Like what?"

"First off, your horse broke her leg helpin' us haul in this heavy piece of equipment to fix the sluicing machine. Then the confounded thing quit working a few months after the repair."

"Why didn't you say that in your letter about Goldie?" Cass held up his hand to stop John—he already knew the answer. Cass was lucky to get what news he had.

"Never mind. What about the company?"

"Most of the boys quit years ago. We're down to five now."

"Blast it all!"

"Cass, without you here to manage things, the

boys never pulled the same amount through the sluices. Plus, I swear the gold's dryin' up. Hell, we don't even use all that fancy equipment you brought in. We've basically gone back to usin' a pan. That's the only way we can find the gold dust anymore. I'm down in the river with them every day. That's why I hardly ever wrote. Or visited ya. Sorry."

"No need to be sorry." Cass swallowed the liquor in his glass with one gulp and poured the rest of the bottle. "It wasn't your fault." He downed that. "It's all my fault. Who was I to think everything would stay the same while I was gone? I should have been more careful about what I did ten years ago." *Not just with Kohler.* "Carelessness certainly has a way of coming back and biting you in the butt." He threw the empty whiskey bottle against the wall, shattering it into pieces. "You got anything to drink?" He needed to drown his sorrows momentarily. He would start to build his business back up tomorrow. Then he would find out about Sarah and his child. Chances were he would never be able to speak with her or their child, but if he could but see them both at a distance, determine they were healthy and happy, that would satisfy the chasm growing in his heart. Somewhat.

"You got a pen and some paper?" he asked John. "I need to write some letters."

"Who in blazes to?"

"I'm not exactly sure."

***

Cass looked up from the river. Wiping the sweat from his brow, he gazed at the red-rock plateau reaching for the blue sky behind his little town of Hite. Only it didn't feel like his anymore. Nothing felt the same anymore. Even the mail didn't seem to work. He'd written everyone he could think of that he knew in Hanksville, carefully wording his prose so as to not arouse suspicion as to his reason for inquiring about Sarah. He'd gotten no response. Also, in the three months since his release from prison, he'd worked harder at pulling together the crumbling Colorado River and Utah Placer Mining Company than he'd ever done in a whole year chiseling stone blocks out of boulders at the state pen. Even the weather felt different.

"This blasted heat," Cass mumbled to John as they worked their old-fashion sluice. "I swear I never remember August being so hot."

John slapped his shovel against the water, causing it to splash Cass. "There, that'll help. Now, quit your complainin' and get back to work."

"I'm just voicing my frustration. Things need to get done if we're going to succeed."

John impaled his shovel into the gentle flow of water down to the sandbar below. "No, you're complainin', and you sure as hell have been doin' a lot of it since you came home." He folded his arms and leaned them on the tip of the shovel's handle. "And it's gettin' tiresome."

Cass let go of the handle of the sluice and straightened up. "Tiresome is right. I need a drink. I'm taking a break." He stepped out of the water and stormed toward his cabin.

"That's gettin' tiresome too—your drinkin'." John's voice came up the hill behind Cass. "I'm worried about you, big brother. You need to cut back."

"I'll tell you what I need," Cass hollered over his shoulder. "I need to get out of this heat. And . . . hire us some more men."

John sloshed out of the water, and Cass could hear him scurry to catch up. "Cass, we don't have the money."

"I know, I know." Cass continued stomping up the rise. "That's why I'm headed to Salt Lake. Right now."

"Now? But it's nearly noon."

"I don't care. I'm going to drum us up some more investors."

"Nobody wants to invest in a dyin' mining company."

"I say it's not dying." As long as he could see it sparkle amongst the grains of sand as he let it sift through his fingers, the gold in the Colorado was *not* drying up. It *couldn't* be.

"All right, then, the gold's harder to find." John caught up to Cass. "Those days back in the nineties are gone."

Cass didn't want to hear that. "I'm still going to Salt Lake." He had to try to bring back something that offered him a shred of happiness. He had to do *something*. "Besides, I gotta get away from this heat, and that blasted store of yours is plum out of whiskey. That bottle in my cupboard won't last me beyond an hour."

Chapter 22

S arah rinsed the warm rag again in the bucket of cool water. As she wrung it out to place on Wayne's forehead, the action reminded her of those days so long ago when she'd nursed Cass Hite back to health. She quickly swept those memories aside—now was not the time to think of such things. That past was in the past. As was the freedom she'd discovered eight years ago, after feeling God's forgiveness. She'd felt as though heavy chains literally had been removed from her body. Her heart had felt lighter too, so much so that she swore it could float away right after that. She'd loved how she no longer had to wear her actor's mask, but those days were returning. Thankfully, not for the same reason—she needed to maintain a happy countenance for Wayne's sake. He couldn't know of her deep concern for his health—nor see how the long hours spent by his bedside wore her down.

She spread the cooled rag across Wayne's

forehead, praying silently for his recovery. She couldn't lose him now. Her love for him had grown tenfold since they'd traveled down to Nyda's funeral eight years ago. Sarah couldn't exactly say she was totally happy, but a sense of contentment filled her soul to where the grass was greener, the sky was bluer, and life took on a flavor that was definitely worth living for. Intense heat warmed her fingers as they touched his skin, heightening her concern. "We've got to bring this fever down," she murmured, more to herself than Wayne. It wasn't like he could do anything about it.

But then again, maybe he can.

"We need to move away from here, Wayne," Sarah spoke up. Her boldness surprised her, but she wasn't going back down now. This needed to be done. "The coal dust is killing you."

"I'll be all right." Wayne's weak voice did little to convince Sarah. "I've got a great nurse," he said, mustering a smile. "Just try to patch me up before the end of the week so I can make it to church, and then to work on Monday."

"There's two more things that will be the death of you. Wayne, for goodness' sake—and your health's sake, it's time you ask to be released as the bishop. You've been serving for over eleven years now. No one will think poorly of you if you step down—not when your health is suffering. As for your job, more often than not, you've said, 'It'll be the death of me.'"

"I don't know . . ." Wayne's voice trailed off. His eyelids fluttered, and he drifted to sleep.

Sarah left Wayne alone for a moment to catch up

on some housework while the girls were at school. But she wasn't going to leave that idea alone.

***

Monday morning after Sarah got the girls off to school, she walked into the bedroom to tend to Wayne. Though he was doing somewhat better, he hadn't felt up to attending church the day before, and that concerned her.

Wayne stood by the side of the bed, buttoning up his good shirt. "Good morning, Sarah," he said in a voice that didn't convince her at all that he was having such a morning.

"What are you doing?"

"Getting ready for work. I know I'm a bit late, but I'm sure Mr. Burns won't mind, seeing how I've missed a whole week already." His fingers trembled as they pushed a button through its hole.

"Oh, no, you don't." Sarah stomped her foot. "You're not any better than yesterday. Mr. Burns can just, just—oh, that man! I dare not say what I think of him."

"Sarah, I appreciate your concern," Wayne said as he pulled on his pants. "But there's no other way around it—I *have* to go to work. October is a week away. We can't afford another late rent payment. I've got to pay it on the first, and I won't have enough to do so if I miss any more work." He buttoned up his pants and pushed past Sarah into the front room, tucking his shirttails in as he walked.

"Don't worry about my breakfast. I don't feel much like eating. Hopefully I'll feel like it when I come home for my break at noon."

He stepped out the front door and closed it behind him before Sarah could gather her thoughts enough to stop him. Unfortunately, she knew he was right. He *would* need this next week's salary if they were to have enough to pay rent, and that meant there would be nothing left for anything else.

She gazed out the window at her garden. Frost had nipped the leaves of her green beans and summer squash a week ago. They no longer produced anything. She'd already dug up what remained of the potatoes, the family having eaten most of them as soon as they came on. Only two meals' worth remained in the burlap sack beneath the kitchen sink. A row of carrots and beets still sat in the ground. Those and the few potatoes would have to last them until Wayne's next paycheck.

She dragged her feet out the back door and headed for the carrots planted along the picket fence on the side yard. Kicking a clod of dry, gray-brown soil out of her path, she thought about the rich red soil of her garden down in Hanksville, and her desire to get her family out of this town revived. That desire gained strength as she remembered how the well in Hanksville never ran dry, allowing her to water her plants all she wanted. The water bill from Price City still sat in that spot in the cupboard waiting to be paid. Her fear of increasing that monthly charge constantly prevented her from tending fully to the needs of her garden. And then there was the matter of its size. Plain and simple, her little garden here just wasn't big enough to produce enough food for her family. Especially if she wanted it to hold them through the winter now that the girls were bigger and their appetites continued to grow.

If only we could move to a place where I could have a big garden, the air was clean, and *Wayne could find a job that treated him better.*

Hanksville would fit two of those three criteria. Unfortunately, she knew nobody was in need of a bookkeeper down there.

Sarah worked in her garden all morning, clearing away the dead beans and squash, preparing the little spot of ground for next spring. Then she harvested enough carrots for supper, along with a couple of beets to add some extra color to the meal in lieu of meat. As she cleaned them in the sink, she remembered she'd used the last of their salt last night for supper. Glancing at the clock in the front room, she realized Wayne would be home shortly for dinner. If she was to make anything fit for a meal, she'd need salt. She ran into the bedroom, pulled open the top drawer, reached beneath her undergarments to where she kept her emergency stash of coins, and grabbed a nickel. Before leaving the house, she removed her apron and then stepped outside into the crisp fall air.

Walking at a brisk pace, she made the three-block trek to the mercantile in good time. She hurried inside and stepped up to the counter. "Good morning, Mr. Steed. I'd like five cents worth of salt." She laid her nickel down.

"Well, a good morning to you, Mrs. Barker. I haven't seen you in a while," he said as he scooped some salt into a brown paper bag.

"We've been living off our garden, so I haven't need to buy much. Sorry."

"No need to apologize. You gotta do what you gotta do to survive in this here town." He pushed the sack across the counter and then picked up her nickel.

"True," Sarah responded, thinking about what else she could do to "survive in this here town." Nothing materialized.

"Will that be everything?" Mr. Steed asked as he pushed a button on the cash register and the drawer popped open with a *ding*.

"Yes, thank you," Sarah said, wishing that nickel could have purchased a slab of bacon or a tub of lard as well. She grabbed the salt and turned to leave, but then spun back around. "There is something else you can do for me. While I'm here, I may as well pick up my mail. Thank you."

"But of course." Mr. Steed moved away from the counter and walked into a back room. Inside the dim room, a network of small shelves hung from one wall, each sectioned off into numerous cubbyholes, many filled with letters. He grabbed a single envelope from one of those sections and stepped out of the room. "Just one letter for you, Mrs. Barker, and it looks like a bill. Sorry."

"No need to apologize. It's not like you're the one sending it to me." Sarah took the letter from his outstretched hand, wondering who else could possibly be sending them a bill. She moved outside before she dared read the return address.

Emery Mining Company, 423 Stauffer St., Price, Utah

was stamped in the upper left-hand corner of the envelope. Sarah let out a breath of relief. This wasn't a bill—it was the same address where she sent her rent checks. But why would they be sending something to her? Could she have possibly overpaid last month and they were sending her a refund? She tore open the envelope with that frail hope and unfolded the single-page letter it held.

Dear Mr. and Mrs. Barker,

This letter is to inform you that as of October 1, 1901, your rent will be increased from $20 per month to $25 per month. We regret that we must make this change, but unfortunately our maintenance costs have increased and thus we must pass part of this expense down to our tenants.

"What maintenance costs?" Sarah covered her mouth, hoping no one out on the street heard her outburst. She clenched her fists and stormed toward home, fuming over the faulty shingles and paint peeling from every clapboard of their house that had yet to be repaired, but they were now being charged for.

For the next three blocks, Sarah's mind grappled for ideas as to how they could pull together the extra money needed to stay in their house. More and more, she wanted to move. But where? Emery Mining Company owned most every house for rent in the town, and theirs was already one of the cheapest places they offered. And as much as Sarah despised Wayne's boss and wanted him to get a new job, it provided an income better than anything else to be had in the town of Price.

After she stomped up the front steps of their house and then through the front room, she barely noticed Wayne sitting at the table when she walked into the kitchen. "Oh, Wayne, you're home early," she said and then took a deep breath. "It's just as well. I've got some not-so-good news." She set down the bag of salt and held up the letter from their landlord.

"I insist I go first." Wayne patted the chair next to him. His face appeared paler than when he'd left for work an hour ago. "Sit down."

Sarah slid into the chair. "What's wrong?"

"I've lost my job."

***

Sarah scurried from room to room, making sure they hadn't left anything of importance behind. When Wayne had announced he'd lost his job last week, her initial reaction had been devastation. After she'd dropped into a chair and wrestled with the bad news for a good five minutes, she looked at it as not-so-bad news after all. It was the motivation they all needed to leave this rundown, high-rent house behind and move.

As she went through the house, she realized even if she were to discover something it probably wouldn't fit in their bulging travel bags and the one large steamer case that carried the sum of their belongings. Of course, the furniture would stay—it was all rented anyway. When her last-minute search found nothing, she ran outside to where Wayne and the girls sat in Brother Willey's wagon waiting for her.

"Hurry up." Brother Willey swept his hand toward his wagon. "Or you're gonna miss your train."

Sarah locked the door behind her, stuffed the key beneath the mat like her landlord had said, and ran toward the wagon. The shabby house of her uncompassionate landlord wasn't worth a single tear. She was taking all that meant anything to her from that house with her. She climbed aboard, stepping past Wayne and sitting down with a harrumph escaping her mouth as she sat in between him and Brother Willey. "I'm ready. Let's go."

Brother Willey flicked the reins, and his horse pulled the wagon forward. "We sure is going to miss you, Bishop, and you too, Sister Barker. Me and the rest of the ward still got our heads a spinnin', what with how fast you and your family are movin' away."

"I sincerely apologize for that." Wayne leaned forward so as to look Brother Willey in the eye. "Unfortunately, we had little other choice. You see, Sister Barker owns a cabin and a nice spot of ground down in Hanksville."

"With a big garden," Sarah added.

"With me losing my job, my health failing, and rent due tomorrow, we all figured it was the best thing to do." Wayne looked over his shoulder "Don't you agree, girls?"

Sarah glanced back to see Beth and Julia wearing long faces, sitting cross-legged in the back of the wagon next to their bags. Maggie sat between them, her eyes lit up as she responded, "Of course we do, Papa."

The train station soon came into view. People scurried onto the platform and then into a train that poured billows of black smoke from its stack into the air. Wayne tried to hide a round of coughing by covering his mouth and then turning away from her.

"I'll go purchase the tickets," Wayne said after his coughing subsided. He crawled out of the wagon much slower than Brother Willey, who was twice his age. "Brother Willey will help you carry our things to the platform, and I'll meet you there."

"Come here." Brother Willey motioned the girls to the edge of the wagon and lifted them and their bags down one by one as Wayne walked to the ticket booth. He then hefted their steamer trunk onto his broad back and walked the girls over to the platform.

Sarah draped the handles of hers and Wayne's bags over each of her shoulders and then grabbed the gunny sack holding what was left of their food and followed. Wayne had tried to get her to leave the food behind, but Sarah was unsure how much of her Hanksville garden would still be alive this late in the season. Mary had moved out years ago. Sarah had her doubts the garden would be kept up like Mary had hinted she'd do. But it was all they had now, along with the carrots and beets in the gunny sack, to get them through the winter. Wayne held on to the little bit of cash they were going to use for rent. She only hoped that after he paid for the train and stagecoach fares, there would be some left over to purchase some flour, sugar, and lard once they arrived in Hanksville.

The porter was helping Brother Willey load their trunk into the baggage car when Sarah stepped onto the platform. "Here, take my things," she hollered and ran them to Brother Willey. She deposited her load at his feet and went over to help the girls board the train, all the while keeping an eye out for Wayne. "I hope your—" *Papa is okay.* She'd cut her words short, not wanting to add her worries to those of her children. They already had more than enough, being pulled away from their school and their friends, having to start all over in a new town—with parents who had no money.

She guided the children toward the southbound train, taking a glance back at the ticket booth. Maybe she should have purchased the tickets and insisted that Wayne take things easy. *No, he would have insisted that he help carry the bags.* She said a silent prayer, asking the Lord to bless Wayne with the strength to do this one small thing so as to bolster his self-esteem and feel worthwhile as the head of their household—albeit in transition at the moment. Sarah knew all too well what it was like to feel poorly of oneself. She wouldn't wish that upon anyone, especially not her husband.

Maggie pulled on her hand. "Mama, which one are we getting on?"

Sarah scanned the row of passenger cars, peering inside through the windows. Each car bustled with people finding seats. "These cars are crowded. Keep moving." As she urged the girls toward the back of the train, her eyes gravitated to a man sitting on a bench with pair of saddlebags on his lap. She swore he looked like Cass Hite. Her first instinct was to approach him and ask him his name, then inquire as to his health, for he looked awfully thin.

Her second instinct pulled her forward, urging her children to move to the end car. She spotted Wayne hobbling toward them with tickets in hand. That part of her, the part with Cass, life lay behind her now. She had three girls to take care of—the youngest barely ten. And an ailing husband. It would be best to leave the past alone.

Chapter 23

Cass sat in his favorite Salt Lake City bar, emptied the remainder of the bottle into his glass, and lifted the whiskey to his mouth. He'd visited every bank, bar, and club where he used to go to find investors—even places he'd never gone to before. No one was interested in his mining company. Especially one run by an ex-convict.

"Whoa. Hold on there, friend." Curly grabbed Cass's wrist, preventing him from partaking of his drink. "Do you think that's wise? You're about ready to topple out of your seat. Besides, you look mighty awful. Is that all you've been doing since you got to Salt Lake is drinkin'?"

"Pretty much." Cass pulled his hand free from Curly's grasp. True, he was grateful to discover that at least this old friend was still around and didn't care one bit that Cass had spent time in prison or that his business was failing. At the moment, however, Cass would rather be left alone. With his drink. And possibly a new bottle to pour himself another. And another.

It was bad enough that he'd wasted ten years of his life in prison, but since he'd come home, everything in his life seemed to have changed and there was little left to enjoy. He'd really tried to bring his life back to normal, but his efforts were getting him nowhere. He might as well be back rotting away in that blasted prison.

A few days earlier, seeing Sarah at the train station in Price with those three little girls, one of them surely his, had put Cass on the cliff of some already shaky ground. Especially when he saw the man he figured was Sarah's husband dragging his feet toward the southbound train, corralling the three girls toward Sarah. He had wanted to scrutinize every square inch of the red-headed man who lived in the place where Cass wanted to be. He very well could have been there—had he turned his life around a little sooner.

That tiny glimmer of hope that one day he and Sarah might somehow get back together had totally vanished. And since he'd taken that northbound train and come to Salt Lake, he'd spent way more money on whiskey than he'd solicited in investments—which wasn't hard, considering he'd collected absolutely nothing. It had tipped him over the edge. What did he have to show for his life? A dying mining company and bittersweet memories of a woman he loved, but could never have.

Cass downed the last of his whiskey. He lifted the empty bottle from the table and waved it at the bartender, intent on ordering another bottle, but he couldn't utter the request. His tongue felt as though it were made of lead. His view of the bartender across the room grew blurry, more so than the abundant cigar smoke could account for. He felt the sensation of falling, and then heard a thud.

***

Cass heard voices, yet saw nothing. He willed his eyes to open, but they failed to respond. Instead, his nose worked beyond what he would have liked. A sickening-sweet smell of carbolic acid made his head ache more. It reminded him of lying in that hospital bed those many years ago. Then came the clink and clank reminiscent of those blasted trays they used to wheel next to his hospital bed. Then more voices.

"Your prognosis, Doctor?" It sounded like Curly's voice.

"Alcohol is killing your friend. It's good you brought him in when you did, but there is a good chance it's too late."

"I know he's pale as a fish's belly, Doc, and thin as a snake, but can't ya do nothin' for him?"

"I'm afraid his heart is seriously weakened, and he's fighting pneumonia."

"Doc, I'm afeared Cass is givin' up inside. Least wise, that's what he sounded like when we talked last night before I brought him in."

Cass finally got his eyes to open. The whiteness of his surroundings nearly blinded him and made him want to close them again. He forced them to stay open, confirming his fears. He *was* in the hospital, and apparently, he'd been here for a while. Things didn't sound too good. But what more could he do? He'd already given everything his all. Now it sounded as though he'd have to endure another hospital stay. For how long? Would he even get better this time? One thing *was* for sure—there would be no angel of mercy sitting at his bedside, nursing him back to health this time.

"He's comin' around, Doc."

Cass could make out Curly's blurry features hovering above his face. He let out a moan, unable to form any decent words. His eyes felt heavy. He blinked them, forcing them to stay open. But why? The black of unconsciousness appealed to him. What did consciousness have to offer him but disappointment, pain, and sorrow? He didn't want that. He let his eyes close.

"Don't let go, Cass." Curly's plea sounded as though it came from far away—like Sarah had oft times as she'd nursed him back to health. "Hang on. Don't give up on yer life."

Blast your begging, Curly. That's exactly what I want to do.

Cass closed his eyes and let the darkness engulf him.

***

Having no sense of time, whether minutes, hours, or days had passed, Cass wondered at the source of the noise that aroused him. He became aware of a rhythm more than he could hear it, a steady thumping like the beat of a drum. Or was it more of a whoosh, whoosh, whooshing sound? He tried to open his eyes. They refused to respond, as did his body when he attempted to sit up. He relented and lay there in the darkness, listening to the rhythm, sliding in and out of consciousness.

Slowly, he became aware that his heart was beating to the rhythm. Over the thump of his heart, he could hear an animal growling, a wild cat or a badger a long, long ways off. Slowly the sound became louder, and it changed. He could tell it was an Indian singing, a low, huffing chant as if the singer was working hard, almost out of breath. The chanting slowed to match the pace of his beating heart, drawing it out, making it beat stronger.

Cass could see through his own closed eyes the figure of an old Indian standing over him. The man danced and chanted with a buffalo tail in one hand and a cluster of eagle feathers in the other. He brushed the buffalo tail over Cass's chest and face, and then leaned down and blew his chanting breath into Cass's nostrils.

Cass could feel his breathing catching up to the rhythm of his beating heart. They meshed, blood and air, coursing through his veins in the perfect rhythm of the old man's chant. The Indian fanned air toward Cass's nose and mouth with the eagle feathers, then brushed his whole upper body with the buffalo tail. Cass looked into the familiar face and recognized Hoskininni.

The next morning, Cass slowly opened his eyes again to white. It startled him. Was it clouds? Was it heaven? It couldn't be. White was such a cold color. Heaven wouldn't be white. Heaven would be soft and colorful like the warm, red sand of Dandy Crossing. But he wasn't in pain, so it must be heaven.

As the whiteness came into focus, Cass recognized it for what it was—the cold, stark walls and ceiling of his hospital room. He lay there for a long time as his head cleared and his vision became more focused. No pretty sleeping woman in a rocking chair this time. Only bedpans and bottles of pills, sterilizing alcohol, tubes, needles, and syringes.

Then wonder filled him when he remembered the vision of Hoskininni dancing over him. *What was that all about? Did that really happen, or am I losing my mind?* It had seemed so very real. He wanted it to be real. It gave him hope—for what, he wasn't sure. He lay there and pondered on the experience for a while. There had to be a reason for it.

He decided not to say anything about it. People might think he was touched in the head. He did, however, pull himself up to a sitting position and leaned back, positioning his pillow to get comfortable. It took some effort, but not nearly as much as it had merely to breathe the day before.

A nurse crept quietly into the room carrying a tray holding a tiny bottle and syringe. Her eyes widened with noticeable surprise. "Mr. Hite!"

"I was hoping that'd be my breakfast you was carrying on that tray. But darn it all if I'm going to eat that."

The door swung open again, and in walked the doctor who had attended to Cass earlier. At least Cass thought it was the same fellow. Then again, he couldn't rightly say—his mind had been in such a blur. "I'm feeling a mite better," he said more to himself than to the other two, who now stared at him as if he were a ghost.

"That's obvious," the doctor said.

The nurse set down her tray next to Cass's bed and turned toward the doctor. "Should I bring him something to eat?"

"Yes. Keep to a bland diet and make his portions small for now."

"Good hel—I mean, good gracious," Cass corrected himself out of respect. Hoskininni never liked Cass's cursing tongue. "I want something worth eating. And plenty of it," Cass called out to the nurse as she headed for the door.

The doctor proceeded to poke and prod and check Cass out until Cass felt as though he were a slab of tough old meat getting tenderized for cooking. All the while, the doctor mumbled under his breath, "Amazing" or "Miraculous recovery." With that darn contraption stuck in his ears, the doctor slid its cold metal disc across Cass's bare chest. "I do believe you might pull through, Mr. Hite," he said with a measure of disbelief in his voice.

The door swung open and the nurse walked in carrying a tray like before, but this time it held a bowl of mush and a small glass of milk. She went to set it down on the table next to Cass's bed, but looked somewhat at odds as what to do about the tray holding the syringe already sitting there.

"You can take that away, nurse." The doctor sent

her a glance as he removed the cold disk from Cass's chest. "He won't be needing that injection after all."

"Very well, doctor."

The nurse slipped out the door. A second later, Curly entered, followed by another fellow Cass recognized from the bar the other night. Curly carried a bottle in his hand.

"Cass!" Curly approached the bed. His eyes held a mixture of surprise and confusion. "You old codger, what ya doin' sittin' up? You's supposed to be dead. We even brought ourselves some whiskey." He held up the bottle. "Was goin' to give you a good Irish wake."

"Well, I ain't dead. Yet. And I don't want a drop of that blasted whiskey."

Curly stared at Cass with one eyebrow raised.

"What I do want is to be shed of this damn—" Cass cleared his throat in an effort to clear his tongue. "Darn hospital." *Little steps at a time. Blast it all, I can't cure my tongue all at once.*

The doctor stood at the end of Cass's bed with his arms folded. "I'm sorry, Mr. Hite, but though you are amazingly much better than you were yesterday, I cannot in good conscience release you from the hospital as of yet."

"Well, neither can you hold me here against my will," Cass said. He'd had his fair share of incarceration, and he wanted no more. And he didn't want to be in this big city one minute longer—he wanted to be home. He cinched his arms across his chest, mimicking the doctor. "So, which one will it be? You sign my release papers all proper-like, or the minute you leave this room, I'll have my friends break me out of here. With the latter, I can't guarantee that nobody will be hurt in the process."

The doctor's mouth sagged open. It took him a second or two before he stammered, "Very well, Mr. Hite. I'll release you this time. But I won't be surprised if you end up right back in this very bed in a day or two. I'll warn you now—next time, I won't sign any release papers unless you are one-hundred-percent recovered." He then rattled off a list of do's and don'ts for Cass to incorporate into his daily schedule. Cass barely listened.

Cass swung his legs off the side of the bed and stood, albeit a little unstable on his legs. "Don't worry, Doc, I'm heading down south, where it's warm and the air is clean, and I have no intentions of ever coming back."

Within an hour, Cass stood in the lobby of the hospital, gazing out the glass of its double doors as Curly and his friend pulled up to the curb in one of those horseless carriages. Curly hopped out and motioned for Cass to come.

Cass grabbed his bag and stepped outside into the cool air tainted with the smell of coal fires. He quelled a cough, anxious to get away from all those chimneys spitting out smoke, and crept onto the sidewalk carefully, avoiding the puddles of a recent rain. "We're going to the train station in that contraption?" He pointed to the vehicle ten feet away, where Curly's friend wore a big smile as he sat up front behind a wheel of sorts.

"Sure enough," Curly said with a lilt of pride in his voice. He took Cass's bag in one hand and with the other latched onto Cass's elbow. "It's 'bout time ya caught up with things, Cass. The world's a changin', and ya need to change with it." He helped him down the remainder of the sidewalk and into the shiny black contraption with oily smelling smoke spewing from its rear.

"Humph," Cass mumbled. He knew he needed to change some things in his life, but a darn automobile was not one of them.

With Curly's help, Cass climbed into the back seat, and Curly tucked a thick woolen blanket around him. The automobile headed down the newly paved street—no ruts to follow. Cold whipped Cass's face, and he pulled the blanket higher to shield himself against the fast-moving air.

Once at the station, Curly purchased the ticket while Cass rested on a bench under the cover of the new awning that ran the length of the platform. Still very weak, he pulled himself up off the bench as Curly approached. "Thanks, my good friend." Cass took the ticket and gave Curly a hug. "I guess this is goodbye, then."

"Ya say that like you'll never see me again." Curly hugged him back and then stepped away. He motioned for Cass to board. "Yer goin' get better, Cass. An ornery ole cuss like you will be up and at 'em in no time. And next time yer back in Salt Lake, the drinks are on me. Okay?"

"Okay," Cass said as he crawled up the stairs into the Pullman car. He wasn't worried about setting Curly straight on that drink—he figured this would be the last time he ever set foot in this city.

Chapter 24

Sarah noticed a plume of dust rise above the junipers west of the cabin. "It looks like a wagon is heading our way," she said to Wayne, who sat in an old kitchen chair she'd hauled outside so he could enjoy the fresh air while she and the girls set to the task of unpacking their scanty belongings.

"You don't suppose it's someone coming to visit already, do you?" Wayne shielded the sun from his eyes with a raised hand as he looked to the west.

"I couldn't say." Sarah doubted it. She'd had no time to tell anyone they were here.

A semi-new wagon rounded the bend, and Edna's distinctive face came into view. She rode next to a young boy at the reins—one of Edna's grandsons, Sarah surmised. The wagon slowed to a crawl and came to a stop in front of the cabin. The boy hopped out and helped Edna down, who immediately ran toward Sarah with outstretched arms.

"Sarah, I'm so glad to see you've made it okay." Edna pulled Sarah into a hug. "I barely got your letter the day before yesterday. Me and my grandson, Chester here, have been working hard to get the place ready for you." She released Sarah and stepped back. "My, but you're looking good."

"So, this was your doing?" Sarah pointed through the cabin's opened door.

Edna and Chester nodded.

"Thank you," Sarah responded. "For both your kind deeds and your kind words, Edna." She wiped some gathering moisture from her eye. "I'd expected the cabin to be full of cobwebs and dust when we got here. To open the door and find a tidy house, well, I can't thank you enough." It had been a definite lift to her spirits after the rushed move and tiring journey.

"How'd you know we were here?" Wayne spoke up. "We barely arrived a half an hour ago. The stagecoach driver dropped us off right there," he swept his hand toward the wagon, "it being practically on his way into town. They'd never do that for you up north."

"I don't suppose they would," Edna said. "Neither would they drop by your house and tell you they'd just delivered your family to their cabin." She nodded. "Gus did that too—came by on his way out of town to tell me you were here. That's how I knew."

"He's the nicest of all the stagecoach drivers," Chester spoke up. "I like him a lot."

"So do I, Chester," Sarah said as she grabbed Edna's hand and gave it a squeeze. "It's so good to be here, Edna. We had nowhere else to turn."

Edna returned the squeeze. "Your letter nearly broke my heart, dear, what with Wayne losing his job and all. Don't you worry—you got family here, and we'll help you all we can." She let go of Sarah's hand and leaned to gain a view of the side of the cabin. "Have you noticed the apples we left for you on the trees?"

"No, I haven't had a chance to look at the garden."

"You caught us barely in time," Edna said. "Another day, and Mary would have had all your trees picked clean. Oh, and the raspberry bushes she planted years ago are still bearing. And she left you some carrots and beets in the ground."

"That's wonderful," Sarah said, overwhelmed by gratitude. Her choice to move back to Hanksville was definitely one of her best.

***

A month after they had moved into the cabin, Sarah took advantage of the uncommonly warm November day and chose to clear the garden of its weeds to get a jump on her spring planting. She pulled some big weeds next to the remaining beets and carrots, careful not to disrupt the soil any more than she had to. Those vegetables were best stored in the ground until they were needed. As she impaled a shovel into the tap root of an enormous mallow plant far away from her carrots, the fall of footsteps on hard-packed dirt drew her attention to the trail running along the far side of the garden. A man approached from the south. His gait held a familiar swagger. She abandoned her task and stood erect to see him more clearly, holding her hand above her eyes on one side to shield them from the afternoon sun. He stopped suddenly, as if catching sight of her startled him. Then his face came into view and it startled her. *Cass.*

Why here? Why now? Sarah had finally found a measure of happiness. She didn't need to dredge up painful memories from her past.

Yet a part of her came alive at the prospect of merely speaking with him.

***

Cass had seen smoke rising from the chimney of Sarah's old cabin the entire two days he'd stayed in Hanksville. That morning when he arose, it was still there. Now, at dinnertime, he could still smell the smoke, detecting a hint of juniper wood as it wafted his direction when he opened the door to get a better view. He ignored its beckoning call, shut the door, and made himself a meal of dried apricots and just as dry biscuits. As he sat and washed them down with a cup of weak coffee, the smoke beckoned him again, seeping through a drafty crack in the windowpane. He deliberated as to whether he should head back down to Hite or stay put a little longer.

Why stay put? He had yet to muster sufficient courage to see if it was Sarah and her family who now lived in the neighboring cabin. There was no reason for her to be here—out in the middle of nowhere. It was most likely she'd just come for a short visit—if that was even where she'd been heading when he'd caught sight of her at the station. The smoke coming from the chimney could very well be from someone else's family now living in her cabin. Surely, she had returned to Price by now.

He bolted out of his chair and headed for the door, feeling the urge to be neighborly and merely ask about Sarah's well-being. Whoever lived there most likely knew who she was—everyone in the town was related one way or the other. He wouldn't mention that he'd seen her at the train station on his way up to Salt Lake. Only that he happened to be in the neighborhood and thought he'd inquire about the kind woman who had once nursed him back to health.

As he approached the cabin, his feet stopped and planted themselves in the road. There Sarah stood in her garden, as beautiful as ever, staring at him in obvious recognition. He couldn't move—except for his jaw. He felt it drop. Grateful he hadn't trimmed his moustache in some time and thus having a means to cover his gaping mouth, he gazed at the incredible sight, unable to speak, unable to take his eyes off her, and unsure what to do.

"Good afternoon." Her voice touched Cass's ears like music. It held no malice, but sounded amicable.

That lent him courage. "Good afternoon," he returned.

"It's been a long time."

"Yes, it has." He braved a few steps and moved to the outside of the picket fence surrounding the yard.

"How are you?" She remained where she was in the garden.

"Things could be better." Cass cringed at his reply. Now was not the time or place to reveal the pathetic state of his life. "Then again, things could be worse. And you?"

She hesitated for a second. "The same."

"You living here now?" Cass held out his hand to indicate the cabin.

"Yes."

"Really?" Cass struggled to suppress the delight in his voice.

"The mine raised our rent, so I told my husband that we had a cabin that's paid for in Hanksville."

"That's the mine's loss."

She smiled. "I don't know about that, but thank you nonetheless."

Three young girls engaged in a game of tag ran around the opposite side of the cabin. They stopped playing when they sighted Cass and rooted themselves firmly to that spot like the apple tree behind them. Then the middle-sized girl stepped away from the others and cocked her head to one side as if sizing Cass up. She looked to be about ten or eleven years in age, definitely the prettiest of three, with her striking dark hair and dark eyes.

Sarah motioned to the dark-haired girl to come and took a few steps closer to Cass. "I want you to meet Maggie." A peculiar expression touched her eyes as she spoke.

Cass broke out into a cold sweat. He knew. He'd looked in a mirror often enough to recognize the girl's eyes and mouth as his own.

"Maggie," Sarah said the moment the girl reached her side. "This is Mr. Cass Hite. He's a good man who lives way down by Dandy Crossing on the Colorado River."

Good man. Cass's heart lifted to his throat at her declaration.

"How do you do, Mr. Cass Hite?"

Cass's words caught in his throat, and he had to try twice before he could say, "I'm fine, young lady. You are as pretty as your mother."

"Thank you, Mr. Hite," Maggie said with a stiff curtsy and a flush of color to her cheeks.

"How old are you, child?"

"I just turned ten." Her face beamed.

Cass and Sarah's eyes locked, and volumes of unspoken words passed between them. What he suspected, her countenance confirmed.

"Maggie, why don't you go around to the back where Papa's picking the last of the apples and bring a few here for Mr. Hite?"

Papa? But I'm her papa. Cass quickly quelled his jealousy—of course his daughter had a stepfather.

"All right, Mama." Maggie took off.

Cass's head felt light—he had a daughter, posterity. A part of him was in this beautiful child. He couldn't ignore that, nor did he want to. "Things get lonesome down on the river," he said to Sarah. "Can I write to her?"

"Not until she writes to you first." Sarah's tone

sounded insistent.

"Fair enough."

Maggie ran around the corner of the cabin carrying half a dozen apples.

Cass graciously accepted them, stuffing them in every pocket he could find. "I'll be back shortly," he said and took off at a brisk pace toward town. Minutes later, he approached the town mercantile, a fifteen-by-fifteen frame building sided with weathered wooden slats. It looked more like a small barn than a place of business. It had been years since he'd visited this store on the corner of Center and Main. Grateful it was still in business, he hurried inside, hoping jars of sweets filled the shelf behind the counter like before.

Yes, there's candy!

An older man wearing an apron pulled tight across his ample middle bent over a dustpan, sweeping up a pile of dirt. He looked up at Cass. "Sorry, mister, I'm closin' up early today."

Cass's eyes gravitated to a jar of peppermint sticks. "Please, sir, I only need three of those." He pointed to the red-and-white swirled treats, desperate to have them, to give Maggie reason to want to write him.

The old man straightened up and surveyed Cass from head to toe. "Well, well, if it isn't Cass Hite. I haven't seen you around these parts for ages. Where ya been?"

"Busy." Cass didn't want to go into any details. He was just glad the old storekeeper hadn't heard of his whereabouts for the past ten years. In that moment, he wondered if Sarah, too, was oblivious of his stay in prison. He could only hope, if for no other reason than she already had enough ammunition in her belt to use against his character. *But she'd called you a good man.* He smiled.

"Well, I suppose I could stay open a little longer, seeing that you haven't visited my place in years—and you only want few pieces of candy." The storekeeper pulled three of his biggest peppermint sticks from the jar and placed them on the counter. "That'll be five cents."

Cass slapped down a nickel. "Much obliged." He grabbed the candy and rushed out the door.

When he got back to the cabin, Sarah no longer worked in her garden. A momentary wave of disappointment spread through his chest. *Why'd I have to go having these blasted feelings?* He knew she wasn't his—and she never would be. And that husband of hers had to be around somewhere. The three girls, however, continued to play in the yard. He sauntered toward them, coming to a stop outside the picket fence.

"Still playing tag, I see," he said loud enough that all three girls turned and looked at him. "I wish I was a few years younger and I'd join you. Ain't nothing funner than a game of tag on a pleasant afternoon." He looked around to indicate the blue sky full of tiny white clouds and sunshine.

"Howdy, Mr. Hite." Maggie waved. "Me and Mama thought you'd left."

So, she actually gave me some thought. Cass noticed Sarah watching him through the window. He wondered if she was giving him another thought, or watching over her children as they conversed with an ex-convict. Warily, he held out his bag full of candy. "I went to the store. Would you girls like a peppermint stick?"

The three girls ran to him, Maggie crying out, "Yes," while the other two nodded.

Cass handed each of them their piece of candy and then looked at Maggie. "You ever write letters to folks, like to your grandma and grandpa?"

"I don't have a grandma and grandpa."

"Who are living," the biggest girl corrected Maggie.

"But I do like to write." Maggie took a big lick on her peppermint. "My teacher tells me I have very good handwriting."

"Writing letters is a good way to practice your penmanship," Cass said, considering his words carefully. To be able to correspond with his only child, the only silver lining to come out of his lapse of judgment those many years ago, would be akin to a thirsty man drinking from a cold spring of flowing water in the middle of a hot desert. "And it ain't such a bad thing to get letters back in return—give you a chance to help practice your reading."

Maggie's eyes opened wide. "We talked about that in school just last week. My teacher called it having a pen pal."

Finally, a bit of luck. "I'd be willing to be your pen pal, if'n you'll have me."

"Uh, all right." She sounded a bit hesitant.

"Tell you what—think about for a while. I'll wait to hear from you first before I write to you, in case you decide you don't want a pen pal." Cass hoped that wouldn't be the case. "My address is easy. It's just Cass

Hite, Hite, Utah. Stick a penny stamp on the envelope and you're good to mail it."

Maggie giggled. "You have a town named after you?"

"A dubious honor, believe me."

As Maggie scrunched her eyebrows, obviously not understanding, Cass noticed a man emerge from behind the cabin. His eyes caught notice of Cass, and with visible suspicion etched on his face, he approached them.

Sarah came from the house and hurried to Cass's side, arriving before the man. "Wayne, this is Cass Hite. Cass, meet my husband, Wayne Barker."

Cass cautiously extended his hand. The man named Wayne took it with cool indifference.

"Nice to meet you, Mr. Barker." Cass mustered the most amicable voice possible, seeing that he really didn't care to meet this skinny fellow. Rather, he wished the man didn't exist. "I do hope you don't mind my speaking to your wife earlier on. It's just that she saved my life several years ago when I was dying of pneumonia, and I feel a true sense of obligation to thank her every chance I get."

"Yes, she told me about that once." Mr. Barker's expression was hard to read. It was almost like he was piecing together a puzzle.

Does he know? Cass swallowed to ease his tightening throat. "I do hope you will forgive me for giving your children candy. But there is so little I can do to repay my debt to this whole community."

"It's all right." Mr. Barker readjusted his hat. Awkward silence followed.

An uncomfortable feeling permeated the air. Cass had to say something to lighten the mood. "You're a lucky man, Mr. Barker. You have a lovely family." The truth of his words only served to slice into Cass's heart.

"Thank you, sir."

Silence filled the air again. Cass couldn't think of anything more to say. The three girls stood innocently looking up at him, quietly munching their candy. Sarah remained by their sides, her arms folded and her mouth pinched shut.

"Well, I must be on my way. I have things to do before I start for Dandy Crossing in the morning." Cass had little to do before he left. In fact, up until a few minutes ago, he wasn't even sure if he was going home. Now it was certain. He didn't need any more reminders that things weren't what they used to be.

"Good day, Mr. Hite."

"Good day to you, Mr. Barker, ma'am, children." Cass tipped his hat, turned on his heel, and walked away without looking back.

Chapter 25

Cass climbed out of the stagecoach in Hite and took a deep breath of the warm, clean air, glad to finally be home.

"Here ya go." The stagecoach driver lowered Cass's bag down from the top of the coach.

"Thanks," Cass said. He felt yet another wave of dizziness come on as he reached up to take his bag. As he lowered it, he looked around to see if he could spot John. He was going to need his brother's help to get past this annoying illness.

John was nowhere to be seen, but plenty of other men were. "What in tarnation is going on?" Cass muttered. With his bag in hand, he headed to John's place first. Hopefully, he'd have the answer as to why five new tents sat on the edge of town and the place swarmed with a dozen men he'd never laid eyes on before. Some of the men sat in the red dirt playing poker, one hung out laundry on a rope strung between two of the tents, and the others weren't doing much of anything.

Two men filed out of the store as Cass approached. He tipped his hat at them. "You fellows are new around here."

"Yep," said a clean-shaven young man with hair the color of straw.

The other fellow sported a straggly brown beard that reached down to his chest. "We all got here a few days ago. Been haulin' in the material to build Mr. Stanton's new barge."

"What the—a barge? Here on the Colorado?"

"Yep." The one with the straw hair nodded.

The other guy scratched his beard and said, "It's goin' to be a huge floating dredge. We're startin' work on it tomorrow, settin' it up a mile or two north of here. It's goin' to revolutionize the placer minin' industry along this here river, you just watch." He extended his hand out to Cass. "By the way, the name's Sam. What's yours?"

"Cass." He shook the man's hand with the energy of a near-dead fish. His body ached to lie down, and his mind begged to talk with his brother.

"Cass Hite?" Sam asked. "*The* Cass Hite?"

"Yeah, that's me, but I don't recollect ever having earned a 'the' in front of my name."

"Heck, you're legendary, Mr. Hite," the straw-haired boy spoke up. "Just ask Mr. Stanton."

"Love to. Is he here?" Cass willed his dizziness to abate—he needed to talk to this Stanton fellow and see what this was all about. See if he could stop this madness that threatened his quiet spot along the mighty Colorado.

"No, he's up north getting more parts."

"That's too bad," Cass said. "Well, if you'll excuse me, fellows, I need to speak with my brother—the man who runs this store." He pushed past the two men with great effort and stepped into John's place.

Cass grabbed onto the mail counter to steady himself. "John, we need to talk."

John looked up from where he collected a silver dollar from the hand of yet another stranger. "Cass, you're back!" His expression changed from one of delight to one of concern. "My, but you look somethin' awful. What happened while you were gone?"

"I might ask the same thing. In fact, that's exactly what I want to ask."

"Let me finish up with this customer, and we'll talk." John placed the silver dollar in the cash box, pulled out a couple of two-bit pieces, and dropped them in the stranger's hand. "Fifty cents is your change. Thanks for your business."

The man pocketed the coins and laughed. "Where else we gonna go? This here sorry excuse of a store is the only one for fifty miles. Thank *you*." He grabbed his canned goods and bag of flour and moved outside.

"Okay, John, time to talk. What's going on?" Cass dropped onto the chair John kept by the front door.

"Cass, I promise you, it's not as bad as it seems."

"How can you say that? I hear that some man named Stanton's building a huge dredge upriver a piece. He'll ruin the river. He'll drive us the rest of the way out of business. First Kohler, now this!"

"Calm your horses, Cass. First of all, business in the store has never been better. Second of all, he won't hurt our gold minin'. He'll only help it."

"How on earth can you say that? And who the blazes is this man Stanton?"

"He came here a few years back—while you were in prison. He and some other fellows were surveyin' a possible railroad route down the Colorado. There were a few nights where we played a couple friendly games of cards and shared a bottle of whiskey. He told me of his dreams and I assured him the gold dust was there, but it was a blasted chore to pull it out. That's when he came up with this floating barge idea. Cass, imagine it—forty-sixty large buckets revolvin' around a boom that sticks out of the barge and into the river bottom. It'll be able to dredge up more sand in a half an hour than our old team of boys could scoop out all day."

"And how on earth are you supposed to sift through that much mud?" Cass couldn't keep the skepticism from his voice.

"The rotating buckets will carry the sand and gravel to a large circular iron screen on the deck where the large stuff is separated and poured back into the river. The fine stuff will fall into the hold of the barge. Then Stanton has this fancy system he'll put in place usin' amalgamating tables lined with mercury, and somehow it'll separate gold from the mud and sand. It's an expensive venture, but a great idea, Cass."

Cass's head ached. "Even if this venture worked, I can't see why you'd be excited. There's no way in hel—I mean, in the world—it could benefit our little mining company. We can barely afford to pay our boys as it is."

"He'll let us borrow the contraption." John stepped around the counter, pulled a chair over from the table, and sat in front of Cass. "The barge is mobile—it can move up and down the river to whatever spot we want. We just have to pay Stanton a small percentage of what gold we haul out each day. Don't you see it, Cass? This can totally revolutionize the placer minin' business. We could finally become rich off that old Indian's gold. And it's about time."

Cass bristled at the mention of Hoskininni in such a way. "No, I don't see it. And I don't like it. I made a promise to my Indian friends to take care of the river and tell no white man about the gold, and I intend to keep it. Stanton's contraption no way, no how fits with my promise!"

John wagged his hand at Cass. "Ah, you'll change your mind once you see it up and workin'."

"I doubt it." Cass wobbled as he stood. "I'm heading to my cabin. It's been a long trip and I've been ailing. Right now I just need my bed and a cup of willow bark tea."

"I thought you looked a bit peaked when you walked in." John stood and latched onto Cass's elbow. "You want me to help you on home? I'll bring a bottle of whiskey—that always makes you feel better."

Cass batted John's hand away. "No, it doesn't—it never did. I was just fooling myself all these years."

John's eyebrows rose. "Are you sayin' you don't

plan on drinkin' no more?"

"Exactly. Now move aside before I faint on your floor like some frilly back-east woman." Cass hurried outside the best he could with his head swimming in a mire of fog.

***

Cass stayed to his bed for a week, slowly gaining strength.

One evening, Cass lay on his bed with the window open, letting the unseasonably warm autumn breeze wash over his body. Unfortunately, it wasn't as peaceful like Novembers in the past, not with all those extra men in town cursing at each other in the background, constantly causing a ruckus. He had, however, felt pretty good during the day, almost back to normal.

"It's about time I return to the land of the living," he said to himself as he crawled out of bed. A friendly game of cards over at John's sounded inviting.

It felt good to stretch his legs. The thirty-yard stroll to his brother's cabin invigorated his body. When he opened the door to John's place, the smell of alcohol saturated the air, and he braced himself. He saw three men seated around the table, along with his brother. "I came over to see if you wanted to play some cards tonight," Cass said, "but it appears someone else has beaten me to it."

John jumped up, grabbed a three-legged stool from the corner, slid it under his behind, and motioned for Cass to take his chair. "Not at all. We'd love to have you. Mitch here is about to deal another hand." He looked to a young fellow on his left with a long nose and close-set eyes. "This here's my brother. Deal him in."

A round-faced man on Mitch's left reached across the table with a bottle of whiskey in his hand. "Here, John's brother. Swig yerself a drink."

Though Cass had sworn off alcohol, he still longed for a drink. The sour odor stimulated his saliva, and intense cravings reared to life. "The name's Cass, and I'll pass."

"Aw, come on." He pushed the bottle closer.

"I said no, thanks. The stuff almost killed me!" Cass glanced at Mitch. "Hurry and deal the cards."

"So yer Cass Hite?" Mitch said as he dealt the first card. "Yer the one who's friends with that Indian named Hoskininni?"

"How'd you know that?"

"Hell, everyone knows the story about Hoskininni's gold." Mitch slapped another card down in front of Cass. "That's why Stanton's building the barge."

Cass glared at John.

John hunched his shoulders. "What can I say? I was drunk." He winced. "I admit, I told him about you, and your Indian friend, and how the old chief told you about the 'gold sand' in the river. But Cass, don't worry about it—everything's goin' to work out fine. I figure it was a blessin' in disguise. I promise, it's not only goin' to help us out, but a heap of other folks as well."

"Yep." Mitch dealt another card. "The way

Stanton figures it, there's plenty of gold in this here river for everyone." He picked up his three cards, peered over them, and locked eyes with Cass. "Like yer brother said, don't worry none about it. Stanton's named his operation the Hoskininni Mining Company for good luck. So there." His eyes moved from player to player. "Okay, who's in?"

Cass picked up his cards, and without looking at them, slapped them back onto the table. "I'm out." He stood, knowing he couldn't stay there if he wanted to remain sober and civil. "And I'm going."

"You just got here." John gave Cass a sideways glance.

"I decided it's time to pay my Indian friend a visit. I'm going to head out first thing in the morning, so it's best I get to bed." Cass walked out the door.

As he shut it behind him, he wondered why he hadn't visited Hoskininni sooner.

It's because you were sick.

Well, I'm not sick now.

The vision of the old chief dancing over him in that hospital bed still lingered with Cass. Had it really happened? He wasn't sure. While living with the Indians, he had witnessed the old chief/medicine man casting spells and healing sick people with his sand paintings and chants. He had been told that Hoskininni oftentimes left his body to go somewhere else to scout for game or answer questions about what the white men were up to. Cass knew the old man possessed some strange powers, but had he actually brought Cass back from the brink of death?

Cass had to ask him.

***

The sun had barely begun to set as Cass drew close to his destination. About a mile outside Hoskininni's village, he spotted a Navajo sheepherder on the precipice of a juniper-covered hill. He must have seen Cass because he sent a young boy off in the direction of the village by pony. As Cass approached, he could see the villagers expected him. The women and children ducked out of sight, and half a dozen men loitered about innocently with rifles close at hand, leaning against trees or doorways. Hoskininni came running, beckoning Cass to get down from his horse and come to the fire. The villagers then trickled out of hiding and gathered around Cass. He tipped his hat to the women and saluted the warriors with a raised fist. A young man stepped forward and took the reins of Cass's horse. Overwhelmed by this reception, a lump rose in Cass's throat.

A young girl rekindled the fire while women scurried to prepare food. Cass sat down at the fire opposite Hoskininni while the villagers went about their lives. He noticed his friend had aged greatly since their last visit. "I have come for a long overdue visit with my friends, Hoskininni and Tahoma."

"Tahoma not here. He has gone south to Kayenta to visit family."

"I'm sorry I've missed him, but I am glad to see you, my old friend."

"As am I." Hoskininni nodded.

He and the Indian chief ate fried cornmeal cakes and venison, and exchanged gifts of coffee and jerky. It being a treat to have the old man to himself, Cass talked late into the night. With the sparkling Milky Way dividing the night sky and the orange embers of the fire glowing soft and still, Cass and his dear friend spoke of the changes they each faced.

In the shadows of the campfire, Hoskininni looked old, his back hunched over and hair streaked with age. Cass figured his friend must be in his nineties by now.

"Are you well and happy?" Cass asked.

Hoskininni looked up and smiled. "No other white man has ever concerned himself with my health. That is why I like you, Hosteen Pish-la-ki." He gazed at the stars. "As for your question, my heart is at peace."

"Your family doesn't seem to be doing as well as before," Cass said, probing the bounds of their friendship. "The children are ragged, and you have fewer horses."

"Yes, we are poor." Hoskininni's voice held no sign of being offended. "We have but a little meat to serve an honored guest." His hand lifted toward Cass. "In the old times, we would have raided the Mexicans or taken new horses from the white men beyond the San Juan. But we cannot do that now. We buy food from the white people when our corn doesn't grow. They end up with our blankets, silver, and horses."

The two of them sat looking at one another across the embers of the fire. Cass dropped his gaze and changed the subject.

"I have been very sick," he said.

"I know."

"I saw you in a dream," Cass added, still unsure if it was real or not.

Hoskininni smiled.

"In my dream, you were standing over me, and you were blessing me in a sacred way."

"Have you found peace in your heart, my son?"

"I was dying and you brought me back," Cass whispered.

"Sometimes a man should live a little longer to catch up on things he has missed in this life." Hoskininni's weathered face emanated a look of wisdom. "You have been given a gift, my son. What will you do with it?"

"I have stopped drinking whiskey, and I have made peace in my heart with the Mormons," Cass offered.

"That is well, my son. Search your soul and see what other things the Creator might want you to do."

The two of them stood from the fire. Hoskininni retired to his hogan, and Cass to a teepee where they housed their guests. Sleep refused to come. Cass had thought he'd been doing good enough with his efforts to reform. Obviously not. But what more could he do? Had his old friend been alluding to God? Cass blew out a long breath. That would be a tall mountain to climb.

Cass stayed a few days amongst his Navajo friends, enjoying the peace and acceptance they offered. And thinking. The moment he got back to Hite, he headed to his brother's store with a new idea that had come to him.

"John, you want to make your store bigger?" Cass said when he stepped through the door.

"Well, that's a fine how-do-you-do. I haven't seen you in days, and that's what you ask me."

"Sorry. How you doing, John?"

"I'm doin' fine. The store's doin' even better, what with another dozen men Stanton brought in. So as a matter of fact, yes, I could really use the room." John's eyes bore into Cass from beneath his wrinkled brow. "Why do you ask?"

"I'm proposing you move into my cabin and turn your entire place into a store."

"That's all fine and dandy, and I appreciate the offer, but you and me would be at each other's throat after a day if'n we were to bunk together."

"You'd have the place to yourself," Cass said, breathing out a cleansing sigh. "I'm moving out."

"Where to? Minin's in your blood. You don't want to move away from the Colorado—especially now. You just watch. We're goin' be rich men, Cass."

"I'm staying on the river—just moving south a mile."

"To Ticaboo? There ain't nothin' down there but—"

"I know, that old beat-up cabin I first built when I came here—before I found Hoskininni's gold." Cass couldn't believe he was doing this, but deep inside, he knew it was right for him. His time with Hoskininni had brought him to this decision, and his soul had confirmed it.

"What are you goin' to live off down there?"

"Don't worry. I'll have enough for my needs." Cass dropped onto a chair at John's poker table, doubting he'd ever be sitting there again—at least to gamble. "It's not that far from your store, maybe an hour by horseback," he continued. "And it's quiet down there, not a bunch of blasted wanna-be-rich-quick ruffians keeping me up at night and wagging their bottles of whiskey in my face."

"I mean, for money. You can't run our minin' company worth beans from that far away."

"She's all yours, John. All's I want in return for my share is enough for some building materials to fix up the old cabin at Ticaboo. And if I should need more money after that, I'll just walk twenty feet out my front door to my personal bank, the sandy one at the river's edge. I'll pan myself some gold the old-fashioned way—just enough to live on. I don't want to be rich anymore, John, just happy. And I'm working toward that. Moving away from this—" Cass swept his arm toward the window and the new tents and men filling the town. "—is just another step."

Chapter 26

Sarah carried a basket of carrots and beets toward the cabin. The garden lay almost bare now. The cold nip in the air told her there'd most likely be a hard freeze that night, and nothing more would grow until spring. She glanced at the garden, making sure the girls kept to their task of gathering all the remaining carrots and beets. "Keep up the good work," she urged. A spot warmed in her heart for the Good Lord and the rain He'd sent to this desert town this season and for Mary planting an extra garden this year.

She stepped inside the cabin, contemplating the other blessings He'd showered down upon her since she'd found His forgiveness. True, she and Wayne were poor as church mice, but they always managed to get by. They would make it through the winter this year. She could see now that Wayne losing his job had been a blessing in disguise. Otherwise, they would have never moved back to Hanksville, where the air was clean for Wayne and the garden was large for her.

Wayne sat in the overstuffed chair, his feet propped upon the footstool. He looked up from the book he read and smiled at Sarah. "You want me to scrub those carrots for you?"

"That would be lovely." Sarah walked over and set the basket on the table. "But just enough for supper. I'll put the rest of them in the root cellar first thing in the morning. Right now I should go help the girls finish gleaning the garden."

"It's the least I can do for you—and something I can actually do." He grabbed her arm as she walked past and tugged her toward his lap. "Sarah, how can I ever thank you enough for all you've done for me? First taking on my children after they'd lost their mother. Now taking care of me after I've lost my job and my health."

"You make it sound like it's a real chore." Sarah sat on his lap and brushed his forehead with a kiss.

"I promise, I'll get better. And come springtime, I'll find a job helping one of the ranchers around here. I'll pull my own weight soon, I promise—and more than that. I'll provide for our family again, I swear."

"Former bishops shouldn't swear." Sarah's grin moved to one side. Then it fell away as she realized once more Wayne was struggling with his self-esteem. She knew that dark feeling all too well and didn't want him to venture down that path. "You are pulling your weight just fine. You're the one who reminds the girls to say their prayers, and leads us in family prayer. You're the one who helps them with their arithmetic. If I had to teach them, they'd never learn their multiplication tables." She gave him a loving smile. "Now take your time with those carrots. There's no hurry." She pointed to the basket on the table. "You always do such a good job scrubbing them—thank you."

Wayne stood and hobbled toward the sink. "No, thank *you*, Sarah. I appreciate you so much. I really mean it. I don't know what I'd do without you."

"I'll go fetch you some water." Sarah grabbed the bucket they kept by the door and offered him a sincere smile before she walked outside. She appreciated Wayne too. He'd not yet recovered from that bout of pneumonia he'd contracted in Price. She only hoped her skills as a caregiver could help him make a full recovery. Not necessarily for her—she loved being needed. But for him—for his ability and need to provide for his family.

As she walked toward the pump, feeling grateful for Wayne's kind words, she thought about their marriage. She couldn't exactly say it was the one she had daydreamed about as a child, the storybook marriage of her parents, but she was content and at peace. After half-filling the bucket, she hauled the water inside the house.

Wayne sat on a chair next to the sink snapping the top off a carrot. "Thank you."

As Sarah leaned over to set the bucket of water in the sink, she turned to Wayne and kissed him tenderly on the lips. "I love you, Wayne," she uttered as she stood straight.

"What was that all about?" Wayne's eyes shone with a hint of surprise.

"Just telling you what I feel." Sarah had found that expressing love always made her feel good. Perhaps it could work the other way around and help Wayne feel a bit better. "I'll be back shortly," she said and stepped back outside.

Maggie looked up as Sarah approached. Her face beamed. "Mama, you want to see all I've gathered?"

"I'd love to." Sarah surveyed an orange pile of good-sized carrots with their tops lopped off. "Did you get them all?"

"I think so," Maggie said with a hint of pride.

Sarah picked up the burlap bag she'd set out earlier. "Here, let me hold the bag so you can fill it up." She glanced to where Beth and Julia worked together filling a bag with beets. "I'll come help you two in a minute."

Maggie dropped a handful of carrots into the bag, grabbed another two, and then stopped, carrot still in hand. "Mama, we've been talking about writing letters in school this week. Our teacher says it's a good thing to learn." She dropped one carrot into the bag. "That got me thinking about Mr. Hite. You remember him? He stopped by and said hello back when we first moved in."

"Yes, I remember him," Sarah responded, the familiar ache accompanying that memory feeling manageable now.

"He bought me and Beth and Julia each peppermint sticks. Did you know that?"

"Yes, I did."

"I got to thinking—when my teacher talked about writing letters—that Mr. Hite said he'd like me to write to him. I imagine he gets lonely all the way down there in that tiny little town."

"Yes, I imagine so too." The thought pained Sarah.

"Well, I do want to be pen pals with him. Every time you say nice things to Papa, I can see how happy it makes him. I want to do the same thing for Mr. Hite, Mama. Would that be okay with you?"

"Yes, that would be more than okay with me." Sarah remembered how pale Cass had looked when he'd stopped by. If anyone could lift the spirits of one feeling poorly, it would be her Maggie Mae—*his* Maggie Mae.

***

Cass stuffed the wild goose he'd caught that morning into a gunny sack and mounted his horse. He enjoyed the smile he felt curling up the ends of his mouth—it would be good to bring John something this visit instead of always being the recipient of his brother's gracious discounts.

It'd been difficult, no longer just helping himself to the commodities on the store's shelf, now paying for everything he took away. But it'd been worth it. In the few weeks he'd lived in Ticaboo, he'd discovered the pink and gold clouds of a serene sunset as satisfying as a day's haul of gold dust—especially when framed by a multi-layered silhouette of the western plateau. And having his head cleared from the fog of alcohol was more satisfying than two days' worth of gold. He'd even found himself talking now and again to the Big Man upstairs. He kind of liked it. It felt good.

The only drawback of living in Ticaboo, as Cass saw it, was that it got a mite lonely at times. That's why a visit to his brother was just what he needed right now—and why not take it? He had no deadlines to meet, no investors to please. The thought prompted a smile.

About an hour later, Cass rode into Hite. The place reeked of tobacco, whiskey, and sewage. More tents had been added to the half-dozen that were already there last time he'd come into town. He also spotted what looked to be the foundation for a new log cabin. Spitting distance from Cass's old cabin lay carefully cut red stone placed end to end, forming a ten-by-ten square. "Yep, glad we moved. Dandy Crossing's getting too crowded for me," he said to his horse.

Cass went directly to John's store, confident that's where he'd find his brother.

When he stepped inside, he saw that John was alone. *Good.* Cass plopped the gunny sack on the table. "I caught this here wild goose this morning. I thought I'd bring it up and share it with you for supper, seeing that tomorrow is that new national holiday ole President Lincoln made."

"You talkin' about Thanksgivin'?"

"Yep. And since there's not many wild turkeys in these parts, I thought this here goose would do just fine."

"We've never celebrated the infernal holiday before." John peered into the gunny sack. "Why you startin' now?"

"Just 'cause." Cass gathered the top of the gunny sack back into his hand. "Besides, it don't hurt to be thankful. I'll just take this girl outside and pluck her now. And I'll cook her up for us." He stepped to the door.

"Oh, while I'm thinkin' about it . . ." John moved over to the counter and sorted through a pile of mail. "There's a letter that came for you yesterday on the stage. It looked kinda interestin'. You'll want to read it before you mess your hands up with all that pluckin'." He pulled out a cream-colored envelope and handed it to Cass.

"Interesting?" Cass took the letter and looked at it. The words *Mr. Cass Hite* blared themselves across the front of the envelope in large, semi-neat block letters, obviously penned by a child. *Maggie?* His eyes darted to the return address in the corner. *Margaret Mae Barker, Hanksville, Utah.*

"Who's it from?" John asked. "It looked like some kid wrote it."

"You'd be correct." Cass opened the door.

John leaned toward Cass, trying to get another look at the envelope. "So, you goin' to tell me who it is?"

"Nope." Cass had contemplated telling John that Maggie was actually his daughter, and thus John's niece, but gossip had a way of traveling. He'd never do that to Sarah, or Maggie. They had respectable lives and deserved to keep them that way.

Cass stepped outside and shut the door behind him, anxious to see what his daughter had to say to him. He dropped the sack with the goose on the ground and lowered into the chair John had set out front of his store. His hands trembled as he tore open the envelope, thinking he still shouldn't be considering Maggie Mae his daughter. No one else did—not Maggie, not even Sarah. Maggie was a Barker—she'd always been.

He didn't care. He could think what he wanted—nobody need know.

He pulled out the single-page letter and opened up the folded paper. It held only two short paragraphs of writing. To him, it was as good as any lengthy epistle filled with literary prose. He read,

November 23, 1901

Dear Mr. Cass Hite,

We are learning about writing letters at my new school. When my teacher said we should find a pen pal to practice on, I thought about you. You said you would like to be my pen pal. I hope that is still all right with you.

Ever since me and Mama and Papa and Beth and Julia moved here to Hanksville, Papa's not as sick as he used to be. That makes me happy and not miss my friends up in Price so much. Mama says the air is better down here. I have a cat now. Her name is Patches. I like to pet her white and peach color fur. She makes me smile when I listen to her purr. Do you have any pets, Mr. Hite?

Sincerely,

Margaret Mae Barker

Cass carefully folded the letter back up and tucked it into its envelope. He sat there on the chair in front of the store, and with the letter still in hand, he gazed off into the distance, basking in good feelings. He smiled at her reservation that he might not want to be pen pals with her any longer. *If she only knew.*

Cass stuffed the letter into his shirt pocket and set to the task of plucking and gutting their Thanksgiving goose. Gratitude swelled inside him, making the normally unpleasant job pass quickly, as did the occasional "howdy" from a customer or two as they approached John's store. When he finished, he stood and stuck his head in the door.

"I'm heading over to the cabin to put this goose on to cook in the Dutch oven. You got any carrots or spuds I can add to it?"

"Yeah, I do." John set the pickle he was munching on upon the counter and scrounged through a crate of root vegetable at the back of his store. He pulled out a huge carrot, then two potatoes, and set them next to his pickle. As he straightened, he looked at Cass. "What do you say we head upstream after you get our supper on to simmer and go take a look at the progress of the barge?"

"I'd say I wasn't interested." Cass stuffed the potatoes into one pant pocket and the carrot into the other.

"What?" John wrinkled his forehead. "Aw, come on, Cass. You're missin' out. I saw it just last week, and it's a sight to behold. It's as big as all three of Hite's cabins put together."

"I noticed you've got a fourth cabin on the way," Cass said, changing the subject. He didn't care to discuss that monstrosity belonging to the mining company that was a sacrilege to Hoskininni's name.

"I'm not talkin' about cabins; I'm talking about the

dredge. Cass, you of all people I would think would be interested in the marvel of machinery that's goin' to set the world of minin' on its end. You've loved gold and silver as long as I've known you."

"That's not my idea of mining—only of making a mess of the river. And it'll be Mr. Stanton's folly, mark my words." Cass shut the door and trudged over to his old cabin, shaking his head most of the way. He knew in his bones, from years of experience, that there was no quick way to get rich in the mining business—unless by sheer luck. And tying the name Hoskininni Mining Company to the barge that ruined the river would hardly bring Stanton luck.

Originally, he'd planned on staying a day or two. Now tomorrow morning sounded like a good time to head back to Ticaboo.

That evening, Cass and his brother ate a tasty supper of roast goose, potatoes, and carrots. "No whiskey for me," Cass said for the fourth time. He placed his hand over his cup to prevent John from pouring him some.

John hiccupped and then glared at Cass. "I'm just tryin' to be gracious. This here's the store's best whiskey. What the hell is wrong with you, Cass?"

"Nothing's wrong with me." Cass stood from the table. "At least, not as much as there used to be." He stuck his plate in the sink. "I think I'm going to bed. I'll help you clean up the dishes in the morning."

The next morning, after Cass did the dishes and got ready to leave, he made a pot of extra-strong coffee for John's hangover. As he poured his brother a cup, he glanced out the window and noticed a yellow tabby cat dart across the dirt. Its fur looked to be the color of gold. "Say, John, has that ole she-cat of yours had her kittens yet?"

"Yeah, done had them over a month ago."

"I think I'll take one down to Ticaboo with me when I leave, if you don't mind. I've got some mice that've been bothering me. Oh, and I'm going to need to buy a few sheets of paper . . . and a couple of envelopes."

Chapter 27

Sarah pushed the front door shut with her hip as she unwrapped her scarf from around her ears. "It feels like winter's finally here," she said to the girls.

Beth sat at the table doing schoolwork. She glanced up from her book and twisted her face in an expression of annoyance.

Julia, sitting cross-legged on the rug playing dominos with Maggie, frowned at her tiles. "I don't like winter."

Maggie looked up from her game and smiled at Sarah. "It is December, after all. Will we get snow down here?" Her words sounded rich with anticipation.

"Sorry, but we don't get very much snow in Hanksville." Sarah deposited the dry mustard she'd purchased on the cupboard next to the sink. "But if and when we do, I promise I'll go outside and play in it with you girls. At least once." She knew she should spend more time with her girls—and reach out to her adult children now that her shame had diminished with God's forgiveness—but . . . She sighed to relieve some of the pressure of the burden on her shoulders.

"That would be grand! Thank you, Mama." Maggie's face reflected the delight in her voice. "You're the best."

"You're welcome." Sarah took a mixing bowl from the cupboard. "Is your papa resting?"

"Yeah," Beth said very matter-of-factly. "He's still in bed, asleep."

"I don't know how he's sleeping," Maggie added. "He coughs a lot."

"Oh, dear." Sarah poured the dry mustard into the bowl and put a kettle onto the stove to heat some water. "I'd better get this poultice on him right away." She glanced at the bedroom door, worry weighing heavy on her shoulders. Wayne's cough never seemed to heal fully, and that day, it had returned in force.

While the water came to a boil and Sarah peeled some potatoes for supper, she remembered the letter sitting in her skirt pocket. She rinsed and dried her hands, and turned to Maggie. "While I was at the store, I picked up the mail. You've got yourself a letter, young lady." She pulled the letter from her pocket and handed it to Maggie.

"Thank you." Maggie grabbed it, glanced at the front, and ripped open the envelope.

"Who's it from?" Julia's lower lip jutted out. "Why don't I get a letter?"

Maggie extracted a sheet of paper from the envelope. "You've got to write a letter to get a letter. This is from my pen pal." She smiled as she read.

When she'd finished, she held it out toward Sarah. "You want to read it, Mama? It's from Mr. Cass Hite."

Sarah froze. She would have loved to read it at the moment. A diversion from her worries sounded like good medicine for *her*. "Hold on to it for right now, Maggie. I'll read it after I get Papa taken care of."

That night, after Wayne's cough settled down and the girls were all asleep, Sarah spotted Maggie's letter resting on the kitchen shelf. She picked it up and settled into the overstuffed chair, thinking she should read the letter and approve of it before Maggie continued being Cass's pen pal.

The handwriting scrolled upon the page in strong, boldly formed lettering. It prompted a smile—it fit Cass so well.

December 1, 1901

Dear Maggie Mae,

I deem it an honor to be your pen pal, and I would like to thank you for your thoughtful letter. I received it on the day before Thanksgiving while I was visiting my brother. It gave me one more reason to be thankful. I hope you enjoyed your Thanksgiving holiday too.

Sarah lifted her eyes from the page and let out a sigh of pain for her daughter. How would Maggie respond to that? Their Thanksgiving dinner had consisted of a tiny chicken Edna had given them, a small scoop of mashed potatoes each, and a few slices of cooked carrots. It had been tasty enough, but Wayne's illness had put a damper on the day. Sarah had spent her whole day tending to his needs, and so the girls had cooked their own holiday dinner.

She returned her gaze to the letter.

In your letter, you asked me if I had any pets. Yes, I do. I have a tomcat named Tom. I have high expectations of the young fellow. I've recruited him to catch this pesky mouse that's seen fit to occupy the same cabin as me. Speaking of cabins, I've got myself a new one. Actually, it's an old one I've been fixing up. I no longer live in the town of Hite. I've moved down river a mile or so to a place called Ticaboo. It's not a town, just a wide spot in the river bottom with a high spot twenty feet from the bank where my home sits. I'm Ticaboo's only resident. I like it that way. There's too many fights and too much whiskey in Hite anymore. I needed to get away from that. I guess I'm not the same ole cuss I used to be.

But this ole cuss sure enjoyed getting a letter from a gentle young lady like you. It made my day, and my week. I hope you will continue to write to me. I can't think of anything I'd enjoy more than having a pen pal like you. (Even more than panning for gold.)

Sincerely,

Cass Hite

Sarah folded the letter back into thirds and tucked it in the envelope, thinking how Cass was still rough around the edges, but time had apparently tempered him. Warmth spread out from her heart. *Good for you, Cass.*

***

Cass looked up at the gray clouds billowing overhead. Maybe he should have waited to ride into Hite and come on a sunny day. It wasn't like he really needed the bag of flour he intended on buying. *Aw, tomorrow's Christmas. You need to at least go and wish your brother well for the holiday.* He kicked his heels into his horse ever so lightly and prompted him onward.

Cass couldn't see his brother when he stepped into the store, but he heard hammering coming from the back room. "John, is that you back there making all that racket?"

John appeared in the doorway. "Cass! Good to see you."

"You make it sound like I've been gone a great while. I was here just last week." *And the week before that, and the week before that.* Cass wished there was mail service out to Ticaboo.

"Well, it's Christmas tomorrow. Are you planning to stay a spell?"

Cass looked out the window, exaggerating his action. "I don't think I'd better. The weather doesn't look too good." He returned his gaze to John, extended his arm, and gave his brother a hearty hug. "Merry Christmas, John. Okay, so it's a day early, but best grab my pound of flour, check my mail, and be on my way before the snow comes—because that's what those clouds look like they're fixing to do."

John returned the embrace, and then measured out a pound of flour into a paper bag. He pushed the brown bag across the counter to Cass and glanced at the mail shelves. "And as a matter of fact, you actually have mail this time." He stepped over and pulled a letter from one of the cubbyholes. He glanced at the front of the envelope before handing it to Cass. "You're someone's pen pal?"

Cass accepted the envelope, anticipation energizing the action. He read the first line, written in block letters and much larger than the rest.

To my pen pal Mr. Cass Hite

"Yeah, I am." Cass jutted out his chest. "What of it?"

"Ain't that something school girls do?"

"Yeah, and one them is writing to me. And I'm writing to her."

John bellowed out a laugh. "Wait till I tell the boys."

"Go right ahead. I don't care one lick what they think." Cass flicked his hand toward John's poker table. "'Cause I dare say I enjoy reading her letters a lot more than wasting my evenings playing cards with a bunch of foul-tongued men too drunk to make decent conversation." He grabbed the flour and the letter and moved over to the table. "Now, if you don't mind, I'm going to put this table to good use." He dropped into a chair and opened his letter, ignoring John, who stood there open-mouthed and staring at him.

December 20, 1901

Dear Mr. Cass Hite,

I hope you are as excited for Christmas as I am. Mama says we're not going to get much in our stockings this year, but I don't care. This year, we have a Christmas tree to hang them on. Mama took me and my sisters up in the hills on the other side of town to cut a tree. We found a real pretty one. Mama said it was called a juniper tree, but I told her it was a Christmas tree. She said

*it was that too. Mama seems so much more fun to be with ever since
we moved to Hanksville. She's happier, and that makes me happier.
I hope you are happy, Mr. Hite. I don't like it when people are sad.*

>*Have a merry Christmas,*
>*Sincerely,*
>*Maggie Mae Barker*

"Well, I'm certainly happier now," Cass whispered as he refolded the letter and stuffed it back into the envelope.

"What's that you said?"

"Nothing." Cass peered out the window again. "But I definitely won't be staying till Christmas Day. I don't care to get snowed in here. If I'm stuck inside for any length of time, I'd just as soon be at home."

"But ain't this the same as home?" John indicated the store's cabin with a sweep of his hand.

"Not quite." Cass knew that come evening, that table would be filled with men who wouldn't take "no" for an answer as they forced whiskey into his gut and poker cards in his hand. That didn't feel fitting for Christmas Eve—or any other evening, for that matter.

Minutes later, Cass rode away from Hite and Dandy Crossing, thinking about Maggie's letter. *I hope you are as excited for Christmas as I am.* Her words replayed in his head with the same childlike enthusiasm that had first jumped from the page.

"Yep, Maggie Mae, I'm excited for Christmas," Cass said into the wind. He would read her letter again tomorrow—two or three times, perhaps. He might even pull out her previous letter he kept in a small wooden chest beneath his bed and read it too. Then he'd write her a letter.

Rain fell from the sky in icy droplets as Cass approached Ticaboo. He led his horse into the corral, removed his saddle, and hurried into his cabin as the rain turned to fluffy flakes of snow uncommon in this neck of the river. With the early hour of the setting sun and the darkness of the storm, Cass immediately lit the lamp he kept on his table. He put away his bag of flour, sat down at the table, and pulled Maggie's letter from his pocket, ready to read it again. Then he thought of a better idea to brighten the holiday in Ticaboo.

He stepped over to the small set of drawers in the corner of his one-room cabin and pulled out one of his best stockings. He stuffed it with things he'd like to wake to on Christmas morning—Maggie's letter, and a new envelope with a blank sheet of writing paper. "There, that'll be two dandy presents," he said to his cat, Tom, who lay curled up on the rug in front of the fireplace. He sandwiched the top of the stocking between the stone mantel and his kettle, and stepped back to admire his first Christmas stocking since childhood as it hung from his fireplace.

Chapter 28

Sarah shut the door behind the girls. She hated sending them out in blowing snow after their Christmas break, but she preferred they spend their day at school. Holidays and weekends were hard enough for Sarah to keep her spirits up and appear as if Wayne's illness took no toll on her. Every day would be impossible.

She pulled the latest letter from its envelope, having waited until the girls went to school to do so. Maggie had received it on Saturday, and had even encouraged Sarah to read it right after she had, but Sarah chose to wait until she could be alone. Wayne's heavy breathing from the bedroom told her he'd succumbed to his usual morning nap. She settled into the overstuffed chair, chiding herself for the excitement at which she unfolded the single sheet of paper that held Cass's correspondence to her daughter.

December 25, 1901

Dear Maggie Mae,

Today is Christmas, and I am having a lovely day because of you. When you told me about how excited you were to hang your stocking on the Christmas tree and how much you looked forward to Christmas, even though you knew there would be little inside your stocking, it brought a smile to my old face.

Sarah looked up, letting her pain and relief mix together in a sigh. She'd been heartsick at what little she and Wayne had given their children on Christmas two weeks ago. And here was her sweet daughter, with her outlook as bright as ever, looking forward to the holiday even though she knew it wouldn't be filled with gifts and good food.

See, it was *a good idea to read this letter.*

Things were still *much* better than the times she'd felt low because of her sins. Thank heavens that was behind her now or she could have never endured. And then what of the children if her redemption had never happened? She shuddered to think of it and returned her eyes to the page, anticipating more words to brighten her day.

I had a wonderful Christmas as well. I placed your last letter in one of my stockings and hung it on the fireplace. It made for a delightful Christmas morning, even though I already opened your letter the day before. After I re-read your letter, I sat by the window of my cabin and gazed outside at the blanket of new snow covering the ground. As I watch the water of the Colorado cut a winding path of blue-green in the white, I thought about how the Big Man Upstairs is quite an artist, and how I appreciate Him a whole lot more than I used to.

My cat, Tom, is getting bigger every day. I guess there were more mice in my place than I thought. That's okay because it made me keep Tom inside my cabin and I've found I like his company. It does get mighty lonely at times, living here in Ticaboo all by myself. How is your cat, Patches? Does she like to curl up in your lap at night and purr?

I hope all is going well and I look forward to your next letter—whenever you choose to write one.

Sincerely,

Your pen pal, Cass Hite

Sarah folded the letter, placed it back into its envelope, and remained sitting in the overstuffed chair, not the least bit anxious to begin her housework. Her mind wandered. Wayne's rough breathing led her to that corner of thought where concern weighed her down low. Would he ever recover? How much longer would he need her constant attention? Could he ever be fit enough to work? Her thoughts shifted to her children, her grandchildren she was closer to now, and how much joy they all brought to her. Especially Maggie.

Then the image of Cass took form, and memories from over ten years ago flooded her mind—some good, some bad. But mostly good this time—she'd forgiven him fully the day she'd found forgiveness for herself. The way he made her laugh, without the least bit of seeming effort on his part, brought a smile to her heart as she relived some of those moments. His dark hair and brown eyes had attracted her and made her heart beat quickly those many years ago. She had to admit, even now she found Cass handsome the few times she'd seen him passing through. Her mind wandered farther, treading on ground she knew to be precarious. *What would my life be like now if I had married Cass instead of Wayne?* The thought was delicious, and she dwelt upon it for more than a moment. Surprisingly, before enjoying it fully, she found herself pushing the thought of Cass aside and contenting herself with the kind man who slept fitfully in the adjoining room and who she loved in a different way.

"Sarah." Wayne's wispy voice reached into the main room. "I need you."

"Coming," Sarah called out. Concern for her husband swept all other thoughts away. Wayne was her husband now. This was her lot in life—one that could have been much worse—and she accepted that.

***

"Yes, you've got a letter, Cass."

Elated, Cass snatched the letter from John the second his brother pulled it from the mail cubby. He'd been braving bad weather every other week for the past three months with nothing to show for his visits to Hite except another pound or two of flour. The last two times he'd checked his mail, he'd feared Maggie had grown tired of the whole pen pal idea.

"Much obliged," Cass said and walked outside the store with a lilt to his steps to read. He settled onto the stool John kept by the front door and opened his letter, letting the March sunshine add to the delight of the moment.

March 23, 1902

Dear Mr. Cass Hite,

I hope you are enjoying springtime as much as I am. It's so pretty and green with all those new leaves coming out. I helped Mama plant peas and onions yesterday. She is so excited to have such a big garden and all those fruit trees. I love to see Mama happy because she has such a pretty smile.

Cass envisioned that smile. "I know," he said.

"You know what?"

John's voice pulled Cass's attention from the page. He looked up. "Nothing you need to know."

"That's another one of those letters from your pen pal, ain't it?"

"Yeah, so what of it?"

"Nothin'. I'd of thought you'd of grown tired of that foolishness by now. Holy tarnation, Cass, you're a grown man. You went and turned a half a century old this month." John slowly shook his head. "First you give up whiskey, then gamblin', and now you look forward to these blasted letters like they were the motherlode. What next?"

"Nothing much, I reckon." Cass returned his eyes to the letter. "I'm content with how things are. Now, if you'll excuse me, I'd like to get back to reading. Why don't you go back inside and dust your shelves or something?"

John stomped back into the store. "Well, of all the—"

Cass couldn't hear his brother's entire string of profanity, and that was just fine. He didn't care to taint the moment. These letters from Maggie Mae were like a gold lining in these lonely, aging years. Not only were his days brightened by his daughter's cheery outlook on life, but in her innocence, the child also provided a small window to view the high point of his life—the only woman he'd ever loved. Sarah.

His insides warmed at the sound of her name ringing in his mind, and a pleasant smile curled his lips. He couldn't see himself loving another.

He returned to reading, anxious to sop up any and every morsel of detail about the lives of these two gals he cherished above all else.

Mama promised me and my sisters that if we helped a lot, and we made the garden big enough, there'd be no more nights of going to bed hungry next winter. I worked extra hard. Have you ever gone to bed hungry, Mr. Hite?

"Yep, I have, Maggie Mae," Cass whispered, not proud at all for having done so. "It was only because I was too drunk to know better."

I hope not because it's no fun at all, he read.

His heart swelled with pain that she had suffered. "No, it wasn't fun," Cass continued to whisper to his daughter. What would it have been like to have her to raise and to talk to every day, to tell her of the foibles of his youth and warn her to take a better pathway? What would it have been like to work hard every day, making sure there was enough food on the table to feed his beloved child and dear wife? That certainly would have been a better use of all that gold dust than the whiskey and poker games he'd wasted it on.

I'm sorry for not writing to you sooner. Papa is still sick, and I had to wait for Mama to buy me paper. She did some mending for folks in town and got some money. She took me to the store with her. It was fun. We bought sugar and flour and lard, and then she let me buy some writing paper and envelopes. She told me she wants me to write to you. I hope you don't mind if Mama reads your letters too. I think she enjoys them because she is as excited to get them as I am.

Have a wonderful springtime,
Sincerely,
Maggie Mae Barker

Cass's heart thumped rapidly, ignited from the mere idea that Sarah read his letters too—and was excited to get them. He carefully refolded the letter and tucked it safely inside its envelope. Words for his response formed in his mind as his mouth formed a smile. He knew, however, that he must hold himself back and only write one letter for every letter he received from Maggie—for decorum's sake. But he could include extra paper and an envelope in each of his letters.

***

Sarah accepted the folded letter the moment Maggie offered it to her. A thrill of excitement shivered through her at the touch of the paper. She couldn't bear waiting until the girls were in school to read it. What would he say this time? "You girls see to the needs of your papa for a minute or two. Make sure he doesn't overdo." She motioned to Wayne, sitting there in the overstuffed chair with his legs propped up on the footstool. Her eyes met his. He'd been out of bed and helping around the house here and there for going on a week now. She hoped he was on the mend and didn't want him to jeopardize his progress. "I'm going to take a short walk. I need to stretch my legs and relax for a minute. I hope that's all right."

Wayne waved her toward the door. "Yes, by all means. You deserve a break."

"Thank you, Wayne." Sarah stepped outside.

The moment she slipped behind the cluster of juniper trees so there'd be no chance of Wayne seeing her through the window, she pulled the letter from her pocket. The last thing she wanted to do was upset her husband's delicate health by leading him to believe she was still in love with Maggie's natural father. True, a soft spot for Cass remained in her heart. But she had that under control. She merely enjoyed reading Cass's letters—that was all. Perhaps she *should* tell Wayne that she read Cass's letters, tell him she did so to make sure they were appropriate for Maggie. She realized then that Wayne still didn't know Cass had fathered Maggie, only that Sarah had conceived illegitimately.

If Cass wrote Maggie again, she'd do that—she'd tell Wayne about Cass. For now, she'd read this one with only the junipers swaying in the breeze behind her knowing what she was doing and then go inside and tell Wayne about Maggie's pen pal.

March 30, 1902

Dear Maggie Mae,

I sure enjoyed your last letter. No need to apologize for not writing to me for a while. I understand about not having paper. Sometimes I run out too, so I sent you some extra I had. And I understand that in time, you might grow weary of writing to an old man like me. That is why I promise I won't bother you with my letters until I first receive one from you. That way, I'll know being a pen pal is something you still want to do.

I'm glad to hear that you are helping your mother with the garden. She is a good woman and works hard, but I'm sure with the size of your place, she needs help, so make sure you give her plenty. You're a thoughtful girl, so I know you will.

Sarah paused for a moment, her heart swelling with appreciation for Cass's praise of Maggie. She let the tender feeling warm her insides and continued.

I planted myself a garden just last week. I have a small row of peas and one of carrots. It's not as big as your mother's garden, I'm sure, but it's enough to feed me. If I get extra hungry, I just wander down to the river and catch myself a fish and fry him up for supper. I like living here in Ticaboo. Its only drawback is that it gets lonely sometimes. Those times, I pull out your letters and read them again. That helps. Thank you.

Tom is getting bigger. He's a good companion. I talk to him all the time when I'm down on the river panning for gold. He sits on the bank, curled up in a ball, warming himself in the plentiful southern Utah sun. I hope Patches is a good companion for you. I'm sure she is because you are a good companion for her—as you are to everyone.

Thank you for being one to me.

Sincerely,

Cass Hite

Sarah folded the letter back into thirds and returned it to the envelope, hoping Maggie would continue to write to Cass. She could tell the man benefitted from the correspondence. She only hoped that once summer came, what began as a school assignment would continue.

When she walked back inside, Wayne still sat in the overstuffed chair, his eyes focusing on her. "Oh, by the way," she began, "I forgot to tell you that Maggie has a pen pal. It's part of a school assignment."

"That's nice. Penning a letter is a good skill to develop."

"I hope you don't mind, but she's writing to Cass Hite, the gentleman I nursed back to health years ago. I believe you met him shortly after we moved here. He bought the girls peppermint sticks. Do you remember?"

"Yes, I remember," Wayne said without any hint of his emotions.

"Don't worry, I'm reading every one of his letters to, uh, make sure they are appropriate for Maggie. That's what I was doing just now." Sarah held Cass's letter up. "You're welcome to read it too, if you wish," she offered hesitantly.

"No, thanks. I trust you."

Nearly Two Years Later

Chapter 29

Cass brushed the dusting of snow from his coat. Warmth emanated from the potbelly stove as he entered John's store, and he gravitated to its side. "Got any mail for me?" he asked his brother more out of habit than anything. He hadn't received a letter from Maggie Mae for the last twenty-one months.

John barely glanced at the cubbyholes where he stored the sorted mail. "Nope."

"Well, then, give me a pound of flour and a half one of lard." Cass dropped into one of the chairs set around John's poker table, the disappointment stinging less than his last trip into Hite. Maggie had obviously moved on from her fascination with pen pals.

"Hold on." John picked up a bundle of envelopes sitting at the back of the counter. "I got yesterday's mail here. Haven't had a chance to sort it yet. You want me to look?"

"Sure—why not?" Cass stretched out his legs and settled into his chair. "I got time." *Plenty of time.* So far, this December had proven to be a cold one. His hands stiffened more and more in the winter weather. He had sufficient gold dust in his pouch—so why pan for more? And he was in no hurry to get back to Ticaboo only to watch the fire burn in his stove.

John shuffled through the stack of varying-sized letters, stopped abruptly, and pulled out an envelope. "Well, what do you know?" He wagged it at Cass.

Cass's heart took an extra beat. He swore it was the same shade of creamy white, and the exact size—just a little crumpled—as the one he'd included in his last letter to Maggie. "Give it here." He jumped to his feet and snatched the letter from John's hand. Sure enough, Maggie Mae's name was neatly penned in the upper left-hand corner. *She's grown up a bit.* Not caring to wait for a private moment, he settled back into his chair and opened the envelope. The sheet of paper inside was folded differently this time, in quarters instead of thirds. He smoothed flat one of the folds to reveal a juvenile drawing of a babe wrapped in swaddling clothes and lying in a manger. A five-pointed star was drawn in yellow above the manger. Below the manger, neat red block letters spelled out the words "Merry Christmas."

John peered over Cass's shoulder. "Looks like you got yourself yer first Christmas card, Cass."

"Christmas card?"

"Yep, they're all the rage right now—leastwise in

the big cities." John tilted Cass's hand, apparently so as to get a better look at Maggie's drawing. "That's what some of the fellas tell me, at least. I wouldn't know—I got no one to write to and no one to send me one." He motioned to a stack of cards on his counter. Each was about the size of three poker cards placed side by side. The top card lay face up. It held a picture of an angel dressed in white with gold and green trim along with the words "Merry Christmas" in red. "But I ordered in some fancy postcards in case the fellas wanted to send some out to their gals. I seriously doubt they could make their own like your little pen pal did."

"That's nice," Cass muttered, having barely listened to his brother. "Shhh, I'm reading." He opened the folded paper and read.

December 15, 1903

Merry Christmas, Mr. Hite,

We learned about Christmas cards in school, so me and my friend decided to make some and send to people to brighten their holiday. She got a set of these coloring sticks called crayons for Christmas from her grandparents. She and I used them to make our cards. It was fun. I could never, ever imagine receiving such a fancy gift.

Cass peered over at John, busy now straightening cans on a shelf. "You ever heard of crayons? They're for children."

"Cray-what? Is that some sort of new poker game for kids?"

Cass rolled his eyes. "They're toys—some sort of coloring sticks. I was going to have you order me some in, if you could," he said as he continued to read.

But that's okay, I have a fine gift in store for me this year. Papa is feeling better and he promised to string popcorn, sing carols, and play checkers with me on Christmas.

"Never mind." Cass knew no store-bought present could top her *papa's*. Nor should Cass have even considered trying to win her affection that way.

"I could look in my catalogs and see if I could find them."

"I said never mind."

"Okay, okay, don't be gettin' your long johns in a wad."

Cass wagged a hand at his brother and returned his attention to the letter.

My friend sent her card back to her grandparents to say thank you. She also made another card and is going to send it to her other grandparents. I don't have any grandparents, so I decided to send it to you. I hope you don't mind that I made you a homemade Christmas card.

Cass glanced up toward Hanksville, toward Maggie Mae. "Of course not," he said under his breath, loving this card more than she would ever know.

"What's that you say?"

"Nothing, John. Get back to work."

I also hope that you have a wonderful Christmas down in Ticaboo with your cat, Tom. Cats can be good company. I know. I talk to Patches and let her curl up in my lap and listen to her purr when I'm feeling alone. I've run out of room, so I'll say goodbye now.

Sincerely,

Maggie Mae Barker

Cass carefully folded Maggie's Christmas card and slid it back into its envelope. "John, how about you put one of those angel postcards on my bill? I'm going to write and send my first Christmas card."

***

Sarah sprinkled some sugar on the top crust and placed her apple pie in the oven. This Christmas was going to be a good one. She could feel it in her bones and couldn't hold back the smile forming on her lips. Wayne had more good days than bad as of late, the garden had produced enough to hold them through the winter, and her trees gave them enough apples to sell some to pay for a comfortable amount of sugar, flour, and other essentials. She closed the oven door as her eyes turned toward the door in response to a gust of cold air.

"Maggie!" Beth hollered, stepping inside and waving a card in the air. "I was down at the store and fetched the mail. You got yourself one of those fancy Christmas postcards."

Maggie abandoned her popcorn string and stepped away from the Christmas tree. "Really? So fast?" Her face beamed as she took the card from Beth and headed toward the bedroom.

Julia darted to Maggie's side. "I want a Christmas card."

"You've got to send one if you want to receive one," Beth stated.

Maggie showed Julia her postcard. "Next year, you want to come over to Emma's with me when we make our

Christmas cards? I'm sure she'd let you use her coloring sticks, if you're careful. They're so fun—it's almost like magic, the way they put color on paper."

Julia's eyes lit up. "Really?"

"Who's it from? Mr. Hite?" Sarah asked, not imagining who else it could be.

"Mr. Hite?" Wayne's voice rose slightly in pitch. "Is he still writing to you?'

"Yes, Mama, it's from him."

Gratitude touched Sarah's heart that her daughter chose to stay in contact with Cass without even knowing the truth of her heritage.

Maggie turned to Wayne. "And yes, Papa, he is, probably because I sent him a Christmas card first. Mama gave me the idea."

Wayne's eyebrow rose.

Sarah caught her breath. Wayne still didn't know. It was well past time to tell him about Cass. She'd put it off and put it off, and then with Maggie not receiving a letter for nearly two years, she hadn't seen the need to approach the subject.

Sarah nodded Wayne to head into the bedroom and she followed, closing the door behind them. "It's time for you to lie down and rest," she said, pulling back the quilt. "And it's time I told you something—something I should have told you years ago." She stared at her feet and let out a heavy sigh. "I'm sorry."

Wayne lay down and slid beneath the covers. "Sarah, it's all right. You have nothing to be sorry for." He closed his eyes like he was feeling pain. "It is I who should be sorry."

Sarah sat on the edge of the bed and gathered Wayne's hands in hers. "Sorry for what?"

"For this." He pulled a hand loose and swept it down his frail body toward his toes. "For sentencing you to years of taking care of a sickly husband." Sunlight poured through the window and lit his features to where she could read agony on his face—not of labored breathing, but something much deeper inside him. He looked away. "Mr. Hite . . . he is Maggie's father, is he not?"

Sarah sensed that his question was more of a statement. He knew. Yet he didn't appear angry. That choked her up such that the words stuck in her throat. She nodded her response. But what did he feel? She struggled to find her voice. "I've always . . . meant to tell you. How . . . did you know?" she said in a near whisper. "The Christmas card?"

"I've known since that first day you introduced him to me," he responded, still not meeting her gaze. "The way he looked at you, and looked at Maggie, I could see the pain of loss in his eyes." Silence fell between them. Finally, he added, "I know because I felt that with Genevieve." He turned to Sarah and took her other hand. "You helped me heal, though," he said, squeezing her hand, "and you still work tirelessly to try to fill the void Genevieve left behind."

Sarah returned the squeeze. "Shush. You make it sound like such an arduous task."

"It is."

"No, it's a privilege." She let go of his hands and pulled the quilt up to his chin.

"You are too kind." Wayne gazed into her eyes and then looked away. "If only I could have helped you heal as you have helped me." He breathed deep, and a fit of coughing ensued. When at last it subsided, he said softly, "If only I'd been healthier, perhaps I could have filled the void Mr. Hite left." He returned his focus to her. "I have seen the pain of loss in your eyes too."

"No, Wayne, no—at least not anymore." It ripped her heart up to see Wayne feel sorry for being a burden rather than being angry for the connections to Cass she'd held on to. "You are my life now. I promise."

***

With the girls back in school and Wayne taking a nap, the house felt overly quiet. Sarah hummed Christmas carols to liven things up as she took down the juniper tree. She moved it out to the south side of the cabin so it could dry out and be used for firewood later. When she came back in, she moved on to the pine boughs Maggie had placed on the mantel and tied together with her red, green, and white hair bows. Behind them, she noticed Maggie's postcard. The artistry of the angel drew her eyes toward it. The fact it came from Cass was *not* the reason her hand took it from the mantel and she settled into the overstuffed chair. In fact, reveling in the past week of holiday festivities, she'd totally forgotten about Cass's card.

December 20, 1903

Dear Maggie Mae,

Thank you for the beautiful Christmas card. I've never received one before. It made my day. I'm going to place it above my fireplace, and I'm sure it will decorate up my cabin right nice for Christmas. I hope you don't mind that I've sent you a store-bought one in return. Unfortunately, there ain't much room to write on. That's probably best for you, as I don't have much new things to tell you about. My life is pretty much the same, except for a few extra aches and pains.

I do like the idea of sending each other Christmas cards each year. But only if you want to. But please know that I delight in our correspondence.

It sounds like you're going to have a wonderful Christmas this year. That makes me happy.

Sincerely,

Cass Hite

Sarah placed the card back on the mantel. She'd let Maggie decide what she wanted to do with it. Perhaps it could remind Maggie of the wonderful Christmas they *did* have. Life promised to be good this coming new year. *Finally.*

Still, Sarah had appreciated hearing that Cass was doing well.

***

One Year Later

Cass headed straight to John's store the moment

he arrived in Hite. The town that bore his name held nothing else of interest to him anymore—only his brother and the store/post office he ran. The influx of strangers there to work on Stanton's dredge, along with their horses, gambling, and whiskey, appealed to Cass about as much as an abscessed tooth. During the past summer, at best he made it into town once a month. But ever since Thanksgiving, he'd journeyed into Hite once a week. He held to the hope that Maggie Mae had picked up on the hint in his postcard last year and chose to send him another homemade card this holiday. With a week left until Christmas, he walked into John's place holding his breath.

"Any mail for me?"

"That's all I get from you?" John wrinkled his forehead as if he were pouting. "Not a howdy, hello, or even a Merry Christmas?"

"Merry Christmas." Cass slapped John on the back and then pulled him into a hug. He let go and stepped back. "It's not like I never see you."

"I know, I know. I'm just givin' you a hard time." John reached into one of the mail cubbyholes and extracted a letter. "That's because I know this must be why you been comin' in every week, checkin' your mail."

Cass glanced at the envelope as he took it from John. Seeing Maggie Mae's name in the corner evoked such a wave of excitement, Cass would have thought he was a kid again. "You'd be correct," he said and sat down at the poker table.

He opened the envelope to find another homemade card. On this one, a green Christmas tree decorated with multicolored dots practically filled the front of the card. Inside the card in beautiful red cursive lettering were the words "Merry Christmas." Beneath that in blue-black ink was the body of a letter. His hand trembled as he brought it closer to his eyes to read, not helping his marginal eyesight one bit. He steadied his hand and read.

December19, 1904

Dear Mr. Hite,

As you can see, I was able to use my friend Emma's crayons again to make you a Christmas card. Julia came with me this time. She enjoyed making Christmas cards. I had told her it was fun, only she didn't know who to send hers to. She doesn't have a pen pal like me, so she decided to give it to Papa. He's not feeling too good. I made an extra one for him as well. Maybe two Christmas cards will help him feel better.

Emma said she felt sorry for me and Julia, that we had no grandparents. Then Julia told her she did have a grandma, on her mother's side. Emma looked at her funny because she didn't know we were stepsisters. So I told her. Then something strange happened that I still don't quite understand. Julia said me and her were technically not even stepsisters—that my father was Jacob, Mama's husband who died before I was born. I had always thought Papa was my father. So I asked my oldest sister, Clara, who doesn't live with us because she's married and has two little boys, if her father was my father too. She said no, that Papa was my father, just like I always thought. Then I asked Mama because I was confused.

Cass looked up momentarily and caught his breath. Was it possible that Sarah finally told Maggie *he* was her father? Dare he hope?

"What's wrong?" John looked at Cass with a concerned expression filling his face.

"Nothing. Nothing at all." Wild horses couldn't keep him from finishing that letter. He returned his eyes to the page.

Mama's eyes got all teary and she told me it didn't really matter, and not to worry about such things. Papa was the one who raised me, loved me, and cared for me, and that made him my father. And more importantly, Papa was the one who needed me right now.

Mama's right—Papa needs me. Papa says I cheer him up when I read to him, and when I fluff his pillow, or take his supper into him when he's not feeling well enough to come to the table. I'm glad I can do that for him because I love him and he deserves to be happy.

I'm afraid Christmas won't be quite as good as last year's because Papa is sick again, but it will still be wonderful because it's Christmas! I hope you have a wonderful Christmas too!

Sincerely,

Maggie Mae Barker

Cass tucked Maggie's card back into its envelope. "John, you got any more of those postcards I can buy? You know, the fancy Christmas ones?"

"Sure thing." John pulled one out of a stack on the counter and brought it over to Cass, along with a pen.

After struggling to fit a decent-sized letter onto one side of that postcard last year, Cass had sworn he'd send Maggie something bigger this year. But a short letter felt to be most fitting right now, for he was near speechless. How Maggie Mae could be such a selfless angel when her flesh-and-blood father was quite the opposite was beyond Cass. And Wayne Barker was obviously more in need of her attention than he was. A simple letter would be best for many a reason.

He picked up the pen and put it to the postcard.

December 23, 1904

Dear Maggie Mae,

Thank you for the Christmas card. It's just as lovely as the one you sent me last year. I do appreciate your thoughtfulness and hope all continues to go well for you. May you and your family have a Merry Christmas. I bid you goodbye until next Christmas season—unless, of course, you choose to write to me before then.

Sincerely,

Cass Hite

***

1905

Cass reveled in his good fortune. Another year had passed. His river bank in Ticaboo had produced enough gold dust for his needs, his health had not declined much, Christmas was here yet again, and Maggie had not forgotten him. He lowered himself into the chair at John's poker table with Maggie's unopened Christmas card in one hand and his purchased postcard in the other, ready to write her back the moment he finished reading hers. Dark clouds approached from the west, and he wanted to get back to Ticaboo before the storm hit.

Carefully, he tore open one end of the envelope

and pulled out the folded sheet of paper. He unfolded the card, wondering what colorfully drawn holiday scene he'd see this time. Disappointment washed over him momentarily. The front of the card held the words "Merry Christmas" written in blue-black ink. The greeting took most of the space. Underneath it, drawn in the same ink, was a striped candy cane. *She must not have her friend's crayons this year.* He opened the card to reveal his favorite part.

Disappointment flooded him this time. The words "Merry Christmas" took the majority of the inside page. The body of her letter was a mere three lines.

December 20, 1905

Dear Mr. Hite,

This year I don't have crayons to make your card. My friend Emma moved. Lots of things have changed this year. Mama needs me more. That's okay—it's time I grew up and helped around the house. I hope all is well with you and that you have a good Christmas.

Sincerely,

Maggie Mae Barker

Cass set down Maggie's card, slid his in front of him, and picked up his pen.

December 24, 1905 he began, determined to keep his letter short as well. Even if their correspondence was kept merely to the exchange of a simple hello in a Christmas card each year, he'd gladly accept that over the alternative—nothing from Maggie

Dear Maggie Mae,

Thank you for your Christmas card. As always, I enjoyed

hearing from you. All is going well for me down here in Ticaboo.

It sounds like you're growing up and becoming a big help to your mama. I'm proud of you. You keep helping her. She needs you.

Cass paused, letting the ache settle down in his heart—he needed her too. But the obvious stared him in the face. Maggie didn't need him. She had a father—her papa. And she was growing up. An uncomfortable knot in his gut told him this would be the last Christmas card he'd ever write to her, for he'd receive no more from her.

Six Years Later

Chapter 30

Sarah heard the chair legs scrape across the floorboards through the wall. She abandoned the potatoes she was peeling in the sink and turned toward the bedroom. It sounded as if Maggie had abruptly moved from Wayne's bedside. The dear girl had been in there all day, giving Sarah a break.

"Mama," Maggie said as she stepped through the door. "Papa's talking strange, like there's other people in the room." She hurried over to the sink and motioned with an incline of her head for Sarah to attend to him. "I think you'd better go in. He needs you. I'll make supper."

Sarah wiped her hands on her apron as she walked calmly toward the bedroom. So many times, she or her girls had thought the next hour would be Wayne's last, but then he'd rallied his strength and surprised them all. Beth and Julia had grown tired of the strain on their emotions. Perhaps that's why they seemed anxious to marry and move away when the opportunity afforded itself. Maggie, on the other hand, didn't seem ready to leave Sarah with the task of tending to Wayne alone, though many a young man had tried to court her and take her away.

"Thank you for sitting with him all day." Sarah gave Maggie a quick hug as they passed. "I really appreciate the break," she added, meaning every word. She'd been able to get some much-needed laundry done.

As Sarah stepped into the bedroom, the smell of stale air and urine affronted her nose. She breathed through her mouth momentarily, knowing from experience that she'd soon get used to the odor. As she sat down on the chair at Wayne's bedside, she closed her mouth, too tired to take the added effort to breathe that way. The smell of lavender mixed in with the sickly sweet smell of the room. She spotted a bouquet of fresh flowers set in the closed window and smiled. Maggie must have pick those that morning when her papa wouldn't let her open the window. Lately, he'd acquired a fear of chills.

"I'm here, Wayne." She took his bony hand in hers, saddened to see it wither further each day. She patted it. "Is there anything I can get for you? A bowl of soup? A clean blanket?"

He turned his gaunt face toward her and shook his head. "No."

"Maggie said you're talking nonsense. You're not teasing the poor child again, are you?" she asked, trying to keep things light. Up until lately, he'd done his fair share of teasing.

"No," he repeated. His eyes looked straight at hers, yet straight through her, it seemed. "She's a good girl. I'm sorry I couldn't give you more. Or a son." His voice trailed off like it had when he first told her he was unable to father more children because of his health.

"It's all right." Sarah patted his hand again, finding his words odd, as if he'd forgotten Maggie wasn't his. "We have a lovely family just the way it is."

"Are you still there?" he asked, weakly gripping Sarah's hand while he continued to stare through her. His breathing grew increasingly more labored.

"I'm right here, Wayne." Sarah's insides twisted. He'd never been so distant before. She felt as though he wasn't really there. But he was. She brought his hand to her mouth and kissed it. "I'll not leave your side as long as you need me here."

"Genevieve." The name fell from his lips and tore at Sarah's heart in unexpected fashion.

"No, dear, it's me, Sarah."

"Tell Sarah I love her," Wayne said in a wisp of a voice, his eyes glassy.

Sarah turned, half expecting to see Genevieve behind her. She saw only Maggie, standing in the doorway, obviously listening in.

Wayne gripped Sarah's hand tighter than she'd have thought he could've mustered. "Tell her thank you for loving me when I was so hard to love. Tell her thank you for taking on our children and loving them like her own. Genevieve, I couldn't have made it without her. I hope you don't mind that she loved me dearly. And that I loved her even more dearly. But I needed her." His hand relaxed. "Will you tell her, please?"

Sarah squeezed his hand as tears rolled down her cheeks like a faucet left on. "Yes, dear, I will tell her. And I know she'll appreciate it. More than you'll ever know. Because she wants to tell you thank you for taking her in and loving her when she was so hard to love. And being a father to her dear Maggie just like she was your own blood."

She could hear Maggie sniffle in the background and the next thing she knew, her daughter knelt at her side. Had she overheard? Of course, but now was not the time to tell her the truth. The facts Maggie knew were obviously inconsistent, but she didn't seem concerned about them.

"Mama," Maggie murmured softly. "That was beautiful." She reached over and took Wayne's other hand. "Mama," she said again, only with a sense of urgency. "I think Papa's gone."

Sarah had been holding his hand so tightly while emotions consumed her that she'd failed to notice the limpness in Wayne's hand. She laid it by his side, leaned over, and listened for his heart to be sure. "Yes, he's gone," she said through emerging tears.

Maggie opened her arms, and Sarah willingly fell into her embrace. "He wanted to go home to heaven, where he'd be free of pain. Why is it so hard to say goodbye when he was suffering so much?"

"Because you loved him, Mama."

"Yes, I did." Sarah swallowed the gathering lump in her throat. "And apparently, he loved me more than I realized."

"Why is that so hard to believe?" Maggie hugged

her tightly. "You are an angel, Mama. Your love is unconditional."

Sarah shook her head, causing the tears to trickle faster down her face. If only that were true. "There was a day . . ." she said, thinking back on her marriage to Jacob, and then to her rejection of Cass. ". . . when I thought I knew what love was. At least, what I wanted it to be. I realize now that I knew nothing of love. I didn't know how give it—that's why I never found it. But he . . ." She turned to the lifeless body of Wayne and repositioned his hands upon his heart. ". . . and the Good Lord helped me learn that you love most those you serve." She kissed her fingers and touched them to his pale lips. "Thank you, dear Wayne."

Chapter 31

After a long day of shoveling, bending, and panning, Cass sat on his favorite rock at the edge of the river jiggling his pan back and forth just below the surface of the water. Specks of gold became visible as the gentle current carried the lighter, muddy sand away. That familiar surge of excitement spread through his body in its short-lived, but satisfying feeling. It was nothing like when he'd first discovered gold a mile upstream on the Colorado—after Hoskininni had pointed him where to go. This was a "Yippee." That had been a jump-up-and-down "Eureka!" Those feelings had been full of greed. Now the gold dust simply represented a withdrawal from the Bank of Ticaboo and a meager wage earned for his day's hard work.

He examined it closely, determining if it would be enough to buy a pound or two of flour, a tub of lard, *and* a new shirt. He hadn't bought himself one in years. Being a hermit had some advantages. John would have to order the shirt in. In fact, Cass might be lucky to find the tub of lard in stock on the shelves of the old store. Why his brother kept that store going for the tourists was beyond Cass.

John made most of his money off his ferry there at Dandy Crossing. With more and more folks coming out this way wanting to see the mighty wonders of Mother Nature, their paper money provided John more income than that million-dollar mistake of Stanton's ever did. Cass tried to tell Stanton that Hoskininni's gold was too fine to extract with fancy machinery, but the man's greed got in the way of listening.

Cass straightened his stiff back and took a break—something he did a lot more of lately. His sixtieth birthday had come and gone last month without a single person's notice, not even himself. But as of late, his tired old muscles reminded him daily that yet another decade of years lay behind him and not many more sat before him. He leaned on the rock. As he arched his back to stretch his sore muscles, he took in the beauty of the red rock cliffs on each side of him reaching up into the blue sky of spring. Swirls of coral stone blended in with the darker shades of red on the canyon walls. Add that to the tuft of dark green provided by the occasional tenacious tree growing out of the sheer wall of stone, and Cass couldn't imagine a more beautiful piece of artwork anywhere—not even in one of those fancy museums back east.

After a good minute or so, Cass returned his attention to his nearly empty pan. He finished washing the rest of the sand from three flakes of gold and then collected the precious metal and placed it into the leather pouch where he stored withdrawals from his bank. He stood slowly and walked toward his cabin, contemplating what to make for supper. That was one thing he really didn't like about living alone—mealtime. He never was much of a cook. And good company always made one's meal more enjoyable.

Tom ambled by and rubbed against Cass's leg as he paused to open the door to the cabin.

"Good thing I've at least got your company, ain't it?" Cass reached down and picked up his cat, rubbing its fur as he stepped inside. The sweet, musty smell of something rotting affronted his nose. "You sure as shootin' can tell there's no woman taking care of this place, can't you?" He held fast to Tom and settled the both of them into the armchair next to the cold fireplace. "That's okay. We don't need no woman to take care of us or keep us company, do we, Tom?" The falsehood of that statement shot a pang of torment to his gut. He stroked his cat's fur with fervor, and Tom squirmed away.

He glanced over to the table, to where the letter sat in its usual spot an arm's length from his chair. Needing a lift more than usual for some reason today, he snagged the yellowed envelope from off the table. With the upmost care, he pulled the worn sheet of paper from the protection of its envelope. It unfolded easily, having done so a thousand times over the last five years. Being the last letter that Maggie Mae wrote to him made this one extra special. The bundle of her previous letters and

Christmas cards remained tucked away in the wooden chest beneath his bed. He read them all from time to time.

He looked at the paper in his hand, thinking back on his frequent visits to John's little post office after receiving this letter—it had been a surprise. When he hadn't received a Christmas card from Maggie that year, he'd figured she was through writing him for good. This letter restored his hope. But week after week, then month after month, he'd returned to Ticaboo empty-handed. While John went through the collapse of the Hoskininni Mining Company, taking his life's savings with it, Cass felt he'd lost something much more valuable—his only connection to the two women he loved.

He brought his other hand up so as to hold the delicate paper with more care, and read.

May 20, 1907

Dear Mr. Hite,

It's been over a year since I wrote last. I'm sorry about that, but things have been a bit hectic as of late. Papa has made a turn for the worse and Mama is so very busy taking care of him, so Julia and I have taken on all of her other duties. That's fine. I don't mind helping and it's good for me to learn how to run a household. I figure one day I will be taking care of my own family. But not for a while. Mama needs me. And if Papa happens to pass on, she will need me even more. I hate to see her live all alone.

Beth got married last month and moved up to Provo. Julia has a fellow she's really sweet on. She's sixteen now and could get married real soon and move away too. Aunt Edna passed away a year ago, so all Mama has is Papa and me. I hope Papa can recover from his illness like he has before. Then I won't feel so guilty thinking of marriage.

I've had a fair number of suitors—at least they've wanted to court me. Mama says I'm too young. I'm fifteen. That's old enough. But I don't care to entertain their attention because Mama needs me.

This month is my last month of school. That makes me sad. I enjoy school. Mr. Olsen, my teacher, said he's got nothing more to teach me. He's the same teacher I had when I first came to Hanksville five years ago. Just yesterday, he talked again about writing letters and encouraged the younger children to find a pen pal. That reminded me of you and pricked my conscience. I wanted to write to you at least one more time and tell you how much I enjoyed being your pen pal. You are a good man, Cass Hite. Thank you for being my friend.

Sincerely,

Maggie Mae Barker

Cass let out a sigh and carefully returned the letter to its envelope. He placed it on its spot upon the table and settled back into the chair. Like so often, memories of Maggie Mae's mother rose to the surface of his thoughts—the way Sarah's smile lit her face, making it all the more beautiful; the music of her laugh when she found his stories amusing; and the softness of her lips as they ignited his soul with fire.

Tom repositioned himself in Cass's lap and nudged his hand in want of attention.

Cass stroked the cat's head. "Thanks for breaking my train of thought, Tom. I don't suppose it's too healthy to spend much time dreaming about two angels that'll never be mine. Next thing you know, I'll be wishing Mr.

Barker would pass on. I know the poor fellow is mighty unhealthy, but that gives me no call to do so. What I should be doing, Tom, is praying for the man. Then again, my prayers ain't that good. I'm not even sure they get past the roof of this cabin, the novice that I am at talking to the Big Man Upstairs."

Cass placed Tom on the floor and stood from the chair. "Well, supper's not going to cook itself."

As he started a fire in the stove, thoughts of Sarah returned—along with that same idea he'd wrestled with a thousand times. "Maybe I should just write that blasted letter," he mumbled to the flames licking the dry kindling.

No, you shouldn't.

The reasoning against contacting Sarah stood there in the back of his mind as solid as ever—how on earth could he pen such a letter? There was no delicate way to inquire whether Mr. Wayne Barker had passed on.

"Besides, Tom." Cass glanced over to the ball of yellow fur now curled up on his bed. "If she wanted me to know, she has my address."

After a supper of fish stew, Cass lit the lamp, collected the only book he owned from off the shelf above the fireplace, and settled into the armchair for his nightly reading. The Bible fell open in his lap as Tom cozied up to his stocking feet and purred. The book's worn leather binding and dog-eared pages told him it had seen a lot of use. The person who left it in John's store by accident was most likely sad about the mishap.

"He was merely passing through Dandy Crossing on his way to New Mexico," he said to Tom. "Then he forgot his book, poor fellow." He recalled the Bible collecting dust in one of John's mail cubbyholes for nigh onto two years before his brother deemed it abandoned and was about to use it for kindling.

"Good thing I came along, Tom, and saved it from the unfitting demise."

One page was all his tired eyes could read. He shut the Bible and reached down to pet his cat. "I ain't no saint, that's for sure. I'm just reading this book because I've nothing else to do at night. Remember that, Tom."

The next morning, Cass rose with the sun. Cold nipped his fingers when he stepped outside, gold pan in hand. Between his beat-up hat and coat, long moustache, and straggly hair that reached past his neck, the rest of him felt warm enough. He walked down to the riverbank, sat on his favorite rock, and gazed at the canyon walls, so gorgeous and vibrant lit by the morning sun. How could he get to work with such a view begging him to feast his eyes? Minutes passed, and he told himself he'd collected enough gold yesterday to take care of his next month of supplies.

The neigh of a horse brought his head around, and he looked upstream. He shot to his feet. "John!" He set his pan on the rock and ambled toward his brother. "What brings you down this way?"

John dismounted. Leading his horse behind him, he walked over to meet Cass. "Can't a fellow make a friendly visit to his brother once in a while?"

"He certainly *can*." Cass gave John a quick one-armed hug. "It's just that *you* don't do it all that much."

"Sorry." John wrinkled his brow. "I have a store and a ferry to tend to."

"Seriously, what bring you down to Ticaboo?" Cass hoped it wasn't bad news.

John pulled an envelope from his shirt pocket. "This came in the mail yesterday. I didn't figure you'd be comin' up to Dandy Crossin' for a while, so I thought I'd do the brotherly thing and bring it down to you." He held it out for Cass. "I recognized the name. It's from that little girl you used to write to years ago."

Cass snatched the letter. His heart swelled to where he swore his chest would burst. "Maggie Mae?"

"Yep, that's what it says."

Cass read every word on the front of the envelope to verify there was no mistake. There was her name, Maggie Mae Barker, in the upper left-hand corner, and "Mr. Cass Hite" scrolled across the middle just like before, only much neater handwriting this time. Ready to tear it open and read it immediately, Cass hesitated. "I'd like to read this alone, if you don't mind."

"Alone? You're always alone. I'm worried about you, Cass. Folks are startin' to refer to you as 'the old hermit downriver.'" John's face twisted into a teasing grin. "I'm one of those folks." He brought the reins back and prepared to mount his horse. His grin transformed into a tight-lipped smile. "But it's okay. I understand you wantin' to be alone this time—I know how long you've been waitin' for a letter."

"Thanks for understanding." Cass tipped his hat to his brother. "I'll come in later today for a visit."

John tipped his hat in return and mounted his

horse.

As John rode away, Cass scurried toward his cabin, rushed inside, and plopped down in his chair. With trembling hands, he carefully opened the letter and read.

April 2, 1912

Dear Mr. Hite,

It has been a long time since we have corresponded, and I hope this letter finds you well. I did so enjoy being your pen pal those many years ago. I consider you as one of my dear friends. And as such, I would love to invite you to my wedding. I am marrying my sweetheart, William Johnson, on April 25. The ceremony will be held in the Hanksville church at 2:00 p.m. A reception in the backyard of the big house will follow. There will be lots of good food and company. I hope you can attend. I would enjoy seeing you after all these years. I think my mother would appreciate seeing you again too.

Sincerely,

Maggie Mae Barker

Cass felt as though a stick of happy dynamite exploded in his chest, sending tingles of joy throughout his entire body. He carefully folded up the letter and inserted it back inside the envelope. "Maggie's getting married," he said to Tom. "And she invited me. Imagine that. And she said Sarah would appreciate seeing me." The very idea warmed Cass's heart and reached up to his eyes. He wiped away a tear before it trickled down into his beard.

As he placed the precious invitation on the table next to the other letter, two words stuck out from the others he'd just read. *I think.*

Cass was a fool to have let his hopes soar like they had. Maggie Mae, the eternal optimist, of course would think such a thing because she was a girl who would herself appreciate seeing an old acquaintance. But would her mother feel the same way? Especially one who had caused her such pain? *I have not yet fully forgiven you, but in time, that will come.* Sarah's words replayed in Cass's mind. Had twenty-one years been enough time? What if it hadn't? And then there was the matter of Mr. Barker. The fact that Maggie was getting married made Cass think maybe her father had made yet another recovery from his lingering illness because Maggie wouldn't want her mother to be left all alone. Or Wayne Barker had passed on.

Cass sat in the chair with his legs sprawled out in front of him, not wanting to move, not wanting to pan for gold, make breakfast, or even read Maggie's letter a second time. More than anything, he wanted to go to that wedding in two weeks, especially if the two angels in his life wanted him there. But he wasn't certain that was the case. He could very well taint this special day for Maggie's mother, and possibly her father—at least, the one she *believed* to be her father. Maggie's letter held no mention of him. Wayne Barker might still be alive—she just didn't mention him. Or she hadn't mentioned him because he had passed on.

Even if Cass were still a gambling man, he wouldn't wager a bet either way.

***

A glow of pink peeked over the eastern rim of the

gorge as Cass left Ticaboo. By the time he made it to Dandy Crossing, the eastern sky offered light enough to see that John had one of his men down there already at the water's edge. The man sat in the crude three-sided shelter in which John ran his ferry business. Cass hoped he'd come early enough that he would escape notice.

Blast it all, now he'd most likely have to explain where he was going all dressed up in the new shirt and pants he'd borrowed from John. He was sure the man would wonder why Ole Cass Hite, the hermit from Ticaboo, was going to a wedding. Who could he possibly know that was young enough to get hitched?

There was no chance Cass was about to tell a near stranger who Maggie was to him. Even when he'd borrowed the clothes from John, he'd downplayed the importance of the wedding. "I'm just going to wish my old pen pal well at her wedding," he'd said, and then added, "And get away from Ticaboo and Hite for a day or so."

The man stood and stepped out of the shelter as Cass approached. "Mornin', sir. That'll be two bits if'n you want to use the ferry."

Sir? Cass smiled at his good fortune—even if he did have to pay this time. With his new haircut and close shave, John's man obviously didn't recognize him. "Will a pinch of gold dust do?"

"Sure enough." The man smiled big.

Cass pulled out his leather pouch, pinched a flat grain, and dropped it into a tin cup the man held toward him. He led his horse onto the raft and let the man guide them across the calm, wide spot of the river, and then Cass climbed out of the canyon on the other side.

Once up top, he kicked his heels into his horse. Loving the feel of the wind on his face, he headed to Hanksville at a vigorous pace. He'd have to maintain the speed if he was to make it there by two o'clock.

Not more than a mile or two passed when Cass's excitement simmered down and he set to thinking—again. It'd taken him a full two days to decide to come, and then every day for the last two weeks, he'd battled second thoughts of not belonging at the wedding.

It doesn't matter if I don't fit into Maggie's life, I'm going there to wish her well in marriage, and that's a plenty good reason in itself.

It was one thirty by the time Cass could see the town of Hanksville off to the west. Amazed he'd made it this far, he headed to his old cabin. He'd talked himself in and out of turning around and missing the wedding completely at least a half dozen times. When he found his spare key hidden under the rock behind his cabin, he still hadn't decided about attending the wedding. At least he'd spend the night.

Cobwebs and the musty smell of rot affronted him as he stepped inside. He dusted off the lone chair, sat down, and pulled out his pocket watch. A quarter of an hour remained before the ceremony started. He gazed out the window in the direction of Sarah's cabin, yearning to see smoke rising from its chimney above the juniper trees. He saw nothing.

That's because she's not there, you fool. She's at the wedding.

Why had that clear blue sky disappointed him so?

Was it because that smoke would have spoken of her presence a mere hundred yards away?

Yes. Just to know she was close would bring Cass a measure of contentment.

Then go, stay in the background, admire her from a distance—enjoy that moment or two—then leave.

Cass glanced at his watch again and stood from his chair. He darted out the door, unsaddled his horse, and secured the animal inside the derelict corral, and ran into town.

Horses and wagons filled both sides of the street around the church, but not a single person could be seen. They were all inside. Cass could hear the organ music filter through the wooden walls of the chapel. He ran, slowing his steps to a crawl as he opened the main door and slipped quietly inside, squeezing into the back pew.

Cass barely had time to settle into place when Maggie walked down the aisle with one hand holding on to the crook of a man's elbow. Cass leaned forward to get a better look, wiping sweat from his hands on his borrowed trousers. What a beautiful woman she'd grown to be! His heart thumped with pride.

Maggie's white gown flowed around a pair of dainty feet, and her face brimmed with the same beauty as her mother—only framed in curls of dark brown hair rather than blonde. The man escorting her had dull blond hair and wore a drab, brown suit—both looked out of place next to her. He delivered Maggie to the front of the chapel, where a young fellow with bright eyes and a wide smile took her hand in his. Cass didn't recognize the man escorting Maggie as Wayne Barker. His face looked too young and his step too vibrant to be that of a man transformed by illness to the point of being unrecognizable. Had Maggie asked a relative—perhaps her stepbrother, Cleon—to give her away in marriage because her father was too ill? Or unable to walk? Or . . .?

Cass felt it unfitting to dwell on the other possibility. Instead, he looked around the small chapel, especially up front, trying to see Sarah—and trying to catch sight of Wayne Barker, who may, or may not, be sitting next to her.

"Women and these darn new-fangled hats they wear nowadays," Cass mumbled under his breath, leaning to one side then the other, attempting to gain a view of the entire chapel. He caught a glimpse of the back of a gray-haired fellow sitting in a wheelchair near a second door up front. He strained to get a look at the man's face.

"Sit still," the fellow next to him whispered as he jabbed Cass with an elbow.

"Sorry," Cass muttered. He kept still and focused on Maggie Mae and the lucky young man who'd won her heart.

His mind wandered during the ceremony, insisting on dwelling upon the man in the brown suit coat. If Maggie needed someone to stand in as her father, Cass would have volunteered in a heartbeat—had he known. To walk his only child down the aisle would be worth more than all the gold he'd ever pulled out of the mighty Colorado. If only he'd realized this back in his youth, maybe he would have been the man walking Maggie Mae down the aisle and sitting next to the mother of the bride—wherever she might be.

The ceremony lasted less than fifteen minutes. Cass had to scramble out of his reverie as the crowd stood while the bride and groom made their exit. He tried to catch sight of Maggie Mae as she practically danced back down the aisle toward the door. Any moment now, she could be gone for good. Would she notice him? He wanted to wave his hat. He wanted her to know that he was here and how much he cared. He prayed she would look his way so he wouldn't make a fool of himself.

As she reached the back of the chapel, her eyes met his, and they lit up even brighter. His throat choked with emotion.

"Mr. Hite!" Maggie held out her hand as if to touch him, but Cass was too far away. Her next words, he could barely hear over people's voices, but could read her lips. "I do hope you're coming over to the big house for the reception." Before he could respond, the throng of well-wishers ushered her and the groom outside.

Cass stood and looked for Sarah in the crowd. He couldn't see her, and allowed the people farther in on the bench to file past him. He would feel uncomfortable joining them and strolling over to the big house with all these folks he didn't know. When he got up the gumption to do so, he preferred to walk alone.

As the last of the wedding guests trickled out of the church, Cass sat back down and basked in the welcome he'd received from Maggie Mae. Her sincere excitement at seeing him truly touched Cass. He wondered how she'd recognized him right off, seeing that she'd only met him once or twice in person. It must have been the photograph he'd included in one of his letters. However, that had been taken in his frivolous younger days. Had he not changed much with age—and a good haircut like he'd worn long ago? Apparently not.

And apparently, she wants you to come to the reception. That's what you're here for, isn't it? Go on and do more than give her one glimpse. Go speak to her.

Cass stood and vacated the empty chapel. With myriad reservations impeding his steps, he crept down the deserted street toward the big house.

More than a block away, Cass could hear the cheerful clamor of people rise from the backyard of Nyda's old house. A dusty memory of strolling by here with Sarah surfaced and sent a pang of longing to his heart. Though he'd been sicker than he'd ever imagined a man could be, those six weeks held some of the happiest days of his life. He walked toward the noise, his gut tensing. Would Sarah recognize him with the same ease as Maggie Mae had? Or would he appear as a stranger? Or worse, as a man she cared not to see? And what of Mr. Wayne Barker? Would he be sitting there in a wheelchair next to Sarah, sickly as always, but with a set of steely eyes strong enough to glare and tell Cass he wasn't welcome?

Cass walked by the front of the big house and then around the corner, staying close to the gray picket fence, heading for the gate that would gain him entrance to either heaven or hell. He reached the gate, undid the latch, and stepped into the backyard.

Maggie Mae easily stood out in her cheerful white dress. A line of people formed off to her side, apparently waiting for a turn to hug or kiss the beautiful bride and shake the hand of her new husband. Cass couldn't bear the thought of standing in that line, conversing with strangers. Living alone all these years had done him no favors in the way of maintaining his social skills. When the line died down, then he'd congratulate the happy couple.

He shifted his attention away from Maggie Mae and scanned the yard. Two long tables covered with gingham cloths and a variety of baked goods sat at the far end of the lawn. After the guests greeted the newlyweds, it appeared they worked their way over to the food, made themselves a plate, and then stood around and talked to each other. How nice that no one was drunk. This wedding proved far different from any he'd ever gone to. It was simple, yet grand in its own way, immersing Cass in feelings of gladness.

Cass noticed a smaller table next to the two larger ones. It held a large glass bowl of orange-colored punch with numerous clear glasses arranged neatly by its side. With the help of the long ride that morning, Cass felt the twinge of thirst scratch at his throat. "A cup of punch sounds good," he said to no one in particular. He headed that way, confident and grateful he could drink the colorful beverage without concern for its content. After a little refreshment, he'd venture a stroll through the crowd, keeping a keen eye out for Sarah and Wayne, and then go from there—depending on what he found.

Cass ladled himself some punch from the near-empty bowl into his glass and stepped away from the table. As he brought the drink to his mouth, he noticed a woman in a flattering yellow dress walk behind the table and pour a large pitcher of punch into the bowl.

She turned, and Cass saw her face—the curve of her cheek, the sparkle in her eyes, and the softness of her lips were as beautiful as ever.

Sarah.

His heart beat rapidly. Her eyes met his, and he caught his breath. He swore delight danced within her eyes as the green-blue of each iris brightened like the morning sky lit by the rising sun.

"Hello, Sarah," he mustered the greeting.

"Cass."

Never before had Cass heard his name spoken with such feeling. In that single syllable, she'd communicated everything he could have hoped for—compassion, joy, attentiveness, even love.

If for nothing more than to hear her say his name like that, his decision to come to Maggie's wedding had been one of his best.

Chapter 32

"Cass." His name fell from Sarah's lips as her heart leaped inside her chest. No other words came, only disbelief. Just that morning, his face had materialized in her thoughts. Last week, memories of nursing him back to health had made her stop washing the dishes and stare out the window in deep reflection—back to some of the happiest weeks of her life.

"Maggie Mae invited me." He rubbed his hands together as if he was nervous. "I hope you don't mind."

"No," Sarah managed to say. She surveyed Cass, from his dark hair streaked with gray—cut short like the way he wore it twenty-one years ago—down his lean body to his freshly polished boots. She found her voice. "You haven't changed," she said slightly above a whisper.

"Oh, I wouldn't say that," Cass responded quickly. "Some rough edges have smoothed out a bit." A curious grin pulled at his lips—one she'd never recalled seeing before. His mouth then straightened and his eyes grew more serious. "It is you who hasn't changed." He took a breath. "You look as lovely as ever."

Sarah opened her mouth, ready to contest his declaration—ready to allude to the effects of her twenty-year refiner's fire. She paused in contemplation instead. Had he been through his own refiner's fire? And changed in ways the eye couldn't see? Daring not to probe, she said, "That's very kind of you to say, Mr. Hite." She felt a slight blush of warmth rise in her cheeks, unused to male attention.

"Please, I liked it much better when you called me Cass." His voice held no hint of teasing, only sincerity. He lifted his glass of punch to his mouth, took a drink, and wiped his moustache with his sleeve. "Mighty tasty. Are you the one who made it?"

"Yes," Sarah responded, thinking how much better she thought Cass looked now with his moustache trimmed to match the width of his lips.

He took another swig. "Like I said, tasty."

"Thank you, Mr.—I mean, Cass. I'm glad you like it. I only wish I could have contributed more to my daughter's wedding. If it wasn't for family, poor Maggie wouldn't have had much of a wedding celebration at all." She brought her hand to her mouth—what was she doing, unloading her woes onto this man she hadn't seen in years? "Sorry, I didn't mean to ramble on such as I did. My life is fine. I really have no complaints."

Cass cleared his throat and seemed to hesitate. "So, is your husband doing better?"

Sarah realized Cass didn't know. "Wayne passed

away a year ago."

"Oh," Cass responded. "I'm sorry to hear that," he said in a voice that held emotions, but ones she couldn't decipher.

"It was a blessing for him, really, to find release from his illnesses." Sarah mixed the new punch she'd added in with the old, not looking at Cass as she stirred. "I'm guessing Maggie never mentioned that to you in her letters?" she asked, though she knew the answer.

"Her wedding invitation was the first I've heard from her in five years." His voice distinctly held sorrow now.

"Oh." Sarah didn't know how to respond. She could feel his hurt. And why not? She'd felt it too. When Maggie had grown up and past her childhood phase of pen pals, Sarah missed reading those letters from Cass. At least Sarah still had Maggie around. From what she'd gleaned from Cass's last letter, he had no one. "I'm sorry she quit writing to you. She grew up rather quickly after she turned fifteen."

Cass turned his gaze across the lawn and toward Maggie, where she stood next to her new husband and chatted with a line of well-wishers. "No need to apologize. She's grown into a beautiful young woman I'm sure you are proud of. I know I would be if I were in your place."

The longing in his voice cut Sarah to the core. Maggie *was* his daughter—his only child, but he wasn't considered her father. The ache he must feel reached inside her and slashed her heart. What could she say to him to ease his pain? She felt the need to offer him something. When she finished mixing the punch, she looked up, ready to tell him how much Maggie had enjoyed his letters—and perhaps even mentioning her own delight in them as well. "Cass," she said, but stopped. Brother and Sister Brown approached the table.

The couple each helped themselves to a glass of punch as Cass shifted his weight from one foot to the other.

"Congratulations, Sister Barker." Brother Brown extended his hand to shake Sarah's.

"We're so happy for Maggie and William—as we're sure you are too." Sister Brown motioned for Sarah to move around the table. "Come, let me give you a hug. You shouldn't be hiding behind that table. Someone besides the mother of the bride should be taking care of the refreshments."

"Thank you," Sarah responded as Sister Brown hugged her.

As she stepped away from the embrace, she noticed two other couples standing behind the Browns. She looked at Cass and then shot a nervous glance toward the people obviously waiting their turns to congratulate the mother of the bride. Her eyes came back to Cass momentarily. "Thank you again for coming. I'm sure Maggie and William are looking forward to greeting you as well," she said, unhappy with sending Cass on his way, torn by how she'd handled things. But she couldn't very well ignore Maggie's wedding guests and chat with Cass the remainder of the day—though for some reason, the idea sounded very inviting. Desirable, in fact.

"Good day, Mrs. Barker," Cass said in a stiff voice, tipped his hat, and walked away.

As Sarah shook the next couple's hands, her eyes focused on Cass across the lawn. Her attention split between the words "Congratulations on Maggie's marriage" and worry about her abrupt goodbye to the man she'd tried for twenty-one years to forget, but could never seem to. Would he come back and talk to her again after wishing Maggie and William well? *Oh, please let him!*

"My, but Maggie makes for a beautiful bride, doesn't she?"

The question came as a female voice without a face. Sarah tore her eyes away from Cass's back and focused on the woman reaching out to hug her. "Yes, she does," Sarah responded, hoping her momentary lapse of attention had not come across as rude. "And thank you, Sister Hiatt, for coming. And Brother Hiatt," she added as she shook his hand, glancing over his shoulder at Cass.

Another woman from church approached, and she tried not to wince. Sarah extended her arms to accept yet another hug, though at the moment everything inside her yearned to run across the lawn and apologize to Cass— and to talk to him some more. "Thank you for coming, Sister Smith."

"My pleasure," Sister Smith said. "Now that Maggie's married and is moving far away, I hope to see you out to our Relief Society meetings more often. I'd hate to see you sitting home alone on a Wednesday morning when there are quilts to make and good company to keep."

"I'll try." Sarah cringed inside. Crowds of people had become difficult for her to enjoy. "Would you care for some punch?" She offered Sister Smith a glass, desirous to change the subject. Taking care of Wayne for so many years had rarely offered her much chance to socialize with the other women of the town. And then Edna died, and she rarely talked with anyone outside of her own home.

Her feet shifted their weight as if ready to bolt, but wedding guests continued to file her way, either wishing her and Maggie well or refilling their glasses with punch and sending her a smile. She felt stuck, wringing her hands when someone wasn't shaking them. Whenever she got a fleeting break, she glanced around the backyard for Cass. He had stood there talking to Maggie and William for some time, making her task easy. But now he was gone. Her heart sank and her eyes constantly skirted the guests standing in front of her, trying to spot him.

"Thank you for coming," she repeated to each person, mechanically shaking their hands or returning a hug.

Cass's white shirt and black cowboy hat caught her eye. He walked toward the front yard. Was he leaving?

Panicked, she looked at the stream of people making their way toward her. A quick glance at the punch bowl revealed that it was nearly empty. She grabbed the pitcher from the table. "Please excuse me, but I need to get more punch," she stated and hurried away.

"Cass," she called out when she was close enough to him and far enough away from the crowd that she could speak his name without others hearing. He turned around. His eyes brightened.

"Sarah." The soft tone in which he uttered her name shot a tingle from her heart out through her fingers.

"Would you mind giving me a hand with this punch?" Sarah motioned with her chin for him to follow her into the house.

"Not at all." He immediately changed his direction and rushed to her side. Placing his hand at the small of her back, he assisted her up the back steps.

Discombobulated from his touch, Sarah had to think for a moment about why she was in the kitchen. *Punch.* "Yes. We need to get some more punch made." She handed Cass a bottle of apricot nectar. "Will you please open this for me while I measure out some sugar?"

"With pleasure," he said with a warm grin. His fingers touched hers as he accepted the jar, and his smile filled his entire face.

Reluctant to let go of the nectar and the feel of his rough hand next to hers, she clung to the jar a little longer. "I really appreciate you . . . um . . . helping me," she said and finally let go.

"Like I said before, my pleasure." He opened the bottle.

Sarah set the pitcher on the table and scooped some sugar into its fluted opening. Her heart beat faster as Cass stepped close. His body brushed against hers as he emptied the nectar into the pitcher. "So, what's Ticaboo like?" she asked, wanting to pick up where Maggie's letters had left off. "Is it pretty?"

Cass gazed at Sarah. "There's only one thing prettier in this world that I know of."

She tore her eyes away from his, embarrassed by the flush of heat that rose to her cheeks, yet relishing emotions his words had stirred inside her. With pitcher in hand, she moved over to the sink and pumped some water into the vessel. "I imagine it would get kind of lonely down there." Why had she said that? "You know, living away from your brother and all," she added quickly.

"Yes, it does." Cass stepped to her side and placed his hand on her arm. "More than you'll ever know."

His touch, though as gentle as a butterfly's lighting on her arm, pummeled her heart with long-forgotten desires. Abandoning the pump, she turned her attention once again to him. She swore a reflection of her own feelings gazed back at her through those sable-brown eyes.

The screen door flew open. Sarah jumped, and Cass backed away.

Mary walked in and promptly hitched her hands onto her hips. "Aunt Sarah, what are you doing in here?"

"Making more punch." Sarah pumped water into the pitcher.

"For heaven's sake, your place is outside greeting your guests, not in here making punch." Mary pulled Sarah away from the sink while sending Cass a confused-looking glare. "Now hurry on outside. I'll take care of the punch."

Cass shot out of the door. Sarah scurried down the steps behind him, feeling Mary's hand nudge her all the way. By the time Mary left Sarah alone, Cass had slipped around the side of the house—obviously heading for the front yard and on his way out. She couldn't let that happen—he might never return. "Wai—" she yelled as someone grabbed her elbow and tugged her back onto the lawn. She turned to see who wanted her to stay when she wanted to leave so badly.

Maggie moved her hand from Sarah's arm and pulled her into a hug. "Mama, where'd you go?"

"I was making punch."

"Leave it for Mary to do. Or Beth and Julia—there out in the yard somewhere. Your place is here with me and William right now."

"You're absolutely right." Sarah returned the hug, reminding herself that Maggie was the most important person in her life at the moment. She then strolled across the grass arm-in-arm with her last remaining daughter to have married.

"Mr. Hite was here," Maggie said. "Did you know that?"

"Yes, I did."

"I invited him without asking you, Mama. I hope you don't mind."

"Not at all. This is your day, and you were rightfully at liberty to invite who you wanted."

"He says he's a changed man since the last time we saw him."

"Oh, really now?" Sarah had sensed that already, but she wanted to hear more.

"Yeah, he says he's given up swearing, gambling, and drinking." Maggie offered a coy smile. "Not that I ever knew him to be such a rough fellow before, but I'm glad he's found peace in his life. He's even turned to God in his old age, he told me."

"You don't say?" Sarah's heart warmed with gladness for Cass.

"Yeah. He said he kind of had to, living out there alone in Ticaboo, because there was no one else to talk to except God—and his cat, Tom." Maggie's smile curved up dramatically in obvious delight. "He said the only reason he got the cat in the first place was because of me—he wanted something to talk about in those early letters that I'd be interested in. In the end, the old cat became his best friend, and he thanked me for that. Do you know, that poor tom cat only lived to be eleven? Cass said he died just last week."

"I'm sorry to hear that." Sarah let go of Maggie's arm as they approached William. Her heart felt heavy. She cared not to think about such things today. "Enough talk about Cass Hite. This is your day and there are wedding guests to greet, and I'm going to help you do that."

"Thank you, Mama, I know how difficult it is for you to talk to people." Maggie squeezed Sarah's hand and then hurried to William's side, where she immediately shook an awaiting guest's hand.

Sarah moved into place next to Maggie and greeted the guests after Maggie finished.

By the time the last of the guests trickled away, the backyard was clean, and Maggie and William rode off together, the sun dipping toward the horizon. Exhausted, and with arms full of empty nectar bottles, Sarah trudged toward her cabin on the edge of town. She gazed above the trees toward Cass's old cabin and frowned—no smoke rose from its chimney. Only blue-gray sky rose above the junipers. The unseasonable warmth of the April evening gave her hope that Cass hadn't bothered heating his cabin, and perhaps his supper had been a cold one. She assured herself it wasn't likely that he'd have headed back to Ticaboo already. He would wait until morning. Then surely he would stop by to say goodbye before he left. He had to know she was all alone now—there'd be no one around to pry as to who he was or why he chose to visit her.

When she stepped into her cabin, it felt empty. She looked around to try to dispel the feeling—first, at the old overstuffed chair sitting on the braided rug in the middle of the floor, next the knick-knacks and mementoes of the last forty years of her life, and then the girls' beds, two of them formerly Clara and Cleon's, pushed to each corner of the room. Tears gathered in her eyes as she finally faced the fact that never again would those beds be filled except by the rare visits from her children or grandchildren—they'd all moved so very far away. She thought back on how Maggie had refused William's first proposal of marriage, not wanting to leave her mother all alone. A year later when William asked her again, she'd assured Maggie over and over that living alone was not all that bad, and she'd be just fine. "You'd better marry the man you love when he asks you and not wait for everything to be perfect," she had said, painfully pulling from her own experience.

Oh, Cass.

Her tears flowed. Without concern for the glass, she dumped her load onto the table and immediately started a fire in the stove. She ran outside and gathered some of last year's moldy leaves once the flames burned strong enough to handle the damp kindling. As she stuffed them inside the belly of the stove, billows of smoke poured into the room. She hurried and shut the door, hoping the plumes that rose from her chimney would be visible from a distance—at least as far away as the neighboring cabin. Maybe if Cass knew she was home, he'd make his way over that night.

She stoked the fire some more, and then sat in the rocking chair and waited, ignoring the rumblings of hunger, too anxious to put the hot stove to obvious better use.

"Why is he not coming?" she muttered to herself.

Her stomach twisted with more than just hunger as possible reasons formed in her mind.

He no longer cares for you, and he was merely being gracious at the wedding.

He simply came to the wedding because Maggie had invited him—he didn't come to see you.

No! That couldn't be. She was not imagining the energy that sparked between them as Cass had helped her make that punch. She saw it in his eyes. It was the same as she'd seen twenty-one years ago. He still loved her.

And she still loved him.

But how could he possibly know that? She'd done nothing to communicate her feelings to him. Then again, she herself didn't realize the full extent of them until just now.

She had to tell him.

She jumped out of the rocking chair, grabbed her shawl, and darted out the door, determined once again to take control of her life.

Still no smoke rose above the junipers in the direction of Cass's cabin. All the more reason to hurry.

Sarah ran, putting herself in Cass's shoes, thinking about how low she'd feel if she were to have traveled down to Ticaboo for a visit and Cass were to have given no indication of his feelings toward her. His appetite wouldn't warrant firing up the stove. And he might very well be lying in his bed, hurting, feeling rejected once again. It must have been difficult to brave meeting her after all these years. But he had done it, done it for her, and she'd given no encouragement in return. The thought seized her chest and inflicted a nearly unbearable ache.

No light shone through the windows as she approached his place. *There's still enough light outside. He's not bothered with the lamp yet, that's all.* She rushed to the door and knocked. "Cass, it's Sarah," she said through a crack in the wood.

A raven cawed in the distance, but no response came from within the cabin.

She pounded on the door this time, her mind filled with worry. Leaning to the side, she peered in the lone window only to see darkness. She ran around to the back of the cabin and located the key she'd discovered years ago when she'd come here as a temporary escape from her woes. The moment she opened the door, letting the light from the setting sun pour onto the empty bed and chair, she knew what was wrong.

Cass was gone.

And there could be only one reason why he'd leave before morning—he was hurting. The sanctuary of his tiny cabin, miles away from the nearest human and now devoid of his cherished cat was the only thing to which he could turn to ease his lonely heart. He'd tried to reach out to Sarah. She'd turned him away. The pain in her heart intensified, and her entire body yearned to collapse into the cabin's single chair and sob. She fought the desire— her happiness was at stake here, and so was Cass's. Action was needed, not tears. She'd done harder things than this before, much harder, so leaving her empty home behind and heading down the trail to Ticaboo would be easy.

Sarah gathered her wits, calmed herself, and took a deep breath, determined to head out first thing in the morning. The smell of smoke lingered in the air. On a whim, Sarah reached out and touched the stove. It was warm. More than warm. Only fifteen minutes ago, she'd looked for smoke from his chimney and saw none. The heat of the metal told her Cass must have extinguished this fire a mere minute or two before that time.

She bolted out the door and down the trail, not caring that he was most likely on horseback and she on foot, not caring that the sun had set and the hazy light of dusk would soon fade into darkness. Cass would make camp soon, hopefully, and if she had to walk all night by the help of the moon that now rose in the east, so be it. And if she had to walk all the way to Ticaboo, so be it. She knew what she wanted now. It was the same thing she'd wanted twenty-one years ago. Only difference was, back then she'd let other people sway her decisions. No one was around to sway her now. Nor would anyone sway her again.

"Cass!" she called out, quickening her pace, knowing he couldn't hear her but feeling the desire to shout all the same. "Cass!" she cried again. The release of penned-up emotions felt cathartic.

The lights flickering from Hanksville disappeared in the distance. No longer were those people there to guide her steps, nor to stop her. But she had a full moon. She had her passion. And she had the trail that would lead her where *she* wanted to go.

"Cass," she cried again. It fueled her steps. "It's Sarah," she added this time—just in case.

She slowed her pace to conserve energy. It was fifty miles to Hite, and a few more down to Ticaboo. If Cass didn't stop for the night, neither must she.

The crunch of rocky soil underfoot echoed in the silence of the wide-open wilderness. She tuned her ear to its sound, concentrating on the rhythm created by her feet. A mile or so down the trail, something interrupted the pattern—the whinny of a horse in the distance. The clomping of horse hooves gaining speed disrupted the silence further. What kind of fool would ride at full gallop at night?

Sarah moved off the tail and walked alongside it, skirting sagebrush and rocks the best she could in the limited light.

The horseman took form, emerging from the darkness down the trail. He slowed his horse to a crawl and veered off the trail toward her.

"Sarah?"

Elation erupted within her at hearing Cass's voice, at hearing her name spoken with such depth of emotion. She ran toward him.

Cass dismounted and ran too, meeting her a few yards from his horse. He tossed his hat to the side, collected her in his arms, and embraced her like he'd never let her go. She clung tightly, never wanting him to.

"I was convinced you didn't want me." He spoke softly, his mouth next to her ear. "I couldn't bear to wait till morning to leave. I had to get away from the memories. But then I realized, that would be all I'd ever have. I wanted more than just memories. So I turned around."

Sarah basked in the warmth of his strong arms around her. "I'm glad you did."

"I wanted *you*," Cass continued, his lips pressed against her hair. "I figured I had to try to win your affection else I'd die a miserable old wretch all alone down there in Ticaboo."

"You have it, Cass. You have it." Sarah tightened her hold around him. "You've always had my affection. I suppose I needed to learn a few things first before I deserved yours."

Cass pulled back slightly and gazed at her. "Sarah." He spoke her name with reverence.

The moon lit his face, but she could tell love lit his eyes. A beautiful feeling filled her soul. Her whole life, she'd yearned to be adored like this—and to be able to reciprocate that same deep love. "Yes," she said in a hoarse whisper of a voice.

"I know I'm old, and I ain't got much gold dust to my name. But God willing, I've got plenty of years left in me. And with His help, I'll take good care of you." He let go of her and lowered onto one knee, his hands holding her hands and his eyes holding her eyes. "I love you, Sarah. I promise we'll do things right this time. And we can live in Hanksville, if that pleases you most." He took a deep breath. "Will you marry me?"

"Oh, Cass, yes." She pulled on his hands, tugging him up to her and then wrapping her arms around him. "Yes, I'd like that more than you'll ever know. And I don't care where we live, so long as I'm with you."

His arms caressed her, securing her to him. Then he kissed her, long and passionately.

Sarah melted against his body, remembering once more how wonderfully happy life could be.

About the Author

Carolyn has always enjoyed writing—or anything that exercised her creativity. She also loves history. So combining her two loves in the form of historical fiction was a forgone conclusion. *The Prospector and the Widow* is her sixth historical novel and her fourth western historical romance.

Other things Carolyn enjoys includes gardening, remodeling houses, road trips to see new places and glean ideas for future novels, and most of all, playing with her grandkids. Carolyn has lived most of her life in the valleys of the beautiful Rocky Mountains. It's no wonder she feels at home with her characters of the old west.

To see other books written by her, check out her website at www.carolyntwedefrank.com

Made in the USA
Monee, IL
26 June 2021